OUT OF
SHADOWS

Jason Wallace

First published in 2010 by
Andersen Press Limited
20 Vauxhall Bridge Road
London SW1V 2SA

www.andersenpress.co.uk

British Library Cataloguing in Publication Data available.

ISBN 978 1 84939 048 4

Mixed Sources
Product group from well-managed
forests and other controlled sources
www.fsc.org Cert no. TT-COC-2139
© 1996 Forest Stewardship Council

Typesetting in Adobe Garamond Pro by Palimpsest Book Production Limited,
Grangemouth, Stirlingshire
Printed and bound in Great Britain by
CPI Bookmarque, Croydon CR0 4TD

'If I stood you in front of a man, pressed the cold metal of a gun into your palm and told you to squeeze the trigger, would you do it?'

'No, sir.'

'Are you sure?'

'Of course, sir. No ways!'

'What if I then told you we'd gone back in time and his name was Adolf Hitler? Would you do it then? Would you?'

For my mother, June, and my stepfather, Richard,
who took us on an adventure

And for Katharine

ZIMBABWE
1983

ONE

Go ahead, shoot, I thought, because I was thirteen and desperate and anything, absolutely anything, was better than the fate to which my parents were leading me.

The policeman sat astride his growling motorbike, one hand on his holster, anonymous behind shades. He was one of the outriders for the new Prime Minister's motorcade, signalling for cars to get off the road. If drivers didn't stop quickly enough he was entitled to shoot. If they didn't move right off the tarmac, he could shoot. If they *did* stop but the policeman thought the passengers inside looked shifty or saw them messing around, he'd shoot. He was nothing like the policemen back home.

Home, I thought. An old ache swelled in my stomach. England. Britain. So far away. For me, this Africa was another world, and as we sat there watching the rider watch us, Britain felt further away than ever.

I sighed.

My father completely misinterpreted it and tutted as he showed me his watch against a sunburned wrist.

'We've plenty of time, I made sure you wouldn't be late on your first day,' he said.

And instantly the fear came charging back. It was here: the day I'd prayed would never come. Any hope that my father might have a change of heart and take us back to our own country flickered and finally died.

The policeman didn't move. With sweat glistening on his

3

black-brown skin he just glared at my mother and father and me as we sat rigidly in silence. It was getting hotter and hotter now the air wasn't rushing through the open windows. Beyond the car, insects clicked and buzzed in the dry grass. We were miles from anywhere. Anywhere but here.

A moment later the motorcade rushed by at a million miles an hour, the cars all secretive and dark. I didn't know which one was the Prime Minister's because you couldn't see behind the tinted glass, though I guessed it was the biggest and sleekest Mercedes in the middle with the flags.

'You see that?' My father spoke with the look of a child gazing through a toy shop window. 'There goes a great, great man. He's given the people freedom – what could be a greater achievement than that?'

He caught my confused look in the rear-view mirror.

'Didn't you read the book I gave you?'

I nodded, lying, but he knew perfectly well I hated history.

'For generations, Europeans have treated Africa like a play-ground. We've carved it up amongst ourselves, stolen its riches and not given a damn about the poor people who live here.'

My mother sighed but my father was in full swing now.

'Britain claimed *this* land and called it Rhodesia, but the black Africans have fought back at last and tipped the balance of power, son. White minority rule is over, thank goodness. Rhodesia no longer exists. This is Zimbabwe. And, now that the fighting has finally finished, that man there's going to do tremendous things for this country, you mark my words. He's a hero.'

I nodded subserviently while inside I was chewing over his words: *tipped the balance of power*. It seemed a strange expression to me because it gave me an image of a seesaw, and when one end was up the other was always down. It was never actually balanced.

The tail of the motorcade whooshed by, followed by yet more policemen on motorbikes, sirens wailing. Our man joined them and left us in a cloud of red dust that filled the car and made a mess of everything.

'Yes indeed, a hero. Do you know something, darling?' My father spoke to my mother. 'If I could meet him, just to be in the same room as him, I would consider it the greatest moment of my life.'

And he made a silly laughing sound as if it were something that might actually happen.

He never did meet Mr Mugabe. For me, it was to be a very different story.

TWO

We pulled off the main road and between huge stone pillars that bore Haven School's name. Up a willow-lined drive, then down and round to where the boarding houses were. A jostle of vehicles had already filled the small car park, a reassuring reminder of life beyond the grounds. The baking January sun glinted off windscreens.

My father stopped the engine and sat a moment without speaking, looking up at Selous House – my house – like it was a monument or something.

'Named after Frederick Courteney Selous, one of Rhodesia's founding figures,' he said at last, as if we hadn't stopped talking about it. 'All five boarding houses in the school are named after Rhodesian founders. Giving names of important people to buildings and places is just one way the white government asserted power.'

He gave me a meaningful nod.

'But that's in the past now. Colonialism is an outdated ideal that was never going to work. It doesn't matter who you are, you can't simply plant a flag and claim rights over someone else's land. This is Africa, for Africans. And black people had every right to rise up and use aggression.'

Even though most of the other parents and boys around us were white I started to feel even more nervous about being here, and I wondered if he knew how he was making me feel. I opened my mouth to speak.

'So was that what the war was about?' I asked. 'Land?'

'*This* is what it was about,' he replied, finding and pointing to a black family standing isolated on the grass. The boy was small and looking at his shoes while his parents tried to appear relaxed. 'The winds of change. Opportunity for all. Boys like him wouldn't have been allowed in a school like this before independence. But you can't suppress people because of the colour of their skin. Or at all, for that matter. Do you think it was right?'

'No,' I said.

'It was utterly, utterly wrong.' I wasn't sure my father had heard me. 'White people should be ashamed.'

He climbed out and walked enthusiastically towards the family. Soon, the three grown-ups laughed, and I noticed some of the white parents glancing and shaking their heads.

My mother sat silently in the front fanning her face. She'd cried almost the whole way here.

'It won't be so bad,' she said, a line she'd fed me on and off all through Christmas – I'd felt safe then, despite the weirdness of unwrapping presents in the heat, as though the start of the school year might never find me. But it had. 'You'll make lots of new friends, you won't have time to be sad.'

We sat and watched my father. Two tall senior boys greeted him politely as they passed. My father puffed himself up and stroked his beard, and responded in the voice he saved for the telephone. He looked strange today, wrapped in one of his London suits as if he was on business. All the other fathers were in short-sleeved shirts, shorts, desert boots and long socks. Their wives wore floral-print dresses like ones I'd seen on old British TV programmes.

'You mustn't blame your father,' my mother spoke again. 'He has a very different sort of background, his parents never had money. He feels very strongly that you should take the opportunities he never had.'

She dabbed her nostrils with a tissue.

'The Embassy has been very kind in offering to pay the fees. We could certainly never afford a school like this on your father's salary.'

'He could get another job.' I spoke petulantly into my tie knot. 'In England. He acts like a stupid history teacher most of the time, he could be one of those.'

'Now, now. Don't be rude,' my mother told me, but with her face pointing the other way.

She blew her nose.

'This country is our home for the time being,' she went on dutifully. I could tell she was forcing her mouth into a smile. 'It'll be better this time. I believe that, I really do. Back at home your father's old department just didn't appreciate his . . . *skills*, but I think he'll finally find his feet with this new job. He's running a whole office. Things will be different.'

'But I don't really know anything about this country,' I said, a plea as I eyed the small boy over on the grass who now appeared to be looking right back at me. 'What if they don't like me?'

She turned round again.

'Then we *will* go back, one way or another. I promise. It's where we belong. We can go and live with Granny while we settle back. She says we're always welcome. She misses us so much since we left.'

Now her smile was real.

'But you have to promise you'll at least try. If you can do that then I'll see what I can do. Your father does listen to me sometimes, he does care. Maybe he can put in for a transfer – I'm sure the Civil Service does that sort of thing all the time. Deal?'

I nodded quickly up and down, knowing I could believe her optimism, and my mother leaned into the back to give me a hug. Beyond, my father waved me out with impatience.

'You're at grown-up school now, Robert, you don't want the other boys seeing that,' he said as I went to him. Until that point I'd always been Bobby. It seemed Bobby had been left at home and I wished I was there with him.

I lowered my head and pulled on the oversized blue blazer that itched my skin.

'We've found you a new friend,' my father went on, pointing to the small black boy. 'He's starting today too. This is Nelson. Nelson, this is Robert. You two are going to be best friends.'

Nelson's father smiled and agreed. Nelson himself didn't move until his father gave him a nudge, and he nodded a silent hello. His eyes cried out that he was in fact having the same kind of day as me, and we laughed anxiously together. It wasn't a sound we would make many times that first term.

'Nelson can give you a hand with your trunk, if you ask nicely,' my father added.

My head went down again and he folded his arms. His shirt had dark blots all over it and was tight across his stomach.

'Come on, stop that. You're thirteen years of age,' I was told as if it were news.

Nelson and his parents were watching me, and I looked away.

'Time to take your trunk in, Robert. Up you go.'

'Can Mum come?'

'Your mother isn't feeling well in this heat.'

'But can't she come up, please? Can't she come and see me before you . . .'

Go, was the word that wouldn't form.

My father stood solid, then eventually uncrossed his arms.

'I'll see what I can do.' He took his wallet and extracted two ten-dollar notes, thought about it, then put one of them back. 'Here. And don't go spending it all on sweets in the first week.'

* * *

When I was little my father always insisted on covering any scrape, large or small, with a lock-tight plaster because he said the city we lived in was filthy dirty and infection spread quickly in hot weather. I hated it because I knew when the time came to take it off again he was going to make me cry.

It was always the same: 'OK, Bobby, I want you to count to five. One, two . . .'

Not once did I ever get to five. Apparently it was for the best.

That's what it felt like the whole of that day: counting to five, waiting for the pain.

The dorm was big and open-plan with about twenty beds – ten beds on each side of a chest-high wall. The floor was an ocean of grooved tiles the colour of dried blood, and the walls were painted a stark white. Louvred glass filled the room with light. You could see right over the lower playing fields and across the bush but it felt like looking out of a cage because all the windows still had grenade screens on them from the war.

We carried our trunks up one after the other. When we were done I sat on my bed and it pushed against me, a mere pancake of foam over a thin board on legs. Everyone had their own wooden locker next to them, and sheets and blankets had been folded and put on the top.

'You reckon we have to make them ourselves?' I asked.

'Guess,' said Nelson. 'Do you know anyone here?'

I shook my head.

'Me neither,' he said. 'I wish I did. Someone to look out for me, like an older brother. It wouldn't be nearly so bad with an older brother. We're from Town. And you?'

I told him.

'Close to Town but just outside. It's really boring there sometimes. My dad doesn't like cities because of all the people.

But we're British really, from England,' I added before I could stop myself. The words were suddenly guilty on my tongue, abrasive. They never had been before. 'Does that mean you hate me?'

Nelson frowned. 'Why should I hate you?'

'Because I'm British. And . . . you know . . . the war.'

'The war wasn't against Britain.'

'Oh.'

'I obviously didn't fight in the war, but even if I had been old enough and you'd been too, I still wouldn't hate you.'

'Oh?' It was my turn to be confused. 'Why not?'

'Because surely wars are about putting an end to a wrong, not making a new one?'

'I guess so.'

'Most black people don't hate white people, and most whites don't hate blacks.'

'So what *was* the war about, then?'

He fidgeted slightly.

'Some of the white people that first came loved Africa and everything in it, just not the Africans. They didn't understand us, so they treated us differently . . . badly . . . and that wasn't fair. That's what my dad says.'

'I didn't realize,' I said.

Nelson shrugged. 'It's all over now, that's the main thing. Hey, at least your folks live close, it won't be difficult for them to visit.'

'My dad says it'll be worse for me if they come.'

'*Ja*, mine too. Looks like it's just us then. Maybe we should look out for each other, hey?'

'Like brothers?'

'*Ja*,' he said. 'Like brothers.'

'Yeah,' I said, pleased. 'You're on.'

We shook hands to cement the deal.

I flipped the catches on my trunk. Khaki shorts and shirts for classes, black trousers and white shirts for evenings and Sunday chapel, socks, shoes, sports whites, pyjamas . . . Matilda, our maid, had ironed, folded and packed my stuff immaculately. Postcards from my grandmother lay safely on top in a protective envelope.

The dorm was filling up. A boy came panting in towards us with flushed cheeks because he was carrying his trunk on his own. He dropped it too early and it clattered to the floor. The name on the lid said *Jeremy Simpson-Prior*.

'You want a hand with that?' I offered, but he shook his head and wiped snot.

Boys were looking over from the other side of the partition. One of them kept staring at me – or maybe at Nelson, I couldn't tell – and eventually he came round and tapped my shoulder.

'There's a spare bed next to mine,' he said.

His eyes were a sharp, intense green. I glanced away to Nelson, who I think was only pretending not to listen as he started to unpack.

'I'm OK here,' I said.

'Are you serious? Next to stinking chocolate-face here?'

Simpson-Prior barked out a laugh. If it was a joke I didn't get it.

'Take the bed.'

'Really, I'm fine where I am,' I replied, feeling a whole new sensation of nervousness.

To my relief, the boy shrugged. 'Your choice,' he said, but then gave Nelson a push against the wall.

I had to do something. Nelson was doing his best not to look at anybody, as if he wanted everyone to go away, but we'd just made a promise.

'Hey! Leave him alone,' I said, not quite knowing what would happen.

The boy with the green eyes blazed at me, and I thought maybe he'd hit me. Instead, he simply pointed at my face.

'Don't say I didn't give you a chance.'

'I'll come,' Simpson-Prior stood eagerly. 'I'll sleep over on your side.'

The boy didn't even pause to think about it and turned Simpson-Prior's trunk right over, spilling everything.

'Why would I want a poof like you next to me? Your breath stinks.'

That was my first encounter with Ivan Hascott. It wasn't going to be my last. Not by a long shot.

We continued unpacking our stuff. I checked my watch and glanced at the door but couldn't hear my father coming, and as the minutes went by I realized he wasn't coming back at all, that this time he hadn't even let me start counting before ripping off this particular plaster.

Nelson kept himself busy, taking his time over everything.

'Are you OK?' I asked him.

He nodded. '*Ja*. Fine. Thanks for helping.'

'Any time. See? We're like brothers already.'

And if someone had told me then how badly I would actually come to let him down – and in the way I did it – I would never, ever have believed them.

THREE

Our official introduction to the house involved us being herded into the common room where Mr Craven, our housemaster, was waiting.

I can't recall exactly what he said that night though. A greeting. A welcome. Some acknowledgment that as the third years, the youngest in the school, we might be feeling homesick but that wasn't anything to dwell on because we'd get over it, there was a lot to take in and a lot to find out so if we didn't know anything we mustn't hide in a corner; we should *ask*.

Then he left and a senior called Taylor took over. He was tall with wide shoulders, a strong jaw and sandy hair. Handsome. Stern-yet-fair. Matter-of-fact without menace. Everything about him said Head of House. His tie was different from anyone else's. In fact, the two other sixth formers behind him – Greet and Leboule – weren't like him at all. They just eyed us in a way that made us feel like intruders while Taylor welcomed us new boys to Selous in a smooth and controlled voice.

'Forbes, Heyman, Burnett, Willoughby . . . Those are the other houses, each named after an important person' – I straightened my back, strangely pleased with my father for telling me that – 'and I daresay the boys in those houses might try and kid you that theirs is the best. But they'd be wrong. Selous House is the best house in the school, in the best school in the country. No one can take that away from us, so take pride and don't let the house down.'

He went on to read out the study room list. There were only ten boys to each room, and Simpson-Prior was already frantically wetting his lips because our names had been read out with Ivan's, while Nelson escaped and was placed in the next study along the corridor.

The parquet floor reeked of polish, instantly establishing itself as the smell of New Term. Simpson-Prior pushed past and grabbed the best cubicle and pointed me to the one in front.

'Go there! Go there!' What Ivan had said about his breath was true, it was as if he had rotting meat in his teeth, plus he followed certain words with a fine spray of spit. But I felt sorry for him because he seemed more afraid than anyone else. I'd thought I was going to be that person, being in a new school *and* a new country, but I wasn't. 'We can swap prep easily,' he said.

I put my tuck box onto the desk, which made a loud creak.

Ivan came in and sneered at us before taking a cubicle on the other side of the room. He had a red mark on his cheek as if he'd been hit.

'Shit. Not you two,' he said.

Before I had a chance to react, a more senior boy – the only black boy in the house I'd seen other than Nelson – suddenly rushed in and twisted Ivan round. Ivan lost his balance and fell to the floor.

'Don't walk away from me,' the senior barked. 'I know it was you. If you ever push Nelson around again . . .'

Maybe he didn't know it yet, but clearly Nelson had someone else looking out for him. I felt strangely jealous, and a little bit alone again.

Ivan was belligerent.

'So what if I did? Why do you care?'

The senior boy glared. His tongue – bright pink against his deep brown skin – darted like a snake's to lick his lips.

'Things are different now. You lost the war. It's not how it used to be, remember? So I'm warning you, white boy.'

And he stole a packet of Chappies sweets from Ivan's tuck before heading out.

Ivan got up and pushed his shirt back into his trousers.

'What the fuck are you looking at?' his voice growled. He marched right up to me, blocking the light from the window while Simpson-Prior slipped back out of the room.

For the first time I consciously registered the murky tanned colour of Ivan's face, which somehow made him look older, and his curling brown hair that was thick and rich and tinted by the sun conversely giving him boyish appeal. But then camouflage and contradictions were one of the dangers of Ivan, something I wouldn't realize until it was much too late.

He was waiting, so I asked, 'Who was that?'

For a moment I thought he was going to get me for earlier.

'Told me his name is Ngoni Kasanka.' He smiled instead. 'Remember it. He's a bastard. I'm telling you, he's going to be trouble.'

'Why was he picking on you? Does he know you?'

'No.'

'Do you know him?'

'No. He's more senior than us and that's just the way shit rolls in a school like this, seniors can do what they like to us. We're just squacks. Bottom of the heap. Don't you know anything?'

Then the smile disappeared.

'But I know he's only doing it because I picked on that Nelson. And I bet he's already dreaming of being Head of House one day, Head of School if he can – I can tell he's that sort – and God help us the day *that* happens.'

'How come?'

Ivan shrugged in a *well-it's-obvious-isn't-it?* kind of way.

'You can't have a Kaffir running things. It isn't right. Don't you see?'

I blushed and shuffled my feet. My father had warned me the merest mention of the K-word was illegal and could send you to prison now.

'Yeah,' I said. Anything to make him go away.

'Don't say "Yeah", you sound like a Pom. Open up.' Ivan pointed at my tuck box and hovered. I did as I was told. 'Jeez, you haven't got much, have you? Your folks must be tight.'

He grabbed the packet of biscuits, the tin of condensed milk and the only two bars of chocolate I had.

The school ate all its meals together. Simpson-Prior and I sat with the other eight boys from our study room, and Ivan made sure we were at the bottom two places. No one spoke to us so I spent much of the time gazing round the hall and at the lines of tables with mostly white faces.

Up on one expanse of wall there were wooden plaques with gold lettering displaying lists of Haven old boys, while another roll of honour was headed 'Brave Boys Who Have Fallen': *Banatar FG, Burnett House 1973; Fearnhead TE, Forbes House 1974; de Beer WS, Heyman House 1976* . . . In total I counted thirty-seven old boys who'd fallen and never got up again.

As far away as possible from this list was a framed photograph of Robert Mugabe, because all schools and public buildings had to have the new Prime Minister on display. His black face beamed like he'd been caught at the end of a joke.

A spoon came clattering to our end of the table.

'Hey!' It was Ivan. 'What are you two gawping at? We need more bread.'

'*Ja*, more bread, stupid,' the boy next to him echoed, spraying crumbs from his mouth. His name was Derek De Klomp, and he hung on Ivan's every word like a new best friend. He looked to me like a gorilla, with thick black eyebrows hanging like weights and swollen lips that never quite managed to meet.

'Put some spoof into it, Simpson-Prior. *Jislaaik*! You are one ugly baboon.'

The table laughed as Simpson-Prior consciously or subconsciously concealed his buckteeth, his small, sprout-like ears burning pink. So I went, but in the steamy kitchen the African workers stared like I was coming to steal, and then one started shouting something I couldn't understand and waved me away.

When I went back empty-handed and tried to explain, Ivan snatched the plate. Less than a minute later he came back with a pile of thick white slices.

'You've got to put them in their place,' he said.

I didn't know if he was talking *to* me or *about* me.

Later, when we were getting ready for bed, Ivan came to our side of the dorm.

'Kasanka says I have to stop pushing you around,' he told Nelson.

Nelson looked scared. 'I didn't tell, Hascott. Honest.'

'Good. So he shouldn't hear about me ripping up your bed, then,' Ivan went on, and pulled Nelson's sheets and blankets until they were in a pile, looking at me as he did it. When I opened my mouth to say something he cut me off with, 'Relax, Pommie, it's only a bit of fun.'

Simpson-Prior laughed like it was something cool, but if he thought it would win him favour he was wrong, because Ivan destroyed his bed as well.

'See?' Ivan said to me, as if that proved he was right. 'Just a bit of fun. Sleep well, girls.'

At nine exactly our light was snapped off and we were told to get our heads down. Two of the sixth formers, Greet and Leboule, menaced the dorm in the dark for a full ten minutes to make sure there was no talking, Greet knocking a hockey stick against the ends of beds. No one dared do or say anything. They were the top of the school, all-powerful; they could do anything they wanted so we lay still and hoped they'd just go away.

Every morning, in the haze before waking, there was a brief moment when I thought I wasn't there, that I was far away somewhere else – at home, in England with my grandmother, anywhere. Those were the best moments of the day.

I wrote to my mother constantly, and almost all the letters started with the word 'Please'.

FOUR

One morning at the end of our very first week we were waiting for Mr Dunn for the start of Geography. He had told us all to go not into the classroom but around the rugby fields and into the bush slightly, over by Monkey Hill, where there was a special rock formation he wanted to show us.

Geography was the only class Nelson and I shared, and as we walked together behind the rest of the class he pointed out what I thought were patches of weed in the grass and told me to step clear of them.

'Why?'

Nelson bent low and put a narrow finger to something growing the size of a large coin, with two points sticking up.

'Devil thorns,' he explained. 'Watch out for those. Tread on one and you'll know about it, it'll go right through your shoe. Hey, look! Lion ants!'

Close by, miniature craters had pockmarked the sandy ground, and Nelson snapped off a blade of grass and gently prodded the edge of one of the indentations.

'What are you doing?' I wanted to know.

'Watch,' he said. 'You won't have seen these in England.'

The tiny grains at the bottom of the hole started to shift. I thought he was making it happen somehow, then suddenly they lifted in a mini eruption and something too quick to see darted out, grabbed the end of the grass from Nelson's fingers and pulled it down and into the sand. The grass wriggled as it went, as if trying to escape.

'That's so cool.' I'd never seen anything like it.

'*Lekker*, hey?' Nelson agreed with a smile.

'You didn't wait,' said another voice.

I smelled then heard Simpson-Prior coming up next to me. His feet landed too close to the lion ants and filled in all their holes, and Nelson got up and stood back slightly.

Simpson-Prior hovered accusingly, sweating. The brown grass was taking a particularly harsh beating that day, and even though the sky was full of clouds they seemed too afraid of the bullying sun to get in the way.

'I thought you were going to wait,' he said again.

When I didn't say anything he took my elbow and led me a few feet away.

'Sorry about that,' he went on, meaning the yellowing bruise that Ivan and De Klomp had taken turns in kneading into my arm the night before.

I hid my annoyance and made as if it was no big deal. Simpson-Prior had been caught whispering to see my work during prep and everyone in the study room had got a Task for it. As far as Ivan was concerned it had been my fault.

'Hascott's right, we should have been more careful,' I said.

'That's not why he picks on you. He's only like that because . . . You know.' Simpson-Prior checked over his shoulder and made his voice low. '*Jislaaik*! You've got to be careful what you say these days. He's only like that because you're friends with that Ndube. He hates him.'

'Nelson? Why, what's he done?'

'He hasn't *done* anything.' He smirked horribly. 'He's just, you know . . . I don't know what it's like in England but you don't really make friends with *them* here. You will let me copy in tests, hey?'

A bee flew close by and he ducked and swatted like a mad man. Some of the other boys from the class jeered at him.

'I'm always getting stung,' he explained to me proudly. 'Once, when I was eight, a bee flew into our car and stung me five times and I didn't cry.'

'I thought bees could only sting once,' I pointed out.

He paused before shaking his head. 'This one stung me five times.'

Suddenly the whole class erupted into commotion. I thought there were more bees but something rustled through the brittle scrub and I felt it move over my foot. By the time I looked I saw the green markings disappear into the trees. I yelped and staggered backwards into a bush just as Mr Dunn appeared.

'Jacklin!' he bellowed. 'What the hell are you playing at? I said, *No talking*.'

The snake had slipped deeper into the leaves. It moved quickly, tail flicking. Everyone rushed around and talked at once.

'Where did it go?'

'What sort was it?'

'Must be a python,' Ivan declared. 'We get hordes of them on our farm.'

'Or a boomslang. It looked like a boomslang.'

'Hey, Ndube. Catch!' Ivan shouted, flicking something snake-sized at Nelson and making him leap. Ivan and De Klomp cut him with laughs. 'Jeez, it's only a piece of bark, you poof. Do one of your witch doctor dances, that should bring it out.'

All the while no one had noticed that Simpson-Prior was now a few metres away and moving stealthily through the tall grass. He stopped to break off a bit of tree, snapped the end so that it was forked, and then gently stabbed the ground.

'*Eweh!* Check it out,' he called.

We rushed over. He'd pinned the snake down, and we all jumped as it thrashed around, but as soon as Simpson-Prior put his hands to it and picked it up by the back of the neck it suddenly came over all calm – sleepy, almost, like it had been drugged – and gently coiled its tail around his arm.

Simpson-Prior's eyes glazed. He brought the snake frighteningly close to his face.

'Green mamba.' His cheeks glowed, and in that brief moment the usual drawn, tense expression had gone and he looked brilliantly happy. For no real reason I felt irritated by him, perhaps because for the first time he seemed less afraid than I was, and I wished I could be that happy.

'She's a beauty. And you found her.' He turned to me, and I felt guilty for thinking the way I was about him.

'Is it dangerous?'

Everyone laughed at me.

'Deadly,' Simpson-Prior nodded.

'Jeez, Prior, you are bloody *penga*,' Ivan said. 'Kill it.'

Mr Dunn agreed, but Simpson-Prior pleaded and asked if he could just let it go.

'OK. But take it right out into the bush, as far away from the school as possible. And take that clown Jacklin with you.'

The other boys groaned enviously. I asked if Nelson could come with us but Sir said absolutely not.

Nelson was standing on his own, looking adrift and wilting under Ivan's gaze.

'Please, sir?'

Mr Dunn rolled his eyes and nodded sternly.

'Hurry up.'

Simpson-Prior talked about snakes the whole way. I liked the fact that he was so enthusiastic but at the same time felt sorry for him because it made him even more different from most other boys, and anyone who's different in school will always be a target.

When we were far away, he crouched low and gently put the snake on the ground, readied himself, then leaped back.

The mamba had already disappeared. Simpson-Prior laughed with relief.

'Did you check? How quick she moved? *Lekker*, man. And you found her.'

I think, though I can't remember for sure, that it was a green mamba that killed Jeremy Simpson-Prior. Certainly a snake of some kind. But that was much later, when he was a young working man doing the thing he loved in a game park down in the low veld, long after he'd run away because of what we did to him. His death, at least, had nothing to do with us.

'. . . So I look down and this thing's going over my foot, and it feels . . . *weird* . . .'

The five-minute warning for Lights Out had rung. Most of the dorm were in their PJs and on beds while I was still buzzing with words tripping off my tongue. I must have told the story four times that evening and I didn't mind one more in the slightest. Nelson was by my side, and Fairford and Lambretti and the Agostinho cousins listened intently, while Simpson-Prior waited for the part that involved him.

'. . . and I swear, it checks round at me like it's going to graze my leg, one-time.'

I was even talking like everyone else.

'Meanwhile your *machendes* have shrunk to the size of a couple of peas,' one of the Agostinho cousins heckled.

'And let's not even mention the chocolate runway in your gudds,' Lambretti rabbit-punched me. Everyone roared.

'Shut up, guys,' I said.

This was great.

A missile flew across the dorm. A shoe. Ivan was standing by the door.

'You girls stop shouting,' he breathed heavily. 'I could hear you squealing from the top of the stairs.'

Everyone went to their beds but Ivan didn't move.

'You're sounding like a Pom again.'

'Sorry, Hascott,' I said.

'Greet wants tea. He wants *you* to make it for him.'

'Why me?'

He threw his other shoe.

'Because it has to be someone's turn and I told him it should be you.'

Over the last six nights some random boy had been selected to make Greet's tea, and at least three of them had come back crying.

'Get a move on. Two cups.'

My stomach bunched and loosened as I stood up to go. It was a comfort to feel Nelson at my side, coming with me, but Ivan blocked his path.

'Where do you think *you're* going?'

'To help,' said Nelson.

'Greet doesn't want *you* touching his mug. He wants Jacklin. Only Jacklin.'

Greet's study was right at the end of the sixth-form corridor. The gloom seemed to thicken the further I went. His door was open, and as the kettle filled the seniors' kitchen with steam I could hear voices over a watery cassette player trying its best with Def Leppard or Van Halen or someone like that.

When the tea was made I stood at the door and dutifully lowered my head. Leboule was in there too, swinging a bat and practising cricket strokes. Greet himself lay on his bed in the far corner, waving his stick in the air as he broke wind. Above his head, the green and white of the Rhodesian flag clung belligerently and illegally to the wall next to an equally dangerous poster of a white soldier with the words *Rhodesians Never Die*. It was the only decoration Greet had given his room other than a dozen or so empty Castle lager cans along a shelf instead of books.

A fire crackled. It was January, the middle of summer, but I didn't dare think anything strange about having a fire going.

Greet spotted me first.

'At last.' He pointed towards the mantelpiece. 'Put them there.'

The heat of the fire pushed against my trousers as I got near. The smell of wood smoke was strong. There was something mixed with it, and out of the corner of my eye I could see the red of a pack of Madisons peeking out from Leboule's pocket.

Leboule hit an imaginary six. 'Who are you?'

'Jacklin.'

'First name?'

'Robert.'

'Serious? As in *Rroh-bett*? Like our *grrreat Mist-ah Muga-beh*?' he mimicked. 'Your parents must have hated you. Are you a Pom?'

'I was born in England, but—'

'In that case I loathe you. Get out.'

He turned his back. Defensive shot.

I put the mugs down and turned.

'Wait,' Greet called before I made it. He was holding out his hand. My heart thudded. 'Do you expect me to fetch it myself? Bring it to me, you queer.'

One was a Haven School mug, the other was brown and had a picture of a white family looking over a huge dam with *Kariba* above it and *Rhodesia Is Super* underneath. I'd seen Greet drinking from it before and took it to him. He looked pissed off that I'd got it right.

'Think you're clever, hey, squack? How am I supposed to

take it if you're holding the handle? You want me to burn myself?'

'No, Greet.' A tremor had come into my voice.

'Then hold it. Like this. With both hands.'

The warmth spread into my palms and quickly became heat as Greet teased.

'I'm not thirsty yet, go stand by the fire. Nice and close.' He lay back against his pillow. His stick started to swing again. 'So you're a Pommie.'

'I was, but now I live here.'

'So? You're still a Pom. In what way do you think you're not a Pom, Pommie?'

Of course, I didn't know.

'What are you doing in our country?'

'My dad is attached to the British Embassy.'

'Oh, *is* he now.' Greet gave his best English accent, a cocktail of aristocrat and chimney sweep. 'How very *noice* for dear Papa, being at-*'atched* to the Bri'ish Embassy. Must be a *lekker* job, hey? The Bri'ish Embassy, cor bloimey.'

Leboule fed him laughs.

'So what's wrong with Pommieland? Too much rain for you?'

'Yes,' I said too eagerly, fear making me betray the land I'd been born in and yearned to go back to.

'Place is a mess. You let your blacks get out of control, they're all taking drugs and starting riots and shagging white women, and the government lets them get away with it. I could never live in a place like that.'

'Yes. I mean, no.'

'And now people like you think you can come here and screw our country again. Wasn't Lancaster House enough?'

I didn't know what or where Lancaster House was, just that it wasn't good.

Greet let the silence needle me. A log spat. Sweat was starting to run down my legs.

'Or does your old man just enjoy African women?' Leboule wanted to know, swinging the bat towards my groin. Boiling tea spilled over my knuckles. 'Well? Does he?'

I remembered now that Leboule had been one of the seniors who'd walked by and greeted my father while he was talking to Nelson's parents.

'He tried to get a posting in lots of countries,' was my only defence. 'Thailand, Singapore, India . . .'

Leboule scoffed. 'A Kaffir's a Kaffir, whatever the country. Your old man like the taste of coloured women? Or is it because he's crap at what he does and can't hold down a job in Pommieland?'

'He was in the army once,' I said, as always hoping it might give me some credibility.

Greet reacted suddenly. How was I to know the things he'd gone through? In those early days how was I to know what a *lot* of people had gone through while the country was being ravaged by war?

The stick stopped and he glared. Even Leboule seemed uncertain. Then Greet got off the bed and came right up close.

'The British army?' he breathed. I could smell cigarettes and the beef and cabbage we'd had for supper. His eyes reflected the fire like broken glass in the sun. 'They're the worst of the bloody lot. I hate them the most.'

Now I fully expected something bad to happen so I was surprised when he removed his mug from my red and swollen hands. The skin sang merry hell. He took a long sip and I wondered if that was it – he hated me, but I could live with that as long as he let me go.

He put the drink down.

Kneeling, he grabbed the ends of my trousers with his fingers and pulled. I didn't get it at first; it seemed a bit weird. A moment later the black material was gripping my calves. Pain roared and dug in. I could feel the hairs curl and singe under polyester that had soaked up the heat of the flames like metal. Already the blisters I'd have for days were starting to bubble. Fortunately there were no tears, but they would come later.

Greet stood.

'Now piss off, Pommie bastard. You make shit tea, I'd rather have a bloody black do it.'

Leboule sniped my backside with the bat hard enough to push the air from my lungs. The door slammed behind me.

Before I reached the end of the corridor the sound of Don Henley on cassette was drowned by their own gruff voices.

'We are Rhodesians and we'll fight through thick and thin,' they sang.

'Three six six five, please.'

The handset was black and heavy in my hand. I struggled to keep my voice from cracking. I knew I was breaking all the rules but I had to. I didn't care. I needed to tell my mother what it was like. I needed her to take me away.

The operator made a gentle slap with his tongue – a lazy sound. I made up a picture instantly: a friendly black face, half-lidded and drugged with sleep. As I sat in the lightless telephone booth I kept one eye out of the small window, checking, but the school was dead beneath the moonlight. My legs throbbed.

'The tellyphone exchange is closed,' said the voice. I knew the operator room was nearby, at the back of the kitchens where we weren't allowed, but he sounded miles away. 'The telly-phone exchange is open between six eh-em and nine pee-em, you must try again tomorrow, pliss.'

Tomorrow?

'It's an emergency.'

'Then you must speak with your house mastah. The telly-phone exchange is closed now. From nine pee-em in the evening until six eh-em in the morning.'

'I have to get through tonight. Please.'

He thought about it. 'What is your name?'

Maybe he sensed the desperation in my words, or maybe he'd just had too many boys like me in the past.

'Jacklin. Robert Jacklin.'

'*Manheru*, Rhrob-ett. *Tonana mangwana.*'

'Pardon? I don't understand.'

'I said, good evening, Rhrob-ett. But I am very very sorry, the tellyphone exchange . . .'

The receiver weighed like a brick. A hundred metres away Selous House was hulking in the dark, waiting.

'Mastah Rhrob-ett?'

'Yes?'

'My name is Weekend,' he said, 'and I will be here tomorrow.'

FIVE

During the war a number of black anti-Rhodesian fighters had been found on the school grounds and killed down by the squash courts. If you looked closely you could see where gouges made by the bullets hitting the wall (all close together, even though it was claimed the terrorists had been running away) had been filled in and painted over. Mr Bullman, the Head, had discovered the terrorists and called in the Rhodesian Forces, and he'd been given official recognition for diligence and quick thinking.

Ivan took us down to see the gouges one Saturday morning after classes. He'd been acting all friendly for once but I quickly realized it was just a trick because, as soon as we got down there, he and De Klomp started pretending to be soldiers and fired imaginary guns at Nelson: '*Terrorist! Get him! Shoot the fucking gook!*'

We walked quickly away.

'That guy's a jerk,' I said. I could see Nelson was struggling with tears. 'Just ignore him.'

Somehow, he still managed to stay above it all.

'The war only ended three years ago,' he said. 'I guess it can take time to forget.'

He was small, and yet it was such a tall thing to say.

'Yeah, well, he's an idiot. We won't fall for something like that again.'

And at the time I meant it.

Nelson and I went back to the house and hid in the common

31

room. Simpson-Prior was hiding too. He'd failed the maths test and got into trouble, and he slashed a look at me for not having sat next to him.

You said I could copy.

I tried to say something but he just continued reading a copy of *Time* magazine which had pictures of Margaret Thatcher and Ronald Reagan on the front, and no one ever read those. I didn't like the way he was trying to make me feel so I went.

All that afternoon we had house trials for athletics. Taylor split us into groups, and because we were friends he put me in the 1500 metres with Nelson and sent us to the far end of the field to warm up. When it was our turn to run, Kasanka came up and pulled Nelson to one side.

'I want you to show these lame white asses what running is really about,' he said. He seemed angry. Had he found out about Ivan's stupid trick that morning? 'This is our country now. Don't let them beat you. Never let them beat you. You're better than any of them. You hear me?'

Nelson looked to the grass, embarrassed, but we'd all heard it.

Mr Bullman didn't usually take sports but he was the official starter. As he clicked his fingers at us to get to the line, I wondered if the gun was the one he'd used to capture the terrorists all those years ago.

'To your marks, gentlemen . . .'

And we were off. Dry grass filled the air as boys watching from the pavilion roared their houses on.

'. . . Come on, Forbes . . .'

'. . . That's it, Willoughby, keep it strong . . .'

'. . . Burnett's the best . . .'

'. . . Go, Heyman . . .'

'. . . All the way, Selous . . .'

At the end of the first lap I was right at the back. Ivan

yelled at me from the pavilion but Kasanka must have been grinning because Nelson was way in the lead. With two more laps to go I felt I should want to slow down or give up, but I kept the pace, and a lap later I was more than halfway through the order. The crowd was ecstatic. It felt like a race day as boys from all years swelled and cheered. Even Ivan. I saw him in the blur of boys, clapping and urging me on.

'Come on, Jacklin. You can do this. Only five places. You can *do it.*'

This was one of Haven's key lessons, I realized, the one about winning being everything, and for the first time I was more than just Robert Jacklin.

My feet were on springs. Fifth place was mine, then fourth, and on the back straight I climbed yet another rung on the ladder. With eighty metres to go I was on Nelson's heels and almost at the front, and everyone was going crazy, but suddenly my legs turned to lead. Nelson stretched the lead again and there was nothing I could do, and I sprawled across the line in sixth.

I lay in the sun with stars on the insides of my eyelids. I felt shade, and when I looked Ivan was standing over me, panting like he'd run his own race.

'How could you let the Kaffir win?'

The anger was as black as it was deep, and I felt more alone than ever.

To my relief, he turned and marched across the playing fields, shaking his head.

'Good race, man.' Nelson came over and offered a shy arm to pull me up. 'You know, I didn't win because of what Kasanka said. I just love running.'

'It doesn't matter if you did,' I said. 'You're really good and I'm glad. Showed Ivan a thing or two.'

But Nelson still seemed suspicious and watched Ivan storming across the field.

'Was that about me?'

'No,' I lied. But I hated myself for making sure Ivan wasn't looking before I shook Nelson's hand. 'Honest. He's in a mood. I don't care.'

And when we got back to the house I cared even less because waiting for me was a postcard from my grandmother, the first since the start of term. I knew it was from her straightaway; a picture of one of those chocolate box villages drenched in perfect snow.

Darling Bobby, it began. *How is your new school? I think about you every day. Here's somewhere I haven't sent you before. Maybe one day I can show it to you for real, darling, with all the snow!!*

Yes. One day soon, I thought. I imagined how it would be living in that village, away from school and away from boys like Greet and Ivan, and I smiled right up until after showers, which was when the day plummeted with no warning at all.

Funny how good things always seemed to happen before the bad.

'Has anyone seen my tie?' I asked the dorm as I changed into my evening uniform, but already I had a sinking feeling about this.

No one had so I had no option but to line up, ears on fire, with a gap round my neck while Ivan sniggered and trembled from trying not to let it out. Greet was taking roll call that evening. He almost didn't notice but Ivan trod on my toes and made me cry out.

Greet shot back. 'Where the hell is your tie?'

'Floating in the piss trough,' someone further up shouted. The whole line laughed. Everyone except Greet.

'After supper,' he said, 'come to my study.'

Tears needled the corners of my eyes. Only then did he smile.

* * *

'Three six six five, please.'

There was only the sound of the operator breathing. I thought he was going to just tell me the exchange was closed again but something made him change his mind.

'Is this Mastah Rhrob-ett who is speaking? This is Weekend. How are you this evening?' And when I couldn't answer him: 'Is this your parents you are trying to make call, Mastah Rhrob-ett?'

'Yes,' I said. 'Yes, it is.'

'One moment, pliss.'

There was a hum. My eyes were swimming and blurred, my heart throbbed in my ears in time with the pain. Then, after what seemed like eternity, my father.

'Robert.' It was neither question nor statement. 'We spoke about this. No calls. Not this soon. It'll only make it harder for you.'

In the background I caught a noise and pictured a bottle pushing amongst bottles.

'Is Mum there?'

I could hear my father lifting his eyes to the ceiling.

'It's gone nine, you know how your mother gets . . . sleepy.'

'I need to speak to her.'

'About what?'

'I want to ask her. About something she once said.'

He sighed. 'Make it quick.'

I heard the phone being handed over. Then my mother, incredibly near as though she was trying to climb down the wire.

'Darling? Are you all right? I'm missing you so, so much. I mean, we both are.' Her voice was slightly loose, like she'd just woken up.

Suddenly the words I'd wanted weren't there. It had seemed so easy in my mind.

'Mum . . .' It was like there was something in my throat, stopping anything from coming. 'I don't like . . . I want to . . .'

I swallowed hard and had to put my head against the wall.

Gently, she filled the gap.

'You'll never guess who I got a letter from today.'

The corner of my mouth twitched up. 'From Granny? I did too.'

'She received the photographs I sent. She thinks you're ever so good-looking in your uniform. She's shown all her friends, and Marjorie Downe's granddaughter is dying to see you again, by all accounts.'

'Mum!'

'You remember Natalie, don't you? I don't think she knew what a boy was the last time you and her met, but apparently she couldn't take her eyes off you. I'm sure none of the girls at home will be able to when we go back, you're the talk of the town. The mysterious boy from Africa. And so handsome!'

From somewhere I found a laugh.

'That's silly,' I said.

'It's true! Cross my heart.' And then, coming even closer: 'Bobby?'

'Yes, Mum?'

'I haven't forgotten, you know. About what I said in the car. We still have a deal, yes?' I found myself nodding even if she couldn't see. 'I want to go home too but your father assures me he's doing a good job of running the office and we have to give it a chance. We have to be fair. But if you're not happy I will discuss it with him very soon. I promise.'

'Yes, Mum.'

'Good boy. Just hang on in there a bit longer.' The sound of my father's voice rumbled somewhere behind her. 'I've got to go now. I'll write . . .'

Now he was taking the phone from her; I could hear the scratching of his beard.

'It's gone *nine*, Robert.' He carried on from where he'd left off, as if only just realizing what that meant. 'Shouldn't you be in bed?'

'I . . .'

'Goodbye, Robert. Sleep well.'

Clunk.

A few seconds passed. The sound of someone not saying anything, and then a gentle click as the operator closed the line.

SIX

It took forever, but that first term rolled and shuffled and eventually passed by. I couldn't wait to get home. None of us could. Four whole weeks of not being at school was a dream come true.

April turned into May. The rains had stopped and autumn was starting to bite the evening air. The holidays were good, but my father said he had to work all through them because his staff weren't up to scratch. It meant we couldn't go anywhere as a family like we'd planned. My mother met the news with a resigned nod and a long sip of her drink.

About two weeks in I phoned Nelson.

'What you up to?' he asked.

'Not much.' Which was true. The next bit wasn't though. 'This and that. You?'

'I've been selected to run for the National Junior Team,' he said, unable to contain his excitement. 'I've been training every day. It's *lekker*. The best thing ever.'

'I said you were good.' I was pleased for him. Then a drop of disappointment hissed on the flames. 'So you're busy every day?'

'*Ja*. But you can come watch me race if you like. It's not far, about half an hour's drive from yours.'

My mother walked past with an empty bottle and put it in the bin.

'Yeah. I'll ask my mum' I said, knowing I wouldn't. 'Sounds like a plan.'

I put the phone down. Now my mother was out on the veranda again, sighing as she picked up the paperback I could tell she wasn't really reading. She caught me looking at her, and suddenly pretended not to be sad, and waved.

I waved back, then slipped away to my room because there was nothing else to do. I took out my atlas again and looked up Britain, and found comfort by running my finger over the names of places I knew.

SEVEN

Our second term.

The counting of weeks started all over again. June arrived and autumn became winter.

It was another boring Sunday and we were sitting in our study room, drinking Milo for warmth. No one wanted to go out because a thick *guti* had been hanging around all morning and you could barely see twenty metres before the damp air turned everything grey.

'*Ja*, and do you remember the convoys?' Ivan talked towards the ceiling, tipping his chair right back and popping jelly babies into his mouth.

He and De Klomp were reminiscing about the war and they were letting me listen. Ivan let me do a lot of things these days. Nelson had been given special leave to go training almost every weekend, so he never seemed to be around any more, plus I think even Ivan felt sympathy for the amount of attention Greet was still giving me.

'Whenever we went on dirt roads my old man would get the first black he saw and make him sit on the bonnet, because he said they all knew where the land mines were. A lot of them didn't, but that didn't matter. Some of them shat themselves.'

He gave me a wink. Despite the cold, we were in good moods. It was hard not to get excited before half-term weekend, this term seemed to be going so much quicker than the first.

At that moment Simpson-Prior came into the room.

Normally I would have said Howzit but Ivan had warned us that some pictures of *Scope* babes had been found in his locker and so all the seniors were calling him 'Prior the Wire-Puller' now. It wasn't good to get too close to someone branded with a nickname like that in case it rubbed off.

I decided now was a good time to venture out and make the phone call I had to make.

'*Masikati*, Weekend. Three six six five, please.'

'Ah, and good afternoon to you, Mastah Rhrob-ett. How are you today, *shamwari*?' The handset was light with Weekend's friendly voice.

'Good, thanks. Looking forward to going home. And how are *you*, my friend?'

He made a long, drawn-out tutting sound by sucking his tongue against the roof of his mouth. I was smiling already.

'Well, you know, today my wife is ver-ry very unhappy with me, and my girlfriend is also talking no longer with me either.'

'Really? You know how girls are.' I didn't. 'Give them time.'

'You think so?'

'Did you do anything wrong?' I could practically hear the waft of innocence being thrown up into the air. 'Then you've got nothing to worry about.'

'Thank you, Mastah Rhrob-ett. Perhaps you are right. I shall put you through.'

Click. Hum. Then a voice. It sounded as if it was on the other side of Africa.

'Hi. Dad? It's me. Hello?'

But for once it wasn't him who'd picked up, it was my mother. She garbled something incoherent then made a high, strangled noise. I closed my eyes. Had the drinking started this early now?

'Mum? It's Bobby. Can you hear me?'

'Bobby? Bobby! Oh my, thank goodness.' I could tell she'd been crying. 'My little angel. Are you all right? Tell me. Are you?'

'Fine, Mum.'

'You can tell me. Is everything OK? Are you unhappy? Because if you are I can . . .' *Take you out of there?* Was that what she wanted to say? 'Are you coming home?'

'Soon.'

'Good. Because I need to . . . I want to talk to you about . . .' She was weeping again. 'I think we should have gone back. We should. Maybe none of this would have happened if . . .'

She wasn't making sense and I felt scared. 'What do you mean?'

'We should have gone back!' she said again. 'We shouldn't be here, and now it's too late.'

'Mum?' She disappeared. 'Mum!'

The line crackled and then it was my father, voice snapping down the wire.

'Hi, Dad.'

'Oh. It's only you. What do you want?'

'It's half term, Dad.'

'Today?'

'Next weekend. Saturday, after the rugby.'

'For the whole weekend?'

'Saturday until Monday evening.' Just like the term before.

'I see.'

'We'll be free from one. Firsts are playing Prince Edward and the buses are taking us in to support so you won't have to come all the way here to pick me up. We don't get lunch,' I added, because last time he'd been over three hours late.

A faint crash. Perhaps a slamming door.

'Dad? What's happened?'

'Look, Robert, to be honest this isn't really a good time. Your mother's not well.'

My heart raced.

'What's wrong?'

'She's had a bit of bad . . .' The line dropped for an instant. 'She needs rest, that's all. You know how she gets sometimes. You understand.' He coughed awkwardly. 'And besides, the car's playing up a bugger and I can't get the spare parts. It's so difficult to get spare parts in this country! Perhaps you can make alternative arrangements.'

My hand was gripping the handset tight enough to hurt.

Yes, I can make alternative arrangements, I thought. *And so will Mum. And we'll go back to England without you.*

Now, more than ever, that's where I wanted to be.

'Yes, Dad.'

Alternative arrangements.

I felt like crying.

Ivan spotted my face as soon as I went back into the house, and he came and stood by my cubicle.

'What's up?'

As vaguely as I could, I told him. He actually seemed concerned.

'So what will you do?'

What *would* I do? Boys who stayed in school over half terms were the handful that lived abroad, like the Shekiro brothers who came from Kenya, or weirdos like Button, whose mother ignored him most of the time and was shacking up with a businessman somewhere in Zambia. For someone who lived less than an hour away, there was no reason.

'I don't know. Maybe ask someone if I can stay with them.'

My first thought was Nelson, of course, though I didn't dare mention that. Ivan had hardly been angry with me all term and I didn't want that to change now.

Maybe he could read minds.

'Who? That Nelson Ndube?'

I didn't reply. I thought he'd walk off with a huff but instead he simply said, 'Have you ever thought about how he gets to go home all the bloody time while the rest of us only get three weekends a term?'

'To go training.'

'But do you know *why*? I'll tell you why. Because he's special.'

'You mean, because he's a good runner?'

'No, *special*. He's black. And he's got Mr Bullman wrapped round his little finger because of it.'

'You reckon?'

'For sure. Bully's paranoid that if he refuses permission then the government will come after him and accuse him of being racist, maybe put him in prison. Those lot do that to people. But if anyone's being racist it's Nelson.'

'How do you mean?'

'If he wasn't black, would he get special treatment?'

I didn't know and shook my head. Ivan read it the wrong way.

'That's right. He wouldn't. And you know what? That's not fair. He's using his colour to his advantage. Whatever you think of me, or of the country we used to have, it's just not fair.' He patted my shoulder with each word. 'Just. Not. Fair. Is it?'

'I . . . I guess not,' I said.

In his own cubicle, Simpson-Prior turned briefly round, looking like he maybe wanted to ask if I wanted to stay at his, but Ivan snarled and he shut up before he'd even started.

'And you don't want to stay with that poof, either,' Ivan added quietly, still chewing on jelly babies. 'He'll be dribbling over the babes in his magazine and pulling his chain all weekend.'

We laughed at the thought; it was funny. Then Ivan became more serious.

'Besides, he's two-faced. He was the one who put your tie in the piss trough last term. I know you think it was me but it wasn't. I swear.'

'Did he?' I said. I looked at Simpson-Prior, who was grinning and making his lips wet with his tongue as he resumed his hunched position at his desk, feverishly scribbling in an exercise book. I'd let him check out my English prep for one tricky question but it looked like he was copying the whole lot word for word. 'I've got nowhere, then; I'll have to come back here after the rugby on my own.'

'Come to mine.'

I looked at him, doubtful. Surely another trick . . .

'Me? To your farm?'

'No, up my ring-piece. Of course the farm, where'd you think? It's boring on my own now my *boet*'s not there, and if there's two of us my old man will let us go shooting.'

'Wow. I mean, *lekker*.' I found it hard to be casual. 'You have a brother?'

'Had. He was killed in the war,' he said.

My mouth opened and closed.

'Jeez, man, I'm *joking*.' He punched my arm, though only lightly. 'Don't be so gullible. He *gapped* it to Jo'burg before the war ended.' He leaned in to inspect all the postcards stuck to my wall. 'What's the deal?'

'They're from my grandmother.'

'From Pommieland?'

'*Ja.*' I paused, still wary. 'She sends them all the time.'

I hid the disappointment from my voice at only having received one so far this term. Had she got bored? Maybe I didn't write back enough, but my pocket money couldn't afford many dollar-each aerograms.

'Broadway. Chipping Camden. Snowshill,' he read. These were alien worlds. 'Lower . . . *Swell*? Jeez, are they serious? Reckon the chicks all want to live there, hey?'

'I know. Stupid names,' I said, blushing, but Ivan nodded approvingly as he tore the head off another sweet – and I was eight feet tall.

'Can't be any worse than the Kaffir names this country's being forced to use.'

The towns had been changing steadily since independence: Gwelo had become 'Gweru', Umtali 'Mutare', Marandellas 'Marondera' . . . The most significant change happened when Salisbury ceased to exist, although most of the boys refused to accept 'Harare' and just called it 'Berg' or 'Town'.

'Have you been?' he asked.

'We used to visit my grandmother all the time before my dad decided it would be better to work abroad. I'm going to go back one day, though. Maybe soon.'

'You should, if you want to. You should always do what you want.' He chuckled. 'Lower Swell. Man! Jelly baby?'

And he jeered when he saw I'd taken a black one.

That evening, while we waited for the supper bell after chapel, Simpson-Prior was telling everyone that my old man was making me stay at school for the half term. Nelson was back from training, and I yelled at Simpson-Prior in my head to keep his mouth shut.

'Where will you go?' Nelson asked when we were alone, as I knew he would. 'Do you want to stay with me? My folks won't mind. We can go to the movies in town, have a laugh. It'll be fun.'

I stumbled over my words. Over by the table, Ivan was watching.

'Will you have to do training?'

'Yes, a bit. I have to train every weekend now.'

'Don't worry.' It was less complicated to lie, and it came more easily. 'I'll see if I can get my dad to change his mind.'

EIGHT

Firsts lost the rugby. Only just, but the two-point margin might as well have been a hundred because Prince Edward boys always thought they were far superior for a reason no one could remember. They mocked our supporters even before the final whistle, and teased us for having blacks in our school without actually saying those words. In the new era everyone had to have blacks, only that didn't make any difference, they still hated us so we hated them.

Our school prefects were furious and made us do an extra war cry before we could go.

Ivan's dad was in the car park by his pick-up. He was a short, stocky man with big arms and a big belly, and a small Tobacco Farmers' Union hat on sun-bleached hair. His face was brown and coarse. He wore khaki shorts and *veltskoens* with no socks, with the red of a box of Madisons poking out of his breast pocket. With a spiked voice he told us to hurry and get in the back of the truck.

The late-June sky was pale and clear, and the air gnawed into our bare skin as we journeyed through the shade of the capital's architectured valleys. The roads were rivers of noise and exhaust, school seemed so far away.

Mr Hascott needed supplies and gave us ten dollars each to catch a movie. *Return of the Jedi* was showing at the Kine 400 so we went to watch that. Afterwards Ivan had fun walking behind people and scaring them with Darth Vader noises.

As we left town we stopped to get ice creams from the Borrowdale Dairy Den.

'Get me a Coke,' Mr Hascott barked. 'If they tell you they haven't got any cold ones they're lying.'

The Den was empty for a Saturday afternoon. Ivan and I sat at the counter and tried to give our order to the waitress but she looked worried and couldn't concentrate. She had deep furrows stretched across her dark skin because of a white guy over by the window who was opening sachets of sugar and pouring them over the table. It was Greet.

I wanted to leave but it was too late.

'Well, well. Look who we have here. Still wearing the stripes, Jacklin? Let's check them out.'

For the last three evenings I'd been the star attraction in the showers, yet again, thanks to my latest trip to Greet's study. I'd made his bed with a crease. Now I did as I was told and lifted my shirt to uncover the mess across the bottom of my back. I didn't know if he'd meant to miss quite so badly.

It wasn't the worst he'd done to me recently. The week before I'd put a toe onto the grass and he'd made me stand against a wall and fired darts made from paper and six-inch nails through a plastic tube. One had just caught my arm. Before that, for nothing more than fun, he'd squashed me into a trunk, fastened the lid, and sent me skating down the stairs – the trunk had caught halfway down and flipped three times.

He grinned. I despised him and that grin alike.

'Piece of bloody art,' he said. 'So what are you two girls up to?'

Ivan held Greet's eye. I wished he wouldn't. 'Going back to my farm.'

Greet exaggerated his hand to his ear. '*Your* farm? Are you sure about that?'

Ivan said nothing.

Greet swung his legs out towards us and I felt sick.

'Let me give you a bit of advice, Hascott. When you leave here with those delicious ice creams that the filthy Kaffir over there has put her fingers all over, ask your old man what he plans to do when our great leader takes *your* farm. You'd better start paying more attention in class because you'll be getting nothing once Mugabe has finished with you lot. You'll have to get a proper job that requires brains.'

Ivan shook his head. 'Mugabe won't take our farm. He's not allowed.'

'*Ja?* Are you sure?'

'My dad says so. Willing seller, willing buyer. That's what the law says, because that's what Mugabe agreed to at the end of the war.'

'I've got news for you: Mugabe's a liar. He told people what they wanted to hear – anything, as long as it got him in power. Which means, stupid, he'll find a way to take your land. You think the war's over? Trust me, the blacks are still fighting, and they won't stop until they've kicked us whites out of our own bloody country.'

Something my father had once said came to me: *Britain claimed this land and called it Rhodesia . . . It was anything but fair.*

I even opened my mouth but Greet sent my tongue scurrying back.

'You're just a fucking Pom, what would you know about anything? Shut it.' He chuckled to himself and took out his smokes. 'I'm kind of looking forward to it because, once we've gone, the blacks will start fighting themselves.'

'It won't happen,' Ivan insisted.

'"The whites will have to be culled." Mugabe actually said that. Our leader. Has everyone forgotten that we've got a gook running our country? A terrorist. And terrorism is all a terrorist knows.'

He finally turned my way, but only to blow angry smoke rings at me.

'No use looking to your boyfriend here for sympathy, the Poms are on Mugabe's side. Now hadn't you better run along and show him your farm, while you've still got it?'

We ate our ice creams in the back of the pick-up with barely a word, and Ivan ended up tossing his over the side with still more than half left, his appetite gone.

The road retreated in a cloud of diesel and the city shrank beneath the *msasas* and kopjes. His dad was going fast now. Occasionally a cluster of African huts appeared off to the side, where children stopped to wave; and at one stage, when it felt there was nothing but us and dry bush in the world, we overtook an old-timer pedalling hard on naked rims. He wobbled and nearly fell over yet still managed to flash a huge smile at us two white boys in the truck.

This didn't look like a nation still at war to me.

After more than an hour from the city we left the tarmac and hit dirt. The tyres rumbled over corrugated track and red dust swirled around the open cab and got in our eyes. We passed a sign that read *Hillcrest Farm*. We were on Hascott land but it was still another ten minutes before we turned between high-security fences and onto the edge of a green oasis.

The farmstead was an ornate, Dutch-style bungalow, probably over a hundred years old, robed in bougainvillea and with a raised veranda as wide as the house. The garden ran down a gentle slope, the borders of the flowerbeds carving sharp, European order between bursts of wild African colour. And right at the end of the lawn, a swimming pool rippled a reflection of the sinking sun. Beyond, miles and miles of brown-green *vlei* all the way to the hills.

Mrs Hascott was on the veranda. She put down the book she'd been reading and leaned forward as though watching a train come into view.

'Howzit, Mom.'

'Hello, my boy,' she said in an accent that was harsher than I expected and pulled a sweater over her shoulders.

She might have been quite pretty once, with green eyes like Ivan's and jet black hair, but closer up she was tired and drawn. She looked old before her time, and I wondered if that's what living through a bush war – out here, actually in the bush – did to you. I thought of my own mother and wished I was at home with her.

It was strange that she didn't get up to welcome her son, but as we climbed the steps I spotted her crutches. Only one leg found its way out of the blanket on her lap. I tried not to stare.

Mrs Hascott got Ivan to give her a peck on the cheek then ruffled his hair. Ivan made a face.

Over by the gate, Mr Hascott let out a strangled cry and slammed the door as he jumped back into the pick-up. The very tall farm hand who'd been speaking to him had to jump out of the way to avoid getting hit.

'Where's Dad off to in a hurry? Luckmore done something wrong?' Ivan asked.

Mrs Hascott sighed. 'No. Trouble on the perimeter again, you know how the old workers like to make trouble. They're still bitter but if they think they're going to get their jobs back they can think again. Now go on, don't be long. Dinner in an hour. The dogs are out, by the way.'

It was scant warning. The sound of barking erupted and a couple of huge Rhodesian Ridgebacks came bounding round from the back of the house, showing their teeth. I stayed as still as possible while Ivan wrestled them to the ground and played with them until they yelped.

They weren't the only ones happy to see him.

'Mastah Ivan! Mastah Ivan! *Kanjani*.'

A large African woman appeared at a side door. A simple floral dress hung from her enormous bosom, and the baby strapped to her back in a towel bounced as she danced and clapped cupped hands.

'Hey, Robina! *Kanjani*.' Ivan went quickly over to her. He seemed more pleased to see the maid than his own mother. 'I've missed you, the food's even worse this term. What are we having?'

'Tonight you have shep-hedds pie, your favour-itt. I make it special special, number one.'

I was stunned. This wasn't an Ivan I knew. And the surprise went on when he took me to the workers' village and we kicked a football around barefoot with the little piccanins until it was too dark to see. When we left they danced around us, laughing and singing, 'Bye bye, Mastah Ivan.'

On the way back he detoured us to the pool and produced some Madisons.

'You want a *gwaai*?'

I looked around nervously and said no. He fired up a match and lit his smoke, and then we sat in front of the blackness; the vague outline of the hills against a starry sky all we could see.

'Greet's an arsehole.' He took a big drag. The cherry glowed and lit his face, and in that moment I knew what he would look like as an older man. I shivered, perhaps from the cold.

'He's a bastard,' I said.

'That's because he hates you. I wouldn't take it personally, he hates all Poms. Poms killed his brother.' Ivan spoke flatly. 'That's how he sees it. In the war, gooks divided the unit his brother was fighting with, and they found him the next day pinned to a tree with his own cock in his throat.'

'Jeez . . .'

'A few weeks later the Poms signed the country over to the blacks at Lancaster House, when they should have been sending troops to help us.'

'I didn't know.'

'Well, now you do. And don't you dare tell him I told you. Greet's going to keep at you as it is, don't haul me into it.' He took another long drag.

'Does your old man know you smoke?'

'You're kidding, right?' He pointed to his backside. 'If he *gaffed* me he'd lash this so hard I'd have an arse for a nose and sneeze shit every time I got a cold.'

'Your old man beats you?'

'Of course. Doesn't yours?'

I didn't answer and pretended to swat away a mosquito that wasn't there, while inside I felt a strange swell of jealousy. My father didn't do anything.

Ivan lit up a second smoke with the first. I took one, too, drawing angrily and trying not to cough.

'He has this stick he calls Moses,' Ivan went on, 'because he reckons he could part the Red Sea with it. He uses it on the workers, too. It's the only way blacks learn. My old man's good to them, but you've got to keep a firm hand.'

'Is that what your dad was doing earlier?' I asked, shocked. 'Beating them?'

'No, that was the local blacks causing trouble. We only employ Matabele now, you see. That's my old man for you – Mugabe is Shona tribe and the Shona and Matabele have always hated each other, so my old man sacks our Shona workforce and goes all the way to the other side of the country to get Matabele hands. Any chance to piss the government off. The Shona lot come back and stir now and again. Robina's Shona but she's all right, she knows her place. She looked after me and my *boet* during the war.'

'You don't talk about your brother much,' I said. Ivan

strangled his cigarette with his fingers so I quickly changed the subject. 'The war must have been scary, hey?'

Ivan came right up close. His eyes glistened in the light of the quarter moon.

'No, actually it was a laugh and a half. We couldn't stop creasing up the day Mum found a mine.' I was starting to wish I was stuck at school after all. 'Listen. To what's out there. Listen hard.'

I did. There was nothing.

When I looked back, Ivan had gone as if he'd never been. I was completely alone. Then, in the distance, an eerie rustling. Perhaps cattle shuffling over grass. Whatever it was it was getting close. I strained and shapes started to swirl. A snapping twig. A feral grunt. I had to tell myself it was just a warthog, or something, because otherwise . . .

'Now remind yourself there are gooks out there,' Ivan breathed right into my ear. I almost screamed. 'Gooks the colour of shadows with guns and knives, who want to steal your land and think nothing of cutting a guy's dick off and making him eat it.'

He started back up to the house.

I trotted to catch up.

Dinner was round a large mahogany table too big for the four of us. Mrs Hascott asked a few of the usual questions while Ivan's dad attacked his meal.

'Dad?' Ivan had been itching to ask. 'The farm's not going to be taken, is it? You know, by the government.'

'Why the bloody hell would they do a thing like that?' came the gruff response between mouthfuls.

Ivan shrugged. 'To give it to the blacks. Ian Smith isn't leader any more, so who's to stop them?'

His dad met Ivan's gaze with the closest thing to a smile I thought I was likely to see.

'Blacks can't farm. It's a ridiculous idea; I wouldn't lose any sleep over it.'

'But if Mugabe wanted to,' Ivan went on, 'could he?'

Now Mr Hascott put down his fork.

'Look, my boy, Ian Smith might not be our leader but that doesn't mean blacks can just walk onto someone's land and take it. This is ours, we have title deeds. My grandfather bought it perfectly legally and the law is there to protect us. The Kaffirs may have won the war, they've got Mugabe, but this farm still belongs to us and will be ours until we decide to sell. Which we won't. OK? This is our land.'

Yet again, my dad's voice haunted me about whose land it had been in the first place, but no way was I even going to think about saying it this time. I made myself get rid of the thought.

Ivan wouldn't let go. 'Surely it's only legal if Mugabe says? He's in charge. He can do what he wants.'

'Don't be so bloody stupid. He made an agreement when he took over this country, he's not allowed to take it.'

'But he said—'

Mr Hascott had started to take up his beer bottle and cut Ivan off by dropping it.

'Since when have you been a bloody expert in politics? You're boring me now.'

'He said he'd give them land if they won.'

'That Mugabe said a lot back then. Their sort will say all sorts of shit to get what they want.'

'Language, please.' Mrs Hascott tried to intervene. 'We have a guest.'

Only Mr Hascott shot her a glance that made me go back to wishing I hadn't been invited.

'He said he would, though.' Sometimes I didn't know if Ivan was trying to make things worse or was just unaware. 'He said the whites had stolen the land from the Africans and it was their right to take it back. He *promised*. How do you know he won't?'

'He won't.'

'How do you know?'

'I know.'

'*How?*'

'Because if even one Kaffir steps onto my farm screaming land rights I'll slot him with a bullet.' Mr Hascott stabbed the air. He probably didn't know he'd started to shout. 'You see if I don't.'

'And fifty?'

'Enough.'

'A hundred? Five hundred?'

'You're pushing your luck, my boy. This farm will stay in this family for another hundred years, I can promise you that.'

'Ian Smith said the *country* would stay white for another *thousand*, only that didn't happen because we lost. Besides, what if I don't want it? Are you going to leave it to Steven and his long line of children?'

Mrs Hascott gasped and put her hands to her mouth. Mr Hascott was on his feet, chair crashing to the floor. He undid his buckle and ripped the belt from his shorts.

'You dare bring that name into my house.' His voice hissed. 'I *told* you, I won't have it. That boy is dead to me. Get to your room.'

Ivan didn't go. Not straightaway.

'You're scared, aren't you?' he said, perfectly calm, his face a picture of serene clairvoyance. 'You're scared because you think it's true – what he said. I heard it on the radio but you said it was just Kaffir-loving journalists scaremongering. But

Mugabe really said that about culling the whites and you think he still might.'

Mr Hascott threatened a hand to his son's face and stopped just short.

'*Go to your room.*'

Ivan went, and all at once there was just me and Mrs Hascott. She tried to smile but it wouldn't quite work.

'Ivan does push his father. He's turning into a young man so quickly, I think we forget.' Her voice quivered out of control. Then: 'Steven is Ivan's brother. He left home some years ago to live in South Africa with his . . . *friend*.'

She started crying. I didn't know what to do.

Much later, I crept in to see Ivan. He was lying facing the wall, knees curled to his chest, sniffing. I didn't go close because I knew what it was like to have other boys see you trying not to blub.

I stood and looked at the pictures on his wall. There weren't many. On one side, a shot of a massive waterfall spewing torrents above the words *Victoria Falls Is Super*, while in the near corner I spotted photographs of white troops in combat gear, smiling and pulling V-For-Victory signs for the camera as they headed for the bush. In some I recognized a leaner, fitter Mr Hascott with a bullet belt around his chest, a huge gun in one hand and with a young Ivan riding on his shoulders.

'I hate him,' Ivan croaked, making me jump slightly.

I wasn't sure if he meant his dad or Mugabe or Greet.

The silence came back so I moved back to the door.

'Check you tomorrow,' I said.

'*Ja*,' he said.

NINE

My eyes sprang open. The soft pre-dawn light stroked the curtains and I struggled to distinguish the strange shapes of Ivan's brother's room. I'd been dreaming that the war was still on and that the gooks Ivan had put into my head were crawling outside the house; only I was back at school in Selous and trying to run away to England, racing against lots of Nelsons wearing camouflage and carrying guns, and to my side boys were cheering for their houses as they always did.

'. . . Come on, Willoughby . . .'

'. . . Go, Heyman . . .'

'. . . Show us that Burnett spirit . . .'

'. . . Selous is the *best best best* . . .'

Then I woke properly.

Ivan was standing at the foot of the bed. He threw me a tracksuit.

'Here. You'll need this, it's *chilloes* out there.'

Outside, by the garages, he hooked a small rucksack onto his back and asked if I'd ridden a motorbike before. I lied and said I had, so he nodded me to one of the off-road bikes in there.

I copied what he did and kick-started mine into life, but then stalled it four times in a row. He turned his bike round and came back. I thought he was going to shout but instead gripped my clutch hand until it hurt then released it.

'Do it slowly,' he said.

We rode. Out of the gate and onto the farm roads. I felt

a whole new exhilaration as the cold air blew into my face. The track was blood red and bumpy, on either side the fields remained obscure and uncertain as the sun struggled to breach the horizon, and by the time it eventually got there we must have gone miles.

We turned a corner and headed up a steep hill towards a kopje as big as a house – rock balancing on rock like magic and looking like it could topple and roll down on us at the slightest puff of wind. How many people must have gazed with wonder and thought the same on first sight?

We got off our bikes, and as night peeled away the ghostly landscape came to life under a golden mist: cattle, maize stalks, ostriches, blankets of tobacco leaves . . . Ivan must have seen this a million times but even he stayed quiet as it emerged into view. A Lourie bird began to screech its familiar cry of 'G'way', while above, the black and white of a fish eagle swooped low and then out to the almond-shaped dam.

'I fucking love this place.' Ivan spoke perhaps more to himself than me. 'I'll never let them take it.'

Then, nearby, a lone antelope emerged through the trees – a kudu, fawn in colour with thin white stripes down its sides. Young and nervous, it paused with every step, ears twitching, scared by its own sounds. When it was twenty feet away it suddenly became aware and stood rigid, looking right at us.

Ivan had very slowly and very carefully taken off his pack and extracted a semi-automatic handgun. It glinted dully.

He clicked the safety. I'm not sure I'll ever forget the look on his face.

The crack split the morning in two. It made me jump even though it wasn't as loud as I'd expected, and to my relief the kudu was already springing away amongst the branches.

Ivan was kicking his bike back into life.

'Come on!'

We hurtled down after it, twigs and thorns whipping my skin. I tried to keep up, but then a clearing came out of nowhere and I came face-to-face with a barbed wire fence. I jinked left, panicked, and almost sent myself flying over the handlebars as I grabbed the front brake. The bike slid and ended up on its side.

'*Get up!*' Ivan yelled and he slowed past me.

But I couldn't right the bike on my own so now he was really mad. He looked about and the kudu was nowhere in sight.

Ivan parked up at the edge of a tobacco field to squeeze a few frustrated rounds off at some rats, only they were all too quick and he ended up screaming at them.

He jammed the gun into my hand.

'You do it if you think it's so easy.'

The gun was light and fit surprisingly well. The kick wasn't what I'd imagined either, almost nothing, but I'd never fired anything before and my first shot went wild.

'See? Useless Pommie.' Ivan's face was red.

My second went nowhere, too, and when Ivan began to laugh I didn't want to play any more. I was about to hand the gun back when a grey flash caught my eye. I didn't even think. In a single movement I spun and squeezed and the thing scurrying across the road over twenty feet away lifted into the air.

My stomach swirled with disgust and excitement as the rat thumped back onto the dust. Ivan's mouth stayed open but the laughter had stopped.

He grabbed the gun and changed the clip.

'Do that again.'

I felt like I was floating. I took aim, pressured the trigger, and another rat rolled out of the world.

And another.

'Jeez, Jacklin. This is your first time?'

61

'*Ja*,' I said, absurdly proud.

'Well, where the bloody hell were *you* during the war? We could have done with you. You should be in the school rifle club.'

I thought now was a good time to approach what had happened yesterday.

'Your old man was pretty mad last night, hey?'

Ivan snatched the gun back, stamped his engine back to life and shouted over the revs.

'My old man hates two things in life: blacks and queers. My *boet*'s a poof, OK? But if you tell *anyone* there's a faggot in my family you're dead.'

Now we just seemed to be going wherever and Ivan stopped to take pot shots at anything: birds, mostly, a few lizards, a snake . . . He missed them all. I was allowed a go at a bullfrog and obliterated it from fifteen metres. Ivan was getting fed up and I could see the clouds over him getting lower and lower.

We finally started heading back to the house when Ivan stood on his brake and slew to a stop. He stared at the ground with wild eyes.

'Look,' he pointed, and I saw clear imprints of antelope hoofs cutting a path. Alongside, droplets of blood. 'I *did* get it.'

He abandoned the bike and darted off-road. The kudu must have been close; the blood was still fresh. Ivan was making a mad, charging cry. We scampered over rocks, around ant mounds. Low acacias grabbed my clothes with thorny fingers. I wanted to stop only he just kept going.

And then he *did* stop. All at once, crouching low, he put his finger to his lips and pointed to a wall of bristle grass.

'On three.' I could barely hear him. He held the gun tenderly against his cheek. 'Then watch me kill.'

His pupils were dilated and black.

'One . . . two . . .'

If he said three I didn't catch it. He burst through, pouncing in an explosion of leaves and twigs.

What met us on the other side wasn't a dying animal struggling to make a last bid for freedom. It was one of the workers in blue overalls crouching over an irrigation pipe, his tightly curled hair all bumpy and uneven, and with a cigarette rolled from newspaper between his lips. He jumped, spinning as we came, eyes wide and white against his chocolate skin. It was Luckmore, the tall, thin bossboy. I remembered him instantly as the one jumping out of the way of Mr Hascott's pick-up.

'*My weh!*' he yelped. His face was so surprised it was almost funny. Then everything seemed to turn to stone when he saw the gun right in his face.

His cigarette went limp and tumbled to the ground.

A nervous laugh: mine. No one else joined in. Ivan kept holding the gun. I became hyper-aware of everything.

The chill air.

The smell of the worker's cigarette.

The bead of sweat hanging over Ivan's eye.

His finger, tightening around the trigger.

He's going to do it, I thought. For that brief moment, I was sure he really was.

There was a crisp snap of wood. Over the worker's shoulder, the kudu gazed out from the bushes, limping. Ivan shifted his aim and fired a single shot. The worker dropped and covered his head with his arms.

The kudu's legs had buckled. Ivan walked over to it, gazed down with thin lips, then shot it again, and didn't stop until the magazine was empty.

TEN

'We came through the bush and this guy's just *there*, and I swear he almost *kakked* himself.'

Ivan and I told the story together, he perched on the table in the middle of our study room with me beside him. Everyone circled around us and listened intently, desperate to hear what happened next. It felt good, although Simpson-Prior was laughing too long and too loud, which I found a bit irritating, and when he coughed Mazoe orange juice through his nose I knew he was just trying to get attention for himself, and that perhaps Ivan was right about him.

Nelson came in, no doubt to see how my weekend was, and instantly the moment was gone. In all the excitement I'd forgotten about him, and that he was bound to find out sooner or later that I'd lied.

I put my head down and hoped everyone would move away, but if anything Ivan pulled them in further.

'But I tell you, this guy'– he gripped my upper arm, almost like I was going to run away – '*this* guy is the best shot ever. He's a demon. I've never seen anything like it. You name it, he'll sight it and blow it away, one-time.'

I blushed. Nelson looked at me quizzically.

'I thought you were going home,' he said as we walked to supper. 'I thought you were going to get your old man to change his mind.'

I felt bad and uncomfortable.

'*Ja*, well, I didn't,' I said, because I had nothing to defend myself with.

'So you went with *him*?'

'I didn't want to stay here on my own.'

'You could have come to mine. I told you.'

'No, I couldn't.'

'Why not?' he asked, really wanting to understand.

'Because . . .' I began.

Because what, though? Because in hindsight I wouldn't have had as good a half term with him? Because I wanted Ivan to like me and not pick on me all the time? Because Nelson was black and I was white, and the weekend had taught me that this difference somehow made staying with him impossible? Practically no one else would have even contemplated doing such a thing.

'Just because.' I said it flatly, drawing a line. 'Why do you care? It's my life.'

He looked at me with hurt eyes. I don't know why I felt surprised, wasn't that what I'd been after? To do something to make him leave me alone and stop asking difficult questions?

'I just thought . . .'

'Are you my mother?'

'No.'

'So quit telling me what to do.'

'I'm not.'

'Yes, you are.'

'It's just that you said you were going home.'

Over by the wall I spotted Ivan nudge De Klomp and point my way. They both aimed finger guns and then mimed someone being blown away in slow motion. I couldn't tell if it was them marvelling about my shooting again or teasing me.

'Well, I didn't, OK? Big deal. Stop bugging me.'

Without looking back I went to join Ivan, and to my relief

he got De Klomp to budge up so I could sit between them until the bell rang and we filed into the dining hall.

Inside, we discovered the school prefects were still mad about the rugby. Up at Top Table, Portis, the Head Boy, didn't say grace but made the whole school stand while he told us what a bunch of spoofless faggots we were.

'Where was the support?' he wanted to know. He played on the wing and had scored a disallowed try. 'You guys need to learn some respect.'

He made us stay standing until the prefects had finished eating so that we only had a few moments to eat our meal before prep. What we didn't realize right then was that this punishment would go on all week.

Nelson started to avoid me, and now and again I'd catch him staring at me, his face bunched with a lost and sorry frown because he didn't know what he'd done wrong. I wanted to try and explain, I really did, but even in the dorm Ivan seemed to be watching, checking to see what I was doing, so it was far easier to ignore him.

One afternoon I spotted Nelson sitting on his own in the common room, crying quietly. I decided to finally break the stupid silence when some boys from another house came rushing in and stopped me.

'There's been an accident,' one gulped with excitement. 'On the main road just outside the school. It's not serious but you can see it from the fence.'

When he said it wasn't serious, he meant no white people were involved. You could spot the carnage straightaway. A bus full of people had been going one way and an army truck the other, but most of the buses in the country had chassis that were so shot they crab-crawled with their front wheels virtually rumbling off the tarmac while the rear jutted out in the middle of the road. The army truck – a Crocodile, which was an ugly bulk of angled metal and jagged edges and virtually indestructible – had come round the corner too fast, ploughed straight into the side of the bus and ended up on the grass. The bus had stopped being a bus altogether.

Wailing filled the air. A couple of passers-by and police cars had stopped, but no more than that, and even though the ambulance had arrived it could only carry two at a time and it was twenty-something kilometres to the hospital and back.

One of the older boys spotted the soldiers who'd been in the Crocodile by the edge of the trees, their guns slung casually over their shoulders. They were big men, and the only thing they seemed concerned with was finding a light for their smokes. They called over a small man in a policeman's uniform, demanded some matches, and then sent him away without looking him in the face. The policeman looked happy to be going the other way again.

Why weren't *they* doing anything to help? I wondered.

As though answering the question, the older boy pointed out the crimson berets tucked into their waistbands.

'Fifth Brigade,' he said. 'Mugabe's *special* troops. Evil bastards.'

A small commotion sparked further along the line as a boy from our year called Pittman started to climb the fence. Ivan was egging him on the loudest, while for once, I noticed, De Klomp wasn't by his side and had retreated, looking small and pale.

This Pittman guy got up and over, and, with a huge grin he started to creep through the thin trees to where the soldiers were squatting. None of them had seen him.

'Don't,' came De Klomp's thin voice behind us. 'He mustn't. Make him stop.'

I don't think anyone else heard him, and when I looked he'd turned and was heading quickly back towards the house.

Now Pittman was really showing off, jumping and mimicking a gorilla. When his foot found a pine cone the noise crackled like fire, and the next thing we knew the soldiers were all up and rushing towards him. Pittman started to run, his face suddenly a portrait of complete fear, but they were quick. The front soldier knocked him to the ground and pinned him with a boot. The rest flooded around and pointed their guns at him, screaming in Shona and kicking his heels.

Behind the fence, even Ivan looked relieved when the policeman came running back over and begged them to stop.

Gradually they calmed and lifted their guns. One of them spat at Pittman and stamped on his legs as he went.

The policeman hauled Pittman back to the fence.

'You *stay!*' He shook him. 'You are *crazy boys*. Stupid.'

'We were only having a bit of fun,' Ivan protested through the wire.

'*Ja.*' Pittman wiped the policeman's black hand off his skin. 'It was only a game.'

'You cannot do this.' The policeman shook his head gravely. 'Not with them. *Never* with them. Next time maybe I will not be there to help and you will not be so lucky.'

Pittman basked in his moment. He was from Heyman House but he spent the rest of the afternoon in Selous, in our study room. He told everyone what had happened, getting louder and louder. De Klomp was back by Ivan's shoulder, laughing much more than the rest of us to hide the fact he'd snuck away and hadn't been there to see it. None of us had known Greet was in his study above trying to get an afternoon's sleep, but Greet's mood over the mealtime punishments had been steaming for days and De Klomp should have just known better.

He didn't care who it was. Greet simply marched in and

gave us all one solid thump each, then took De Klomp and two others off to the drying room with a cricket bat and ball. Greet spent the next eight minutes smacking the ball around as hard as he could.

The sound echoed around the house.

When it was over, Osterberg and Davidson hobbled back to the study room, fighting tears. In time it would be one of the good stories to tell, but not yet.

De Klomp, meanwhile, hadn't come back.

He still hadn't appeared by supper time. Ivan looked worried.

As soon as the bell for prep went I heard him slipping out. I followed him into the night. If we got caught we'd get whacked for sure.

'I'm coming with you,' I told him.

'No, you're not.'

I felt brave because I wanted him to like me again.

'I'll tell everyone about your brother.'

He thought about it.

'Keep up, I won't wait.'

'Where are we going?'

'The Cliffs,' Ivan answered matter-of-factly. 'He'll be there.'

I didn't ask how he could be so sure, I just knew he must be right.

We ran across the playing fields to the bottom gate.

I hadn't been to the Cliffs before because they were strictly out of bounds. It was actually only one cliff, a disused quarry in the middle of the bush from when the school had been built; a sheer sixty-foot face on one side and a gradual slope on the other. There were no safety fences or anything, of course, but it was an ideal playground where boys could leap off and jump into the murky water below.

We didn't talk again until we got there. Winter was an eerie time in Africa: no chirrup of crickets to electrify the air, no buzz of flying ants to meet the rains. And the dark was always thicker, sometimes tinged with the waft of burning wood from somewhere you couldn't see.

Smoke came that night, too, and Ivan slowed.

'We've got to be careful.'

'Why?'

He tutted. 'You won't understand.'

De Klomp was sitting with a fire at his feet, shivering because he was still in only his sports T-shirt and shorts. We got as far as the tree line around the clearing when he heard us, and he was up in an instant, stepping back into the gloom. I saw angry red marks on his arms and legs where the ball must have hit him.

'Klompie. It's me, Bru. Jacklin's here too, no one else. We were worried.'

It was too late, De Klomp had already turned. One moment he was there, the next he'd just gone, snatched by the night in a way that seemed completely unnatural. We sprinted after him, and it was only when I realized Ivan wasn't alongside me any more that I noticed the blackness ahead. But before I had time to question it everything had suddenly gone, and like in a dream I was floating in nothing for what seemed an eternity as cold air and silence carried me. Then I was falling. Just falling. I could taste my heart in my mouth. With arms spinning and legs kicking, I went down into the abyss, faster and faster until at last I landed.

My final thought was that I would surely die, but the surface gave way and I kept on falling, down and down, sucked from beneath as freezing water filled my mouth and nose.

When I erupted back to the surface something pale bobbed in front of me and I knew straightaway it was De Klomp, face down and unmoving, and without another thought I'd flipped him onto his back. His shoulder and face were bleeding, he must have clipped the rock face on his way down.

'. . . are you doing? Can you see him?' Ivan was shouting from way above. 'Jeez, man, *talk* to me . . .'

I held De Klomp under the chin and paddled him to the other side. I was glad to hear him groan as I dragged him up the slope.

'Dad?' he kept saying. 'Dad, is that you? Don't go in there, Dad.'

He was trembling. For whatever good it would do, I took off my jumper and laid it over him.

'Dad?' He curled into me.

I felt embarrassed. I didn't know what to say so I just answered as any thirteen-year-old schoolboy would.

'Shut up, you idiot, I'm not your old man. You should be glad, your folks would kill you if they found out about this.'

At which point he came round. I could see his eyes focus on me, then he rolled away and started to sob. How was I to know that it was completely the wrong thing to say because, actually, his folks wouldn't do a thing to him seeing as someone had already killed them?

We walked back through the dark mostly without speaking, Ivan guiding De Klomp with his arm around his shoulder and me always slightly behind. Every now and then De Klomp let out a sob and Ivan let him pause.

'I understand, Bru. I understand.'

But *I* didn't.

We'd set off again when De Klomp was ready.

Ivan's caring, fraternal exterior was a side I hadn't seen, but I kept my distance because none of it was for me. This was between them, I wasn't part of it. Ivan wouldn't even turn to look at me so I was certain the steely quiet was fury with me for having made De Klomp cry like that.

We took him to the sanatorium for the night. Fortunately

it was Sister Lee on duty, who was a soft touch, and we told her De Klomp had slipped and knocked his head and fallen in the pool. It never even occurred to her to ask what we'd been doing there at this time, in winter.

Ivan and I went slowly back to the house together.

'You can't blame him for blubbing.' It was a relief to hear him speak to me again, like being released. 'He's not a poof, it's because of his time in the war. Greet's a bastard.'

'You think what he did brought it back to De Klomp?' I asked. 'The war, I mean?'

'The war doesn't *come back*, Jacklin, because it never goes. It's part of us. And we're reminded of it every day: nothing works, you can't buy anything and the blacks walk around like they own the place.'

He hesitated. I didn't dare hurry him.

'Klompie's folks were religious nuts. You know, real God-botherers, and they worked at this Pentecostal Mission up in the mountains beyond Nyanga, so far east they could have opened the window and pissed over the border. When the gooks started to come over on their raids the police tried to get them to move, but the nuns tuned, "No way". They had God on their side, He'd protect them. So they stayed: Klompie, his mum and dad and baby sister, a priest and the nuns. Plus the black workers. They thought they were good blacks but just goes to show you can't trust a Kaffir because this lot didn't just steal food for the terrorists, they opened up the door to them. The gooks slaugh-tered everyone, even the blacks who'd let them in.'

'Why?' I asked. There was nothing else to say.

'Gooks don't need a reason. They shoved everyone in a storeroom and just opened fire.'

Ivan's voice stayed flat and even, his eyes training on some-thing unseen.

'But De Klomp – Klompie – survived,' I said.

'Of course. Only because they wanted him to, though. Africans are born cruel, it's the way they are, but not all of them are stupid. They often made sure someone was left to tell of what they'd seen. That's what terrorists do. As it happens Klompie didn't speak for a full year after that. He lives with his aunt and uncle now in Berg, and he won't step foot on a farm or anywhere too rural, so God knows why they sent him to a school out in the sticks with bastards like Greet.'

'*Ja*, he's such a bastard,' I echoed.

'It's not Greet's fault,' Ivan surprised me. 'He's in his rights as a senior to beat us. It's the Kaffirs' fault really, they're the ones who did this to Klompie. It was the Kaffirs. Don't you see that? Don't you get it?'

I found myself nodding.

'*Ja*. I get it.'

We were almost at the house.

'He'll deal with it,' Ivan said, 'because that's what we all do. Deal with it and move on.'

'For how long, though?' I wondered. 'And what if he can't?'

But he didn't answer that one.

'You showed big *machendes* jumping to save him,' he said instead. '*Huge* gonads, flying off the edge like you couldn't give a shit. You think you're Superman or someone?'

He gripped my shoulder. There it was at last, what I'd been wishing for.

'That's my name, don't wear it out.' I felt proud.

'*Ja*. But you're sounding like a Pom again, don't say things like that. As far as I'm concerned you're one of us now. You belong here. With us.'

That word: *Belong*.

And I thought, *Yes, I do*.

'And if that's the case' – Ivan's grip tightened with meaning – 'you don't want to be hanging around that Nelson bloody

Ndube. I just told you what his sort are capable of, you can't trust him. Steer well clear. Don't you see? Don't you?'

This time I said it. 'Yes, I do.'

'And what's the deal with you and Prior the Wire? You and snake-boy have been hanging around like a couple of bum chums.'

'I guess I feel sorry for him.'

'Well don't, the guy's a wanker. You don't want to stick with him, not if you're going to get through this place. I swear he dreams of taking it up the arse.'

I saw a way of affirming my position at the top of the ladder and took it.

'I think he wets his bed.'

Ivan turned keenly. 'He does?'

'Once. I think. His PJs were wet and he hid them quickly after he got up.'

'We can't have that. I think it's time the Mess Police conducted a little experiment, to see if you're right.'

The Mess Police.

More school folklore, another story of a time gone by when a whole dorm had apparently conspired to make some poor individual wet the bed.

They'd pretended to sleep as normal, and when the one closest to the victim had signalled the All Clear, everyone had crept slowly round. They'd carefully put the guy's hand into a bowl of cold water, and then, very gently, dripped a few drops right next to his ear. It took a while, but when it happened it was obvious. The lights were whipped on, the victim's bedding ripped back, and all he'd ever been from that time on, without mercy, was the one in the school caught with his pyjamas drenched in his own urine. Apparently the guy had eventually left the school because of it.

It was a cruel story, though we secretly doubted it was really true because what kind of idiot would be so stupid as to fall for something like that?

None, I told myself as I followed Ivan's instructions and let everyone else in the dorm in on the plan. It couldn't possibly work, I convinced the voices in my head as I kidded Simpson-Prior into thinking I was making him cups and cups of tea before Lights Out because I was his friend. We couldn't possibly all close in around him, trying not to laugh, without him waking and realizing.

Simpson-Prior slept while we produced a bowl of water and coaxed his bladder into letting go. After a while he murmured and grinned, and we detected a familiar smell rising from his bed.

The lights went on. The sheets ripped back. Simpson-Prior blinked as though coming out of a trance. He hadn't yet noticed his pyjamas were matted to his skin.

'*Prior's pissed himself!*' someone yelled loudly – perhaps Ivan himself – and suddenly our dorm was full of older boys, too. They must have known, someone had told them.

The chant began.

'*Prior's wet the bed! Prior's wet the bed!*'

Simpson-Prior tried to pull the sheets back up but two boys grabbed him and stopped him, giving everyone an eyeful. There was nowhere to hide. Simpson-Prior started to cry but that didn't make any difference, and he was dragged up and then through the whole house like a spoil of war.

I can still see his face today. Surprise? Disbelief? Horror? Hate? There is no word that could describe the harrowing look of betrayal in his eyes as he gazed through tears at each of us in turn – me in particular – in a dreadful search for what was going on, because even though he knew perfectly well, it was just too much for him to face.

*   *   *

Klompie came out of the San after a few days. I'd already swapped beds by then to the other side of the dorm, away from Simpson-Prior and Nelson. I wasn't comfortable over there any more. I felt bad for what I'd done to Simpson-Prior and for the way I'd treated Nelson, but luckily Ivan and Klompie were there to make me forget about all of that.

My friends.

Who knows, maybe that was the plan. Maybe Ivan's idea had formed as early as then.

Ivan was pleased with my decision to move beds without being prompted. When I went down to the showers that evening he shook my hand and patted me on the back like I was a champion boxer. Then he quietly pointed out Nelson, who was standing under the spray.

'That's why we're getting head lice, because of people like him. They can't wash them out. I'm telling you.'

The water was bouncing off Nelson's hair; it didn't get wet like ours. I'd never really noticed that before.

ELEVEN

Because of everything that had gone on it only dawned on me at the end of that term that I'd had just the one postcard from my grandmother, and that had been right at the beginning. That wasn't normal.

I was desperate to ask my mother about it, but ever since I'd come home her bedroom door had remained almost permanently shut and I never saw her. I guessed it was because she was feeling more sad than ever for some reason, though I didn't know why.

Almost a week into the holiday, and I decided I'd just wait for her. I sat at the bottom of the garden where the lawn sloped into endless bush and threw stones at a Coke bottle.

Don't bend your arm so much. I imagined Ivan telling me what to do. Not that I needed the advice because I was hitting it every time from thirty feet away. I wondered what he was doing at the moment. It seemed so long since he'd invited me to his farm and I wished more than anything he'd ask me again.

Then I thought about Simpson-Prior's expression that night we'd made him wet his bed. I found another stone and hurled it, pretending the bottle was the memory, but on this occasion I'd tried too hard because although I waited for the noise, the only sound of chinking glass came from up at the house.

My mother was up.

Our garden was huge and circled with a boundary of jacaranda and avocado trees and tall pines that felt like prison bars sometimes. Our bungalow sat in the middle, with its plain white walls and a grey asbestos roof that hung over a veranda the family hardly ever used.

The grass hadn't seen rain for months and made noises under my toes.

'Herro, Mastah Bobby,' Matilda greeted me, bent double over the washing board yet still managing the biggest smile.

I waved back and went into the cool.

As expected, my mother's door was closed, though I knew she'd been out because a glass by the drinks table had been used, empty before the ice had even begun to melt. He said he hadn't but I knew my father had moved into the spare room, because Matilda made the bed in there each morning.

Daylight was banished in my mother's room and merely glowed around the edge of the curtains while she lay in the gloom, pale and propped up against pillows. I scarcely recognized her any more.

Her eyelids fluttered.

'Darling. Goodness me, what are you doing here?' She raised an arm, another glass at the end of it I hadn't noticed until now, sloshing clear liquid. 'It's so early.'

'It's nearly the afternoon,' I replied.

'Really? Golly, and here's me still in bed. I'm sorry, darling, I haven't been feeling too well recently. You know how it is.' Her cold and damp fingers found my face. It was the touch of a stranger and it made me uncomfortable. 'Look how my little baby's growing up. That school of yours must be feeding you well. What time is it?'

'Almost twelve. Mum—'

'Almost lunch, then. That's good,' she said. Guilty eyes peered over the top of her glass. 'Don't worry, it's only water. Promise. Have the rains come yet?'

'No, Mum, it's only September.'

'I do miss the rain so. Cold, grey, English rain . . .'

A vacant cloud drifted over her. I'd noticed that same cloud almost straightaway on my first day home and it hadn't gone away.

'Mum, have you heard from Granny recently?' I asked.

She stayed silent for a while.

'Your grandmother is,' she began. 'Has . . . Is . . . Oh, it's all too late.'

Too late?

'For what?'

She reached weakly for the bedside table and her bones made shapes under her skin. In her hand she held a tattered envelope with a British stamp on it.

'Here,' she sighed. 'This explains everything.'

As I went to take it I saw it was a handwriting I didn't recognize. The word *URGENT* had been written on it in big capitals and I hesitated. It was enough time for her to change her mind and she took it back.

'Your grandmother has gone away,' she told me in an unfamiliar tone because she was speaking into her glass. She tipped it to take a final swig of whatever it was only to find she'd already finished.

'Where?'

'Does that really matter?' She noticed my reaction to her tone and softened her voice. 'Moved. An old people's home. Yes, that's it. A sort of hospital. She couldn't cope on her own any more, the poor thing. So old, so suddenly. It happens.'

'But . . .' Only at that precise moment I didn't know how to articulate my thoughts. 'But she didn't tell me.'

'She couldn't. Not in her state.'

'But . . .'

'Maybe she forgot where to write to, her mind's not what

it was. Come, come, darling, it's not like she's really part of our lives, we live here now.'

This time I pulled away from her touch without trying to and we looked at each other.

'Mum.'

She hid her eyes.

'Don't argue.'

'I . . .'

'*Don't.*' And when I flinched: 'Please. If only you realized . . .'

Something told me I didn't want to. I wrestled with confusion.

'Do you know where she is?' I asked. 'So I can write?'

'No, I don't. Oh darling, *do* take Mr Glum away. Trust me, she's better off where she is, and she'll only get confused if you start bombarding her with letters. Best to leave her. Things will improve now that it's all over.'

All over?

'Her friend Marjorie has sorted it all out.'

'So you don't think maybe we could leave here to stay with her,' I floundered, 'like you said once? You *said*. I don't like school, some boys do bad things to other boys. You don't think we could live there with Granny? You know, while we settle back.'

My mother – or the woman in front of me who vaguely resembled my mother – ran her tongue over cracked lips. We held each other's eyes, and for a few seconds I thought I could see someone I'd known before fighting to get out. She almost made it before the glass drew her back and she rattled her teeth against the rim. The cloud descended fully and won her from me.

'No, my darling, I don't.' She burst forward and retched a huge, shaking cough into her hand, then raised her energy a second time, dropped the envelope back and shut the drawer with a loud *clap*. 'It's all too late. We belong here with your father. What time did you say it was? Perhaps it's not too early for a drink, then maybe I'll get up and we'll have lunch together. Be a good boy for Mummy.'

Whoever she was, it was then that I started to hate her, and I carried on hating her a bit more each day until she died.

Back to the bottom of the garden, and beyond. I didn't want lunch, I wanted to walk. Just walk. I threw stones at everything: at trees, at rocks, at lizards on the rocks. I even hit an African Hoopoe as it flew away.

'Stupid bird,' I cursed only when I knew it was OK. 'Stupid bird in a stupid country.'

The sun was blaring, the red dust hot under my soles. I must have walked for a good hour before I saw anyone, and even then it wasn't a real person. He was part of an old monument, a weatherworn statue of some up-his-arse white man in military uniform and with a razor moustache. I'd never seen or heard of him before; a pioneer who had apparently discovered gold and built the town, so the plinth told me.

He built? Or the blacks he beat and whipped? I could hear my father. *Not so powerful now, is he?*

Although he looked powerful to me, perhaps because his expression or his pose or something else reminded me of Greet.

'Stupid place for a statue,' I told it.

There was a path that might have been a dirt road once but any sign of civilization had been taken over by the trees. I turned and felt uneasy when I realized I couldn't see any sign of our house or how I'd got here.

'In the middle of bloody nowhere. Stupid.'

A sudden rustling made me jump. For a moment I thought maybe it was an animal but a couple of young men came through instead, each holding a Chibuku carton and clearly fairly drunk on it. They were laughing and swaying and speaking loudly in Shona. When they spotted me they stopped and just smiled, each black face glistening beneath a thick padding of hair that pushed out at all angles. I could see bits of their grey-pink maize drink in their teeth.

I tried indifference and nodded. One of them copied me and giggled. The other said something I didn't understand, his eyes moving from me, to the statue, to me. He wore a sleeveless T-shirt and there was a big scar down one of his well-defined arms from shoulder to elbow. I wondered how he'd got it. He caught me staring and laughed something to his friend, pointing to the monument.

'*Ndipo fojica*,' he called.

I turned away. I heard him make singsong noises while the other blew hysterics.

'*Ndipo fojica*,' he said again.

I just kept walking, hurrying while trying to make it look like I wasn't. Ivan's voice tapped me on the shoulder: *Africans are born cruel.*

My heart beat solidly when I saw them following. I lengthened my stride.

'*Mwana haasati ava nomurangariro.*'

Another reason to laugh. Why did they find everything so damned funny?

I moved faster; so did they. I broke into a casual trot; they dropped their Chibuku cartons and started jogging. Eventually I just ran, I didn't care which way. I barged through twigs and leaves and leaped over scrub. I couldn't ignore the thorns, though, and had to stop to pull them out.

Still they came, their motion smooth and effortless and relentless as they emerged through the bush. Like warriors.

With a small cry I set off again, only I was too preoccupied to notice the rock in the ground and, before I'd got anywhere, I was down and inhaling dirt.

In no time the two Africans were up to me. I scrambled backwards as the one who'd done the speaking walked calmly up to my feet, close enough for me to see the reds of his eyes and draw on his pungent odour. He bared his gums. How many folks had felt what I was now feeling during the war? How many people had this man killed? I wished more than anything that Ivan was with me.

He raised his hand and I just stopped trying.

'*Kanjani, shamwari,*' he said. *Hi there, my friend.* '*Ndipo fojica.*'

And when I made no reaction he gestured his hand to his mouth.

'I want *fojica. Fojica.*'

He only wanted a smoke!

Still smiling, he kneeled low.

'*Shamwari*, why you running a-weh? Do you thinking I will in-ja you?' He pointed to the cut on my leg. 'You run fast-fast and now you are in-jad.'

My mouth opened and closed.

'You must see a doctor. He give *muti* to make you better-better, number one. Yes?' he went on. His friend hovered, yawning and digging his fingers harmlessly into his hair. 'I am looking for wherk, bhas. I wherk very hard for dollars. Does your fatha need good wherkers in the garden like me, my friend? My name is James.'

He stretched out a giant hand. I flinched and he retracted, looking hurt.

'*Leave me alone!*' I threw at him.

Then I was on my feet again, and this time I didn't stop until I'd stumbled onto the strip road that would lead me home.

* * *

I stayed in my room the rest of the afternoon and listened to music with the curtains drawn. Both my Spandau Ballet and Nik Kershaw got chewed because they were local cassettes and instead of trying to fix them I just flung them across the room and listened to my older English ones. Ivan was right, nothing worked in this country. He'd also said Spandau Ballet and Nik Kershaw were gay anyway so I didn't care.

After five o'clock the TV channel started broadcasting. I was bored so I went into the living room and switched on our black and white dinosaur. The picture stretched and I groaned as yet another Special Bulletin came into focus.

There was a group of soldiers, proud and pleased and leaning on their guns. They looked like the ones Pittman had messed around with, red berets in their waist bands, and they joked and laughed for the camera while still managing to look menacing. These comrades, the commentator read, had repelled another attack by rebel forces in Matabeleland, in the south-west of the country.

The picture cut to the roadside, where Matabele bodies lay scattered. Maybe fifty of them, men and women. And children. I couldn't see any of their guns around them, though, only sacks of maize.

My father returned from work. I was going to ask him about the TV report but he seemed irritated so I simply turned off the set.

'Where's your mother?'

I didn't answer, so he knew where. He went to be on his own in his study.

Over dinner, he and I sat at other ends of the table while a tray lay outside my mother's door. The room clattered with the sound of cutlery on china.

'You're very quiet. What's wrong?' My father's beard dripped gravy.

'Nothing,' I replied.

'Did you speak to your mother today?'

'Yes.'

'About your grandmother?'

'Yes.'

'Ah.' He puffed and put his fork down. 'Yes. She said she might. I thought it could have been handled better but there we go. I still don't think she should have . . . I mean, I thought she could have . . .'

He coughed.

'Your grandmother and I never saw eye to eye, and when your mother and I got married . . . Life's complicated, Robert, you'll find that out one day. This hasn't been easy for anyone. Your grandmother's friend Marjorie Downe has sorted it all out, so let's leave it there.'

Sorted it all out? What was to sort out? She'd only gone to a care home. Hadn't she? Why was everyone acting so weirdly?

I wanted to ask but he changed the subject. 'What else did you do today?'

'Nothing much,' I told him. 'I found a statue.'

'That's nice.'

'Right out there, off the strip road. Lieutenant Willington BSAP, or something, he found gold and built the town. I guess this town used to be helluva rich, hey?'

'That's nice,' he said again, 'but only the *whites* in the town would have been rich, the poor Africans who lived here and did all the work wouldn't have got a penny. And don't say "helluva", Robert, it's common slang. Say "very". Maybe you could show me this statue one day.'

'*Ja. Lekker.*'

'When I've got more time on my hands, the office is very busy at the moment. My assistant still isn't pulling his weight.'

'Oh.'

'I don't want to have to fire him. And don't say "lekker", say "great". You sound like a colonial.'

I scooped another piece of meat into my mouth and chewed.

'Dad?'

'Yes, Robert?'

'Do you think the Kaffirs hate us? I mean, they were fighting against us in the war, they hated us then.'

My father pushed his plate.

'First of all, Robert, don't ever, *ever* let me hear you use that kind of language again. We're not sending you to a school that demands the kind of sums it does to raise a racist. Do we have an understanding?'

I nodded.

'Secondly, there is no reason for the Africans to hate *us*. We didn't fight them. Britain and Rhodesia severed ties long ago. Britain was on the Africans' side in the war.'

'Yes, but Britain made Rhodesia. Britain took the land to start with, and you said that was unfair.'

'It was.'

'So the blacks should hate us too, then, shouldn't they?'

He rubbed his forehead. Once upon a time I might have read that sign and stopped, but I remembered how Ivan hadn't stopped the argument with *his* dad and I wanted to be more like him. *He* wouldn't have run away from those two men in the bush as I had.

'You're right. Maybe they should. Europeans treated Africa abominably. Don't get me wrong, I think some good was done during the colonial era, but mostly it was for the extension of power. And, believe me, when power goes to people's heads it all turns very sour, very quickly.'

'So . . .'

'So Mugabe is here to put things right. If there is any hatred in the country, black towards white or white towards black, he's the man to douse it and make sure it never flares up again. He won't tolerate it, I truly believe that. He's proved himself to be a very forgiving man. Sadly there are few like him.'

'Ivan says there were black Rhodesians who didn't want Mugabe, like the Matabele workers on his farm. Some didn't even want the country to change.'

'Who the devil is Ivan?'

'A friend.'

'Well, tell your friend he has a weak argument. I thought even you might have seen that. The people he's talking about had no freedom, no choice, they said what they were told to say.'

'Ivan says it wasn't like that. The enemy . . .'

'I hear what Ivan says and he's wrong. The enemy, as he insists on calling them, were fighting for *freedom*. The real enemy was actually the white government. You can't rule by minority and discriminate against the majority, least of all in a country that wasn't even yours in the first place. It's an unfair, morally twisted and utterly wrong use of power. Like I said, power is a wicked, evil thing. It . . . *corrupts*. It gets under the skin and turns people into something else.'

'So you don't believe the blacks hate us?'

'Of course not.'

'And they don't want to hurt us? You know, for revenge. Because of all that power used against them in the Old Days.'

'Unthinkable.'

'But Mugabe has power now, and you just said power is evil.'

He waved his hand in the air like he was trying to catch escaping thoughts.

'This country is led by a good, unselfish, peace-loving man with the grace and humanity to forgive and forget. He wants the best for everyone. He wants to see a prosperous country because it's in everyone's interest. The word is *Reconciliation*. Trust me, history will remember the name Robert Mugabe for a long time to come.'

I stared into my food.

'Ivan said he promised the blacks he would take all the white land and give it to them if they won,' I said quietly, 'and that all the whites would have to be culled. Will we have to give our house to them?'

'White settlers stole that land by force. They drove families apart and killed innocent people without recrimination. Do you think that's right?'

I shook my head.

'No,' he underlined. 'If there is to be land redistribution in this country it would only be fair. But Mugabe wouldn't do it by force, he knows two wrongs don't make a right.'

'So he won't fight us? Like Ivan says he will?'

My father said nothing for a while, just finished his meal. I could see his jaw muscles working overtime.

'He won't,' he said at last, as though he'd spent all that time thinking about it. 'If you're bored maybe you should ask one of your chums to come and stay. One of your *other* chums. The little chap you bunk next to.'

'Who, *Nelson*?'

'Yes, Nelson.' And then: 'What's wrong with him?'

'Nothing, just that he's a . . .'

My father waited.

'He's not really a friend any more.'

'Why not?'

I shrugged and got a grunt.

'Whereas Ivan is?' He moved his plate to the side and spoke towards the table. 'Friends will only let you down in the end. They always do.'

His face was drawn and sad as he said it, he looked lost. I

ate the rest of my food in silence. When I was done and asked
to be excused, he simply added:

'I'm not sure I think much of this Ivan. I'd even go as far
as to say you'd do a lot better than hang around with the likes
of him. Maybe I should have a word with your housemaster.'

Now, I wish he had. Things might have worked out better
that way.

TWELVE

I tried to find out where my grandmother had been re-homed but my mother refused to tell me and in the end even stopped looking at me when I asked. If she felt bad I didn't see it because she didn't come out of her bedroom again for the rest of the holiday, pretty much, and I didn't come out of mine.

I'd packed my trunk a good twenty-four hours before I was due back. My father merely arched his eyebrows.

'I think you could polish your shoes yourself next time. I see no reason why Matilda should have to do it.'

As it was my last night, my mother made a special effort and joined us for dinner, but my father had to lead her back to bed when she started nodding into her dessert.

'Hey! Jacko's here!' Ivan cried as I walked down the corridor into Selous.

'About time, Jacklin.' Klompie threw a pair of hockey socks into my face so I nearly dropped my tuck box. 'Ivan recks he's checked his wife-to-be, says this chick Adele makes him *jags*.'

'Jeez, man!' Osterberg barked. 'You ever heard of a tan?'

Davidson simply came up and twisted my nipples.

It was great to be back.

I slipped easily into the routine I'd missed: rising, breakfast, chapel, classes, rest, sports, clubs, prep, lights out . . . The solid footing of regularity I didn't get at home, even things like squacks' duties and cold showers. In a bizarre way, Greet was part of it; at least I knew where I stood.

The only real changes were headline sports (cricket and hockey this term as we returned to summer) and afternoon clubs – I got out of having to go to computer club with Simpson-Prior and joined photography with Ivan and Klompie instead. But almost straightaway photography closed because there was no film in the country, so Ivan managed to get us into the rifle club. I've no idea how he managed it.

The other new thing that term was chemistry, or rather the chemistry teacher, because old Mr Pines, who must have been teaching since the white man first stepped foot in the country, was increasingly ending his experiments with his pupils having to open all the windows. Mr Bullman had reduced his classes and got someone else in to help. However, even private schools couldn't pick new teachers at will without the government having some input.

He was trying hard not to, but I swear Mr Bullman looked distinctly embarrassed as he stood centre stage at First Assembly. Of course we'd all spotted him by then, one shining black head in the sea of white staff.

Ivan nudged me. 'Uh oh. We got a fly magnet.'

'. . . Haven is proud to be able to offer this position to the school's first black teacher,' Mr Bullman was saying. 'A symbol of willing unification as we all look to the future,' he read.

As we jostled out I heard senior boys swearing about fucking government spies and the thin end of a wedge.

If Mr Mafiti was a government spy then he wasn't a very good one because he clearly loved his job, especially the experiments, and he often ran over the bell just so that we could see the final explosion or extraction of gas or whatever it was. That was the only point to chemistry, after all, so the more we enjoyed it the less time he spent on giving us prep or doing boring dictation.

Even when a lesson was dull it would have been hard not to like Mr Mafiti. He had a kind face, and outside the lab he possessed an endearing naivety towards all things, often floating around the school like a dazed child at the fair. Some boys teased him, of course, flicking bits of chewed paper when his back was turned, or patting his jacket with the board rubber so that it went all white. But he never got angry. Not once. He found these things funny. I guess we enjoyed him because he was such a breath of fresh air.

As far as a few boys were concerned, however, he was weak so they were cruel.

Ivan really pushed it and started smoking at the back of the lab, ducking low behind the bench to take drags while Mr Mafiti wrote on the board. Mr Mafiti would pause and sniff the air, but if he suspected anything he never said so.

And then there was Pittman, who once put up his hand in the middle of an experiment and asked, 'Excuse me, sir, are you a bastard black?'

Mr Mafiti's everlasting smile dipped momentarily.

'I . . . ehmm . . . I did not hear. What did you say?'

'I said, are you pleased to be back? In the country? You said you lived in Tanzania while the war was on.'

'Yes, I am very pleased to be back.' The smile reappeared. 'Thank you for asking.'

Another time, someone locked an owl in Mr Mafiti's lab so that in the morning he walked in to find feathers everywhere and an extremely agitated bird of prey banging into the windows.

The culprit was never found; all we knew was that he must have had a tough time catching something like that. What I am sure of is that he was there to get his satisfaction as we watched Mr Mafiti come running and shrieking with tears in his eyes.

'It's only a stupid owl.' I tried to cover the fact that I felt sorry for our chemistry teacher. 'It wouldn't harm him.'

'He's a Shona,' Ivan told me matter-of-factly. Unlike the rest of us, neither he nor Pittman had had much to say about the whole episode. 'And Shona hate owls. Bad omens. Some mumbo jumbo about seeing one during daylight means something really bad will happen. They actually believe shit like that.'

Chemistry was the only class Ivan seemed to enjoy, but that had nothing to do with learning. End-of-year exams were coming, yet, while my own grades hovered typically somewhere between Average and Must-Ask-More-Questions, his rolled around the bottom.

'The way I see it, I can either work hard and sweat or I can take it easy. It won't change anything because you don't need exams to farm. I feel sorry for you guys.'

Around the middle of term a Mercedes with government plates appeared outside the Admin Block and was there for hours.

That evening, Taylor gathered everyone for a house war cry out on the lawn. He said he wanted us to remember which was the best house in the school, that it would always be the best, and that we had every right to feel proud to be a part of it. For a moment it looked like he had tears in his eyes. He wiped them and then told us there was to be a special announcement so the whole school had to go to the theatre hall before supper.

Questions buzzed as we took our seats. When Mr Bullman showed he looked really grey and serious, as if the skin on his face had come loose. He climbed the stage and swept back the longer strands of hair from his forehead. He stared straight out, there were no notes.

'As you may or may not have been aware, my boys' – my boys – 'today was the Annual General Meeting of school governors. And this year we were joined by a special . . . *guest*, the Minister for Education, Mr Chapalanga. The Ministry has decided it should sit with the boards of all schools from now on. It wants, it said, to listen, to learn and to have the chance to provide input of mutual benefit.'

Was this it? Was that all?

'Our school, Haven School, is proud to have been built on a foundation of history and tradition, upon which we have endeavoured to establish a sound education system. It is why the boarding houses are named as they are, after the founding pioneers of our once nation. And we believe that we, the providers of this education, have been successful in delivering this strong foundation as we prepare you for your tomorrows.

'You may not realize it now, but you belong to a very privileged club. This is a special place, and you are part of the granite upon which this establishment was founded – solid, immovable, and here for a bloody long time to come.'

He was smiling broadly so everyone laughed. Bully had made a joke!

'But as solid and unmoveable as we are, we must still adapt to our ever-changing surroundings, as all things must. Change should not be denied. Change should not be feared. Change by its very nature requires malleability. If we are to survive we must embrace it.'

Mr Bullman steadied himself. He swallowed hard.

'This is why we have been made to . . . have made the decision with the government to bring the school up-to-date, and to commemorate the modern era.' He paused. 'Specifically, we shall be renaming all of the boarding houses.'

There was a shared gasp. Heads turned one way and the other.

Mr Bullman had to raise a hand.

'Heyman, Forbes, Burnett, Willoughby and Selous . . .' he spoke loudly over us.

The names peeled off in slow succession, doleful shots into the air.

'. . . Next term, at the start of the new academic year, we shall celebrate the founders of our *current* ruling party and rename the houses respectively: Sithole, Takinira, Nkala, Chitepo and Hamadziripi. Your housemasters have been informed and of course welcome this . . . necessity.'

This time he did nothing to stem the mutterings that rose like a flood.

'All I hope,' he said, 'is that . . . All I ask is that you . . .'

He bowed his head.

'Dismissed, boys. Dismissed.'

'Hamadziripi.' Ivan broke the silence, lifting his head from his hands. 'What kind of name is that?'

We were in shock. Everyone in the dining hall was talking about it, even the tables with black boys on them though in a more jokey way. Outside, the night seemed thicker than usual.

'Hamadzi-fucking-ripi. Fuck.'

'I'm leaving,' Klompie declared, nodding. 'This school is wanked. I'm hauling it somewhere better next year. Peterhouse, or Falcon. Or as far as Plumtree. You watch.'

'What's the point?' Ivan sulked. 'They'll get the same. Didn't you hear what Bully said?'

Klompie chewed angrily on a third slice of bread. 'Then I'll *gap* it down south.'

'Don't be so bloody stupid, if you run away you're just letting them win. Except you, Jacklin.' He turned on me suddenly. 'You're not from here, you may as well piss off to your grandmother in Pommieland now.'

I shook my head. 'No ways. I'm not gapping it anywhere.'

Although I couldn't tell him why. Ivan wasn't really listening anyway. His hands went back into his head, pushing up his fringe.

'Shit.'

At that precise moment, Nelson timed things spectacularly badly and walked behind with a bowl of extras. Ivan leaped up as though he'd been stung.

'Hey. *Hey!* Ndube, you piece of shit. What do you think you're doing?'

Reluctantly, Nelson crept back.

'I'm sorry, Hascott.' He didn't know what he was apologizing for.

Ivan reached across the table for one of the large metal serving spoons and stood with it, but by the time he'd turned back round Nelson had gone and Kasanka was in his place. The rest of us took a sudden interest in our plates.

'Leave him, white boy.' As he spoke, Kasanka's top lip curled like there was a bad smell. 'Didn't you hear Mr Bullman? This isn't your country any longer, and now this isn't your school. It never was. We're taking it all back.'

Ivan stood firm. Kasanka came closer.

'I said, leave him.'

Did I imagine it or had the hall quietened to listen?

Ivan sat.

'Stupid Kaffirs,' he growled, though only after Kasanka and Nelson were well out of earshot. 'Don't worry – one day they're sticking together, the next they're stabbing each other in the back. I'll get him another time.'

The table made agreeing noises. I hid by joining in and nodding, even though I could see Kasanka still throwing glances in a way that made my stomach lurch like a dying animal.

THIRTEEN

Two weeks before the end of the school year and another aimless Sunday.

I was alone in the dorm reading *Cujo* because inside was cool and outside was a cloudless day that rained dry November heat.

Simpson-Prior came in. He went to his side of the dorm and lay down, sniffing. I pretended not to hear. In the end he sat up again and started going through his locker for his tracksuit and tennis shoes.

'I'm going out into the bush,' he said.

After the surprise of hearing him talk to me I thought, *'Good'*, wanting him gone because these days I didn't know how to be when he and I were alone together.

'And after it gets dark I'm going to run away from this place. I'm not coming back.' His nose trumpeted. 'I can't take it any more.'

I continued to give him nothing. Whatever he wanted from me I couldn't give it. Or wouldn't. That's a difference I still have difficulty admitting to myself.

'You should never have done what you did to me last term, Jacklin. It was cruel,' he said, reluctantly easing on his *takkies*, and now I felt angry with him because I knew he was right.

'Well, you shouldn't have put my tie in the piss trough in the *first* term just because I didn't let you copy in the maths test. Remember? You pissed in your bed, so now we're even.'

'But I didn't . . .'

'Greet gave me bruises I can still feel. You know he did, you poof, you saw them.' The words gritted my mouth.

'But I didn't touch your tie,' he replied simply.

'*Ja*? Then who did?'

He just looked at me knowingly so I hurled my book into a corner.

'You're such a liar, Prior. Run away, then. Go and play with your stupid snakes, you weirdo.' It would have been so much easier if he wasn't around. 'See if I care. See if anyone cares.'

The dorm seemed to be closing in, I needed to get beyond it and breathe fresh air. Simpson-Prior did nothing, just sat trying to do his laces and getting his fingers tangled. To this day I don't know if he actually spoke, but as I neared the door I heard, perfectly lucid:

'I didn't do anything to you. I didn't do anything wrong.'

I stopped. Eventually I turned to him and, just as I opened my mouth, three figures appeared at the top of the stairs.

Ivan shouted through cupped hands.

'Hey, Jacko, we're going to the Cliffs. Stop strangling your cock and come with us.'

Klompie was with him, and Pittman had come over from Heyman. Pittman seemed to have become one of Ivan's new best friends. I still didn't know much about him, only that I wasn't sure I liked him and that I was too scared to admit that to anyone.

'What are you waiting for? Are you coming or are you going to be gay?'

Simpson-Prior was a sorry smudge in the corner of my eye. Two steps forward and he was gone, and my sight was clear again.

Klompie was carrying shovels, and when we got there Ivan told us we had to dig long-drops because if this was going to be our camp then we shouldn't just shit in the bush like blacks or the place would start to stink.

The ground was dry and hard and made us sweat, so it wasn't long before we had to break for a jump. The water was crisp but the level must have gone down because we really graunched ourselves on the rocks beneath the surface and hurt our feet even with shoes on, so we only did the one. We splashed around for a bit then climbed back up and hung our shirts out to dry.

Ivan scratched all our names on a tree and produced a packet of Madisons.

'Go on,' Ivan told me. 'Don't be a faggot all your life.'

Pittman muttered something under his breath that made the other two laugh so I took one. Ivan nodded approval.

We started talking about the summer holidays. Klompie's uncle had a new boat so they were going to spend Christmas up at Caribbea Bay.

Pittman's folks were taking them down south, to Sun City.

'A whole month of mini-golf and beach pools and casinos in a country where I'm free to call the blacks what I like.'

'Sounds fun.' I hadn't meant to sound sarcastic.

'Well, what are *you* doing then, Pommie?' He stared at me until I had to put my eyes to the ground.

'Nothing really.'

'Nothing? What kind of holiday is that?'

'I don't know. Just ordinary, I guess.'

'*Ordinary?*'

I was blushing and smoke kept getting in my eyes. Ivan stepped in and I was glad.

'Well, while you guys are pretending to have a good time, think of me feeling Adele Cairns up at the Country Club.'

Thankfully, Pittman laughed. 'Bullshit, man. She's our age, chicks always go for older guys.'

'Not after I feed her a couple of beers. I swear, she's grown serious *nyombies*. Best tits in the world.'

And we jeered as boys who don't know what it's like do.

A bit later Ivan and I were digging together. Klompie and Pittman were off getting sticks for a fire; wood smoke was the best for disguising tobacco.

'Don't worry about Pitters,' he assured me. 'It's just how he is.'

Then he stopped a moment to say something I would never forget.

'But you know your problem, Jacko? You don't stick up for yourself. No life is ordinary. Not yours, not anyone's. Not even Prior's, and that's saying something. Only the blacks'. Don't let anyone tell you otherwise.'

'Sure,' I muttered. I laid my spade on the ground. I felt buoyed up but he'd reminded me of the thing niggling the back of my mind. 'Do you feel sorry for him ever?'

'Who?'

'Prior.'

Ivan looked at me long and hard.

'Do you?'

I shrugged.

'Are you serious? Still?'

'No. Kind of. I don't know.'

'The guy's a chop, man, this school doesn't need his sort. If you want to be his friend, that's your lookout; you can do whatever you like.'

He speared the ground.

'Really?'

'Of course. But know this: you won't be hanging around us if you do. You're on your own.'

Those words, especially, made my heart race. He looked completely different, and I wished and wished I could take back what I'd said. And it was all Simpson-Prior's fault. Why did he have to speak to me that morning?

'But I don't.'

'You don't what?'

'Want to. Be his friend.'

'Doesn't sound like it to me.'

'I swear. He's an idiot.'

Ivan carried on digging, working so hard the sweat came off him like a leaking tap. Suddenly I was in the scary end of a swimming pool and getting into trouble.

The bush behind us rustled. I threw down my cigarette but it was only Nelson, staring back at me like a bushbaby caught in headlights. We mirrored each other's awkwardness for a few seconds – two boys who'd once promised to look out for one another like brothers and now did their best to avoid even being in the same room, let alone talk – before the Agostinho cousins joined him from behind. They'd all taken their shirts off because of the heat.

I started digging again. Ivan, however, wasn't interested in me or the hole.

'Well, well. What do we have here?' He walked slowly over. He picked up a stick off the ground and prodded Christos Agostinho's soft overhang. 'You know, that's not nice, you're scaring the wildlife.'

'*Ja*, put your shirt on, fatso.' I saw Pittman. He and Klompie looked like they'd sprinted to get back. 'What are you doing, girls, don't you know this is our camp?'

Klompie giggled stupidly.

'N-nothing.' Paulos Agostinho shuffled. 'Just came for a swim. That's all.'

'It's hot,' Christos added, as if it would make a difference.

'Well, this is *our* camp.' Klompie waved his own stick but it was too thin and broke. '*Voetsek*! Piss off somewhere else, you can't come here.'

All the while, Ivan and Pittman's eyes were on Nelson. Nelson didn't say a word.

All three started to leave. Maybe it was imagination, but both Ivan and Pittman seemed to move without sound as they cut them off. The sun was bouncing off the ground and making me squint, and I felt the start of a headache.

'Jump,' Ivan told them. 'If that's what you want to do. Seeing as it's so hot we'll let you. Go on.'

And when they didn't, Ivan only had to flick his eyes and Pittman and Klompie had the cousins on the ground, ripping off their *takkies* and flinging them into the bush. A scramble of dust, and they were dragged to the edge. Pittman went first, shoving Christos; Klompie sent Paulos right behind. We watched as they windmilled then smacked the water, then came up crying.

Nelson tried to move away.

'You fancy a dive?' Pittman gripped his arm. 'Go on, give us a show.'

Nelson gasped as his toes curled over the lip.

'Just don't hit the ledge as you go down, you'll make a helluva mess.'

'OK, enough. Don't be cruel,' said Ivan. 'His sort don't like water.'

Everyone turned. I may have sighed with relief.

But then Ivan smiled.

He snatched Nelson and pulled him over to the hole we'd made. It wasn't big yet but deep and long enough to hold someone small – a shallow grave. Ivan held him down and started filling. Pittman was quickly there, kicking soil with his feet while Nelson struggled helplessly, his eyes and mouth full of grit. Klompie ran over.

'Well?' Ivan yelled at me. 'Are you going to join in or are you going back to your bum-chum Prior?'

I went to Ivan. Slowly at first, pretending to have thorns in my feet, but with every step I felt myself easing back into the safety of the shallows and I rushed the last couple of metres. I lifted earth and patted it down. Lifted and patted. Before long, all you could see of Nelson was a head and half a foot sticking out at the other end.

I laughed. He looked funny. And, after all, that's all it was: a joke. Just a bit of schoolboy fun.

Wasn't it?

I thought that would be it – it *should* have been it – but Ivan wanted more. He scoured under a tree and came back with a couple of Matabele ants, inch-long and with huge jaws ready to inject sting.

'Are you Shona or Matabele?' he crouched, menacingly gentle.

Nelson's eyes darted. 'What does it matter what tribe I am?' he said earnestly. 'I didn't choose it, and it's only a stupid label anyway.'

'Tell me.'

'I'm Shona, but . . .'

'Really? Are you sure?'

Ivan shook the ants free over Nelson's head. Nelson cried out as they went into attack mode and bit into his cheek and neck.

Ivan clapped. 'Well, look at that, he must have been telling the truth. Those Matabeles sure don't like him much.'

Klompie thought this was the best thing ever and imme-diately went off to find more. That was when he found the scorpion.

It was only small, about three inches, and one of the less dangerous white ones. Its tail was curled ready to strike. Ivan took it and dangled it in front of Nelson's face.

'*Ja*, man,' Pittman whispered excitedly.

My head had started to pound.

'*Ja*,' Pittman said again, licking his lips.

Klompie nodded.

Ivan crouched back down and scooped at the soil.

Nelson cried. 'Hey, man, what are you doing? I'm sorry, OK, I'm really sorry, I didn't mean to . . . Hey, man. Hey. *Hey*!'

Ivan had cleared enough to reveal the top of Nelson's shorts, and with a quick movement he pulled open the elastic and dropped the scorpion in. Nelson squealed, trying to arch his body, only Ivan was already pushing the soil back and stamping it down.

As we ran away, adrenaline pumping, we could hear Nelson's screams fading across the *vlei*; although I could hear them for a long, long time after. Today, even.

FOURTEEN

Kasanka threw baleful eyes down the line.

I put on a mask like I didn't know what was going on, but we'd all heard: Nelson hadn't come back to the house . . . he was in the San . . . the Agostinho cousins had taken him . . . apparently he'd been bitten by something out in the bush and Sister Lee was keeping him in overnight.

Mr Craven wasn't happy. He wouldn't tolerate *any* form of bullying, and if he found out who it was there would be suspensions. And, on another matter, did anyone know the whereabouts of Simpson-Prior?

I looked up and Kasanka was still staring. I felt sick.

Much later, just before Lights Out, Kasanka walked into our dorm. He didn't say anything, just whistled and sauntered so casually it was anything but. He had a big stick and tapped our beds and lockers.

'Don't worry about it,' Ivan told me when he'd gone. 'He doesn't know. Ndube won't tit on us and nor will the fat Portuguese.'

'What if they do?' I asked.

He hit my head. 'They won't. You don't tell on anyone in this school. No one does.'

The following morning Kasanka told me I stank of shit and

made me stand under the cold shower for twenty minutes before breakfast.

'He knows,' I said to Ivan after French.

'Shut up. Everyone thinks it was Prior, that that's why he ran.'

'But Kasanka knows.'

'Not unless Ndube titted on us. I'll have a word with him when he's out the San.'

Only Nelson got sent home, suffering with severe inflammation of the penis and testicles. Mr Craven was visibly angry as he told us. Deadly serious. First Nelson, and now Simpson-Prior's parents had rung him to say he'd arrived home in a state, what had the house done to him?

No one laughed, at least not until Craven was out of earshot. I wished I could join in but all I wanted was for the swirling feeling in my stomach to go away. And wherever I was, at any time, Kasanka was just *there*.

In the dream I was falling and suddenly being caught in this giant web, and a huge baboon spider came rushing out and started turning me over and over as it cocooned me up to die.

I woke, perhaps with a cry. After a moment I realized I was wrapped up in my sheets, bouncing and floating. I heard heavy breathing and someone grunting very near by.

When I hit the ground the sheets fell open and I saw the milky night sky.

Blink.

I was in the middle of one of the playing fields.

Blink.

Kasanka was standing over me with Nyabuta, also a fifth-former, their dark faces gleaming in a faint silver moon. Kasanka's eyelids were half-lidded. Both boys smelled of alcohol.

'Tell me it was you,' Kasanka's voice came out in a slow drawl.

'Me what?' I said, but he knew, and he knew I knew that. He kicked my feet. Nyabuta dug a knee into my back.

'Don't play games with me, honky. Was it you – yes or no? Were you at the Cliffs on Sunday?'

And when I still didn't answer he threw something into my face. A T-shirt, and it had my name tag in it.

I opened my mouth but nothing came. Kasanka loomed close.

'You don't have to lie any more, Jacklin. Tell me it was you,' he said, all calm.

My throat was arid.

'Don't make this worse for yourself. Just be honest and admit you did it.'

And then with more urgency: 'You got him because of who he is. Because he's black. Just like in the Old Days, hey?'

I think I tried to shake my head.

Nyabuta pinned my elbows down while Kasanka grabbed my ankles. He took something out of his pocket.

'Go on, say it. Say what you think. There's nothing wrong with being honest.' He nudged me closer to the precipice. 'Say it. You got him because of his skin. That's how you think, isn't it? It's how you *all* think. Give me the word. The name you and your friends save for the likes of him and me. That's it. Say it and it'll all be over.'

I started to cry. A noise rose from my throat.

'*Say it*, you honky shit.'

'*Stop!*'

The voice cut through the air, not loud but full of authority. The moment stood still. Kasanka and Nyabuta turned and lightened their hold, and I almost floated off the field. Without surprise, I saw it was Ivan.

'Jacklin didn't do it,' he said. 'He wasn't even there. I borrowed his shirt. It was me.'

'Bullshit. You're lying,' Kasanka told him.

'Why would I lie about something like that?'

'To protect him.'

'He can look after himself. If he had done it I would be more than happy to watch this little show, but I'm not going to let him take the flak for something I did.' And when the two seniors didn't respond: 'What's the matter? Are you deaf or did you get vaseline in your ears, you stupid fucking Kaffirs?'

Slowly, Kasanka and Nyabuta stood. I groaned and crawled away. When I got to him, Ivan reached down and helped me up.

'Run your lily-white arse back to the house, Jacklin,' Kasanka shouted over. 'We're done with you.'

Ivan held me. His face was stone in this light, his eyes like distant black holes. Barely noticeable, he gave me a nod.

I ran to the edge of the field, up the granite steps and to the perimeter road. I paused to turn and I could just see they'd made Ivan sit while they stood in front of him.

A few more feet, and the darkness had stolen them completely.

He never spoke about what happened that night, not even to show off the bruises, so I never asked. All I knew was that it had been bad because it took a couple of days before he really said anything to anyone. He just kept himself to himself. Klompie and Pittman both came up to me one afternoon and asked what the hell his problem was because he'd just shoved Klompie against the wall for no reason and told them both to *voetsek* and leave him alone.

But what could I say? So I said nothing and promised myself I never would.

If they asked me the same question today I'd tell them that *that* was the point at which Ivan waved goodbye to everything forever – the school, his friends, his childhood, his farm. His life. He was curling in on himself and starting to die a long, protracted death.

On the very last day of term, and of the academic year, there was an angry clap of thunder. There'd been many in the preceding weeks; this one, finally, held the promise of rain.

I was in the phone booth at the time, the school was almost empty and my parents still weren't there to collect me. The line crackled loudly in my ear a fraction before the thunder came.

'Yes, Weekend!'

'Ah! Mastah Rhrob-ett. *Masikati.*'

'*Masikati,* Weekend. *Kanjani, shamwari.*'

'*Mushi. Kanjani,* my friend?'

'*Mushi sterek.* I'm great too.'

'So tell me, Mastah Rhrob-ett, what is it that I should do? My new girlfriend says she must have also the gift I have given to my other girlfriend, but I have no more money to buy and now she is ver-ry very angry . . .'

Out of the small window I watched a dust devil play with leaves. The air was humming, the giant clouds sweeping in from beyond the classrooms were the colour of charred wood. An almighty storm was on its way.

FIFTH FORM
1985

FIFTEEN

Fairford paused, raised a half-cocked arm like they do in the movies and crouched low. The rest of the line stopped and crouched too, all except Ivan, who stayed standing at the back and rolled his eyes. We thought Fairford had spotted one of the other groups, but as he fidgeted with his pack we quickly realized he just needed to shit.

He hurried round a rise with a bog roll in his hand.

The remaining six of us groaned and rested up, absorbing the sun. The sky was clear but the high mountain air was taking time to warm, and a night of almost constant downpour had made us damp and tired.

Ivan went and sat on a rock and lit up a Madison. Technically, term had started, but for us the start of fifth form meant this survival lesson up the Chimanimanis, and even though there was a handful of masters on the mountains there were hundreds of square miles of high terrain for them not to find us for the whole week.

It had always been an annual thing, to send fifth formers up the Chims – a prelude to O levels to inspire resourcefulness and lateral thinking. The expeditions had been stopped during the war, when it was far too dangerous to be hiking so close to the border. We were only the second expedition to be allowed up here since since the war had ended. The army was fairly confident it had cleared most of the land mines.

'Hey, score us a smoke, china,' I called.

With barely a turn of the head, Ivan tossed the packet over.

The sharp taste bit my tongue as I lit one and I threw the box straight back into his open hand. Ivan continued his own smoke in silence.

We were at one of the highest points here. To the left and right, the way we had come and the way we were going, the line of the green and grey mountains stretched on – the granite outline known as Dragon's Tooth jutted out against the southern skyline. Behind us, craggy turrets of rock hunched and loomed like drunken old men, while ahead the ground plateaued right across to the other side of the range. Beyond, Mozambique lay low and flat far into the east.

I sat next to Ivan, dangling my feet.

'So what do you reck the new history teacher's going to be like?' I said.

Ivan made a noise. 'Who gives a crap?'

I suppose I should have expected that. For the whole of last year – in fact, from the point Kasanka had done whatever he'd done at the end of our first year in the school, Ivan had consistently declared his hatred for the place. He was leaving as soon as he could. Now we were in fifth form, in the year all of us would hit sixteen, and his end was in sight.

'You hear about Bedford-Shaw? Apparently his old man said it's only a matter of time before the government takes all the white farms so he decided to sell up and move to Namibia. They'll be gone by the end of term. Do you think Mugabe will?'

Ivan wasn't listening. He pointed over towards the border.

I counted three women moving away from us across the plateau, bare-breasted and bare-footed, and each one balancing a huge sack of maize on her head.

'I hate those nannies coming over to take our food,' he said, 'but you can't blame them. See what happens when blacks come into power? Mozambique used to be great, the

Portuguese knew what they were doing, but since the Kaffirs won it back the place has crumbled. It's a heap of shit now. You know things must be bad if those three have to cross a whole mountain range for a bag of *sadza* to feed their families, and I bet they didn't pay in cash, if you know what I mean.'

He sighed long and loud. He looked so sad.

'It had better not happen here.'

Fairford came scampering back from his business, waving bog paper over his head.

Ivan sneered, so I said, 'Fairford is such a chop. He even looks like one – check, his T-shirt fits him like a giant fore-skin.'

I was pleased to see the smile reappear.

'*Guys!*' Fairford whispered loudly. 'I found one of the other groups.'

No one moved. Fairford jumped up and down.

'Come *on*, guys. I'm group leader so you have to do what I say. That's what being a leader's all about.'

Reluctantly, we followed him round the rise. Almost without warning the ground fell away and we found ourselves peering over a fifty-foot drop. In the gorge, seven boys were splashing about in dick-shrinking water, their clothes and packs strewn across the rocks.

'Hey, that's Henchie and Davidson. And Rhys-Maitland,' said Arnold, standing up.

Fairford yanked him back down. 'You can't do that, they'll see us.'

'So?'

'So . . . ? They'll know we're here and beat us to Dragon's Tooth, and I want to come first.'

'So?' Arnold was bigger than Fairford. 'You're too late anyway; your mother's been going up there for years waiting for schoolboys and I heard she always comes first.'

We all laughed.

Ivan spotted a load of baboons hiding in the tops of the trees about twenty metres from the pool. Davidson and the rest of the boys from our year couldn't have realized they were there.

Nelson was in that group, too. Ivan grinned.

'Time for a bit of fun,' he said. 'Let's rattle the cage.'

'Are you serious?' Fairford looked worried. 'Have you ever seen a baboon's teeth close up? Besides, there's no path down.'

'Who said anything about going down?' Ivan's brow darkened. I really thought he was going to hit Fairford. 'We use stones, you chop.'

'From here? You'll *never* get them.'

Ivan walked away from the edge and stood his packet of Madisons on a small rock forty feet away. He came back and handed me a stone.

'Show them,' he said.

I looked round. Everyone was waiting.

'Go on, do your trick,' Ivan insisted.

I liked his faith in me. Holding my breath (because that was the only way to be sure of a good shot, keep the body steady), I tossed the stone up a few inches, snatched it out of the air then flung it hard without pausing because it sometimes didn't work if I thought about it too much. Two seconds later the Madisons box jumped and disappeared.

'Shit, Jacklin! *Lekker!*'

'Holy crap!'

Ivan grabbed another stone and walked me back to the edge.

'There,' he said. 'The big daddy in the middle. You check?'

I pulled back a second time and released.

For a moment I thought I'd pushed it too hard, but gravity did its stuff and sucked the stone down, and I stung the baboon right on its ugly backside. Instantly it let out a loud bark and leaped like a crazy from branch to branch. All the other baboons went berserk.

Those boys needed only one glance. They sprang from the water and we were rewarded with the sight of six skinny white arses, one fat one and one black one sprinting down the slope. We couldn't see how far they got because we were all bent double. Only Ivan stayed watching, his face belonging to someone who was satisfying an overpowering hunger. I hadn't seen that face in a while, and I felt both pleased and anxious that I'd helped it happen.

'He's called Mr van Hout.' I tried to distract him and lure him away from the edge.

His forehead blistered into a frown. 'Who is?'

'Our new history teacher. That's his name.'

'So what? Jeez, Jacklin, which bit of "*Who gives a crap?*" don't you understand?'

SIXTEEN

We only had to wait until the fourth lesson to get our first glimpse, but five minutes in and Mr van Hout still hadn't shown. It was all Ivan needed to decide the guy was obviously as much of a complete *gumbie* as his name made him sound and he'd either got lost or forgotten his timetable. Of course, Klompie and I agreed.

I gazed out of the open window, to where the heat had brought ominous clouds.

Suddenly the door burst open.

Our illegal whispers evaporated in an instant and we stood dutifully to attention, eyes front, but no one was there. The door hung limply on its hinges. We stared at the hole it had made and after a long thirty seconds there was still nothing more than the walkway and the area of grass beyond it. We began to swap glances.

'All of you sit down.'

We startled and swung round. At the back of the classroom, outside, a pair of intense blue eyes beneath a thick blond fringe peered over the ledge of the window. Bronzed hands crept over and in the next second he'd pulled himself up and in with one fluid, easy movement.

'Are you guys deaf or stupid?' he said, dusting himself down. He was wearing slacks and a short-sleeved shirt. No tie. 'If the answer is yes to either, then my job just got a great deal harder. I said sit down, you're making me nervous.'

We did as we were told. The teacher marched to the front

and shoved the door shut, kicked out his chair and sat with both feet on the desk, one over the other. He pushed back and lit up a smoke.

'Howzit.'

No one said a word.

The teacher got up with a big smile and took another drag before flicking the cigarette out of the window. He snatched up a piece of chalk and wrote MR VAN HOUT on the board, and HISTORY underneath it.

'OK, guys.' He stabbed a full stop. 'First things first: this is me, and this is what you're here to learn. Any questions?'

None.

'Good, because it's all perfectly simple. Right, harder question coming up. Someone please tell me what this means.'

He underlined HISTORY.

We'd never seen a teacher like him before. For a start, he was years younger than any of the other masters. And then there was . . . well, *everything*.

'*Ach*, man. Deaf, stupid and mute? They've given me a class of bloody vegetables. Somebody . . . ?'

'It doesn't really mean anything.'

A classic Ivan response.

Sir blinked at him. '"It doesn't really mean anything." I admire your courage but you can't say something like that without backing it up.'

'It's in the past. You can't change it.'

Ivan put a grin on for the class while Mr van Hout looked only vaguely amused.

'You honestly believe that?'

'Yes, sir.'

'Then I feel sorry for you. Someone else, an example of history please. You.'

Fairford rocked in his seat. 'The Second World War, sir?'

'Good.' Mr van Hout's eyes flashed. The blue was captivating, like staring into a fire. 'Broad and a little clichéd, but at least we're off the mark, hey.'

'The First World War,' Rhys-Maitland called out.

'Vietnam War,' Osterberg followed right behind.

Mr van Hout acted a yawn.

'If I had a dollar . . . Anyone give me something without "war" in the title?'

A sea of blank. Then: 'The first launch of the space shuttle Columbia,' I heard myself say.

The class rippled and I blushed.

But Mr van Hout clapped. '*Ex*-cellent. Spot on.'

He turned and underscored HISTORY three more times while Ivan slapped me with a ruler and mouthed, 'Bogfly.'

I slapped him straight back.

'Because history,' Mr van Hout went on, 'doesn't just mean wars, and boring kings and queens, and endless bloody dates. It means everything. Everything in the past is history: your breakfast, what you did in the holidays, last year's crap rugby score against Prince Edward . . . All history. The essential element, however, is being able to pick out what's worth remembering because of its importance in the present and impact on *tomorrow*. The launch of the shuttle was a crucial event because it was *important* in the context of Soviet-US relations, and it helped shape the Cold War. History affects the *future*. Remember that. I'll give you another example. My entrance this morning: was that worth remembering?'

'No, sir.' Ivan again.

'You seem very certain of that. So it hasn't affected you?'

'Not at all, sir. I thought it was stupid.' He paused. 'Did you fight in *our* war, sir?'

Mr van Hout perched on the edge of his desk.

'Well, Hascott, I beg to differ – yes, I know who you are.

They told me to watch out for you. For a start, you *will* remember it whether you want to or not because I guarantee no other Haven teacher has come through the window and fired up a *gwaai* to start a lesson. They certainly didn't when I was a pupil here. Secondly, you will deem it important enough to tell your buddies, for the same reason. And thirdly . . .'

We waited eagerly for what he had to say.

'Thirdly, it has formed your opinion of me, and has therefore moulded the shape of our learning over the coming year: already you trust me, consciously or sub-consciously you know I won't regurgitate shit from the textbooks because I'm here to show you what history is *really* about.'

He moved back to the board and began to wipe it clean, stopping when only the *HOUT* part of his name was left.

'One more thing, Hascott: the *course* of history is never set. It's changing all the time. I have no doubt you find my name amusing and intend to circulate a nickname for me on that note I saw you scribbling, probably "*houtie*" or a similar derogatory slang term for an African person. You can make fun of my name in any way you want – I'm a teacher, it comes with the territory – but I advise you at least to be informed. Find out what my name actually means and write it out a hundred times. See? *I've* altered the course of history already.'

A quick swipe and his name was gone.

'And whether I fought in the war is no concern of yours.' He thumped the board rubber down.

We found him in a photograph up on the wall in Burnett House. (We never called the houses by their newer African names except to take the piss, so that Sithole became 'Shithole', Takanira became 'Wanker-Nearer' . . . that sort of thing.) Frozen in black and white, he was sitting in 1973. Those were the days when each house only had about three dozen boys because of the war.

He was in the middle row. He looked different without his moustache and a lot skinnier, and they all had funny straight fringes and shaved temples, but it was definitely him, we could tell from the eyes.

'Looks as much of a chop as now,' Ivan scowled, still sulking, and pressed his middle finger to the glass. 'He didn't fight, he looks like a K-loving objector if ever there was one.'

'What a wuss,' Pittman said.

De Klomp mumbled. '*Ja*, and history's stupid.'

He pretended to punch the young Mr van Hout, only he was standing closer than he realized and almost broke the glass. One of the Burnett sixth formers told us to piss off to our own houses.

We ran back laughing, but Ivan needed to work off steam and said he was going to beat the first junior he saw, then virtually tripped over Nelson in the corridor. Nelson had grown a lot in the last year, not yet sixteen and already a flea's kneecap under six feet. Still thin, but all his training with the Junior Team was making him stronger. Not that it really mattered how strong he was because he hadn't ever forgotten the day of the scorpion down at the Cliffs, and with a sudden look of terror he jumped right out of the way.

For anyone else it would have been a futile escape attempt. Ivan, however, walked harmlessly by as though he hadn't seen him. As he always did these days. I often thought maybe he *couldn't* see him, or if he did he saw Kasanka lurking somewhere nearby, because Kasanka hadn't forgotten the day of the scorpion, either. Kasanka was Head of House this year; he could do whatever he wanted, and Ivan knew he only had to raise an eyebrow at Nelson and he'd get a mauling.

Ivan went to find someone else to pick on instead.

SEVENTEEN

In no time History was the one class we would look forward to. It was different from anything we'd had before, but I got the feeling some of the older masters didn't like Mr van Hout too much because none of them really talked to him and gave him sidelong glances when they walked past him. Every so often our class would erupt in laughter and doors to other classrooms would close. We reckoned they were just jealous.

When we had a double, Mr van Hout let us lie on the grass during the break for ages, and now and again he told us to close our books and he recounted stories of what it was like when *he* was at Haven. The best lessons were when he put his head round the door and curled his finger for us to follow, and we would go and sit under a tree and talk, not about history or about him but about us, because he wanted to know, he said.

Now and again, however, he would come in and we knew straightaway there would be no fun. We just had to sit and wait for those lessons to pass, like when the horizon turns grey and you hear thunder crashing towards you.

One day Mr van Hout threw the door shut with enough force to almost split the wood, and then attacked the board with the rubber. Mr Mafiti had started sharing Mr van Hout's classroom because one of Mr Pines's experiments had almost burned down the chemistry lab. Yet again the board was covered with Mr Mafiti's equations with missing numbers and letters for some other class's test, and the words PLEASE LEAVE across the top.

When it was all gone Mr van Hout slammed the rubber on the desk so hard a huge white cloud blew up.

'Tell me,' he said, 'if I stood you in front of a man, pressed the cold metal of a gun into your palm and told you to squeeze the trigger, would you do it?'

He seemed to be looking at me as he said it. Only me. I felt my ears start to go pink.

'No, sir.'

'Are you sure?'

'Of course, sir. No ways!'

Slowly, he sat. His eyes continued to smoulder.

'What if I then told you we'd gone back in time and his name was Adolf Hitler? Would you do it then? Would you? *Would* you?'

My mouth moved silently.

'*I* would, sir.'

I turned to Ivan, cut by a flash of anger because he'd stolen my answer even though I hadn't known what that answer was. Sir had been talking to *me*.

'I'd slot him one in the gonads, then in the neck so he still knew what was going on, then in the head, but only after he'd begged.' Ivan met my glance and I had to look away. 'What about you, sir? What would you do? Would you have the *guts*?'

The air bristled. We all thought Mr van Hout was going to go *penga* but instead he got up and stared out the window. He seemed calm but we could see his jaw muscles working big time.

In the end he said, 'That's something you can think about yourself while you write me an essay on how much better the world would have been if someone *had* killed the world's most notorious bastard before he came to power. A thousand words by the end of the week. In fact, that goes for the whole class.'

Everyone groaned. Ivan just glared.

Sir didn't like it.

'Stay behind after class, Hascott.'

'He doesn't care.' Pittman stated the obvious as we waited on the low wall in front of the chapel, although it was starting to look like Mr van Hout was going to keep Ivan for the whole of break.

'Do you reck he's beating him?' Klompie wondered.

'What with, you idiot? He doesn't have a cane in there.'

'He might be using his boot.'

'Don't be a dufus all your life.'

'He might be.'

'I said, shut up, OK?' Pittman delivered a swift dead arm. 'You're treading on my pubes, man. If he *is* getting beaten then he bloody deserves it.'

'I reck he's trying to get expelled,' I offered.

Both Pittman and Klompie seized me with a look of fear and loathing.

'He hates school, hates lessons. All he wants is to work on the farm but his old man won't let him until he's finished here.'

They thought about it.

'If he does then he's an idiot,' Pittman said at last. I knew he didn't mean it.

Over by the Admin Block a black Mercedes pulled up, and a chauffeur opened up the door to let out two black men in snazzy suits and shades. We could see Bully coming to greet them as quickly as he could, smiling stupidly.

'Fucking government. *Now* what do they want?' Klompie spoke for all of us.

Pittman grabbed his books and stood.

'I'm going to head.'

'Where to?' I asked.

'Back to *Heyman*, of course,' he said deliberately, no doubt hoping the inspectors would hear. 'Break's over in ten and I'm not getting into more trouble on Ivan's account today.'

By morning all pictures of the Prime Minister around the school had been changed to include an important new detail.

Mr van Hout came into class holding a newspaper and reading about it, shaking his head and frowning.

'"*An honorary degree from Edinburgh University*"' – as though he didn't know we were there – '"*for services to education in Africa.*" Give me a break! They've got to be bloody joking.'

He trailed off, folded the paper and tossed it in the bin.

'A black and mysterious world.' Then he acknowledged us. 'Still, what do the Scots know, hey? Let our great leader have his degree, he can't get one any other way.'

He laughed, so we laughed. Yesterday was a long time ago.

'OK, essays. Hand them to the front.' And when we baulked: 'Jeez, guys, I was joking. Forget about the essays. If you've already started them I apologize, just think of it as a chance to practise your handwriting.'

He started to clear the board – more of Mr Mafiti's equations. I think Sir found satisfaction in erasing them now.

'Except you, Hascott.' He didn't even pause to turn. 'Don't look so pleased with yourself, I still want yours.'

I swear, the guy must have had eyes in the back of his head. Ivan gave him the finger, but only from under his desk.

EIGHTEEN

It was turning out to be an achingly hot term.

Maybe because of it, Ivan walked slowly to class most mornings just so that he could target juniors who overtook us. I remember one day in particular, when he was pushing books out of boys' hands and slapping the backs of their legs with his ruler. One pair tried to take a wide berth, but they were both black and Kasanka was nearby so Ivan let them get away and got the next lot instead.

He shoved one deep into the hedge while Klompie tripped the other one up. I had to do something.

'What's my name?' I demanded of the one in the hedge.

'Jack . . . Jacklin,' he spluttered.

'And don't forget it,' I said. 'Next time, *ask* if you want to pass. You guys get it too easy, we had it harder.'

Pittman joined us. Never wanting to miss out on the chance for fun he bit a hole in the packet of milk he'd just got from the tuck shop and squirted it at any junior or black that came close. When Nelson walked by, however, Ivan suddenly grabbed Pittman's arm because over by the chapel steps Kasanka was still there.

'Leave that one alone.'

Pittman yanked away. 'What are you talking about, man?'

'Just let him go, OK? *Lorse.*'

'Why should I?' Pittman looked keen to battle.

Ivan couldn't say. Only I knew his secret and I was never going to let it out.

'You got new friends you haven't told us about?' Pittman goaded, a challenge to the throne.

Ivan squared up and I thought it would kick off when we noticed Mr van Hout watching, standing with hands on hips.

The bell sounded and he disappeared slowly into his classroom.

When we got there he wouldn't look up or even meet us in the eye, and in the lesson he paced up and down and just read. He sounded bored with it. *We* were bored with it. Everyone was restless and uncomfortable, and I don't think it was because of the heat.

After a while Sir snapped the book shut mid-sentence and flipped it out of the window. We watched in disbelief.

He sat and threw his feet onto the desk. He was wearing shorts that day, and teachers never wore shorts to lessons.

'The first rule of nature,' he told us, 'is inequality.'

He leaned back, scratched the word INEQUALITY in chalk then slapped the board with his hand.

'That's not opinion. That's fact.'

He looked at our faces.

'Jesus, the blinds are down today, aren't they? Bloody idiots. A cheetah can outrun a zebra, a dog can outrun a cat . . . Some things in life are meant to be, the strongest are meant to survive. It's how it works.'

We stayed under the cover of silence and I thought he might throw his chair at us, or something.

'Wake up, people. *Think*, you morons! Have you learned nothing? It's 1914, and Germany has the stronger army and wipes its arse with Europe . . .'

'But Germany *lost* the war,' Osterberg offered bravely.

'Hallelujah! One of you gets it.' Sir slow-clapped, really heavily. 'They did lose, but only because the Brits learned, in their sorry little corner, that *they* were the best and so they'd better get organized and shit right back.'

He shot Osterberg with a finger gun.

'That's called evolution. You have to evolve. The Brits did, and Germany subsequently got their arses severely caned and were left in the ditch. While the world wasn't watching, however, Hitler turned it all around and tried for a second go and the Brits had to prove themselves again.'

Mr van Hout scored about a hundred lines under INEQUALITY.

'None of us is equal. Yet everyone's fighting for the top of the pile. The sooner you learn this the better, or you'll spend the rest of your sorry lives at the bottom of the heap and not where you belong. Shit back!'

He let that settle around us. I found myself thinking about my grandmother, and England, and my mother and how she had broken her promise, and I saw how I should have stood up to her. I *should* stand up to her – she shouldn't have done what she did – and I decided then and there that the next time I saw her, finally, I would.

I felt better about myself already. Sir was right.

He went on.

'Look at our own country. The Poms came shooting guns and the blacks tried to defend themselves with soft fruits. Quite rightly, only one side was ever going to win that battle: the *superior* side. But years later the blacks saw that what *we'd* built was good and wanted what *we'd* worked so hard for, and they tried to take it. They became violent, and because no one was willing to help us they struggled long and viciously and dirtily enough to steal what was *ours*. Now look where we are.'

Mr van Hout stood and put a smoke between his lips.

'The question is, when are we going to turn it around again and fight for what rightfully belongs to *us*?' He stopped and stared right at Ivan. 'Or are they just going to keep pushing you around? Maybe you don't know how to stand up for yourself.'

I could see the flames in Ivan's cheeks. He gripped his pencil so tightly I thought it might splinter.

'Ultimately, it's all about self-respect,' Sir said, 'and integrity. If you have some, there's still a chance. If you let them take it, we're screwed.'

'At least some had the integrity to fight in the first place.' Ivan spoke through taut lips.

Mr van Hout appeared to find that amusing.

'Oh, Hascott . . .'

He took a couple more drags then trod his *gwaai* into the floor. He walked towards the back of the class. Everyone kept their heads down.

The next thing we knew there was a scrape of metal, a clatter of chair, and we jumped round to see Mr van Hout pinning Ivan's wrist to his shoulder blade.

Ivan was struggling even to breathe.

'Just a little extra twist and you won't be able to palm off for a month,' Mr van Hout spoke calmly into his ear. 'But in all honesty, snapping your neck would be easier and quicker. Does *that* answer your question?'

Ivan made a gasping sound into his desk.

'I didn't hear you.'

'. . . Yes . . .'

Sir let him have his arm back.

'You've earned yourself another hundred lines, this time on the meaning of respect,' he said. 'And I want it by end of prep tonight. Bring it to my home.'

It was those words, I guess, that marked the beginning of the end.

*   *   *

We returned to Selous in a group but without talking. Ivan just watched the ground. I was going to say something to him when suddenly I spotted a car outside the house, and it took a couple of seconds to realize I knew it well.

My father and Mr Craven were by the bonnet, politely side-by-side with sombre hands behind their backs. When they saw me my dad took a single step forward, and no more.

'Robert?' he said. Mr Craven seemed embarrassed, as though he shouldn't have been there. 'Can I have a word?'

I started towards him then stopped the moment I noticed that my mother wasn't in the passenger seat of the car. Instantly I didn't want him near me. I wanted him as far away as possible. He didn't belong here. This was *my* school, not his, he had no right.

'It's about Mum.' My father stood with a stupid expression on his face.

'No,' I told him. I shook my head.

'Robert, please. Don't make a scene.'

Only it was *his* face that creased and started to cry. I resented him for that.

'No!'

He came another step with his hand reaching. I moved out of his range.

'*No!*'

I stumbled, falling back into the huddle of my friends, wanting them around me, needing them to protect me from what I knew he'd come to say. And almost predictably it was Ivan who was there first; I've never forgotten the comfort of his hands as he held me steady while the world fell apart.

NINETEEN

The hollow sound of the earth hitting the coffin was what finally brought me out of it. Before that, I wasn't really aware of anything.

I couldn't recollect coming home from school that day with my father, nor what I did in the six days up to the funeral. I didn't even remember getting dressed that morning or walking the road from our house to the cemetery, where two workers waited amid the cool of the trees, resting on their shovels. The tears hadn't come yet. I wasn't really thinking anything. I just stood as the talking and prayers went on, because that was all you could do, and when the vicar was done I watched the men with shovels then come forward and start filling the hole they'd put my mother into.

I fought the urge to tell them to do it quicker because the sound of the stones hitting her was too loud and all I wanted was for it to stop.

A dry wind pushed through the trees. I glanced up. I'd thought the day had been overcast but actually the sky was vivid and pure, and suddenly I noticed a load of other people standing around the perimeter. They must have been from the village. I didn't know when they'd arrived nor did I recognize any of their faces yet they looked on with genuine feeling. A woman started to sing in Shona, a clear, cheerful voice that was somehow sad, and I wrangled with the pain it stirred.

My father and I stood side by side, not touching and not talking. Listening. Just him and me around the grave, there was no one else. The Ambassador and another man I didn't know from the Embassy had retreated to the gate earlier. Now I saw the Ambassador check his watch before coming back to shake my father's hand. He seemed embarrassed and out of place.

'Again, my deepest sympathy,' he said in the end.

He was tall and thin, with a kind face and thick grey hair parted down the centre. His suit looked expensive, his shoes shone through the dust on them. He didn't speak like my father.

'If there's anything we can do, old chap, and I mean anything, you let my secretary know.'

From within their grey circles, my father's eyes expressed gratitude as he bowed a little.

The Ambassador turned to me. I was in my uniform because I didn't have anything else smart.

'And how *is* that school of yours? Teaching you everything you need, I hope.'

School, I thought. It seemed so long ago. I wished I could go back, to have it and everything in it occupying my mind. Not *this*. I didn't want *this*.

I began to say something and had to close my mouth quickly because I didn't know what might come and was afraid I might not be able to stop it.

He pumped my hand and returned to his car. Now it was the turn of the other man. He straightened his tie and started towards us; his round cheeks glowed and sweat had glued the remaining strands of his hair to his head.

'Who is that fat man?' I asked quietly. I'd never seen him before.

'Perkis,' my old man answered, still looking into the hole. 'He's my assistant. But keep your voice down.'

'What's his first name?'

He took a moment. 'Harold, I think.'

But when this Harold Perkis got to us he told my father: 'Come back when you're ready, there's no rush. I'll get someone else in for a while, I'm sure we'll manage without you.'

Which I thought was an odd thing for an assistant to say. I looked to my father but he wouldn't meet my eye.

Mr Craven rang to say I could be excused the last two weeks of term. I didn't want to be, but out on the veranda, all alone, my old man sat with a slight hunch and suddenly looked much older than he ever had done.

So I stayed.

I didn't sleep well at home any more. The bed was too springy, the pillow too soft. Most of all, I missed Ivan. I regretted my decision to stay at home almost straightaway but it was too late, time had passed and all of a sudden I was marooned in the middle of the holidays with endless days of drinking tea and watching my old man being unable to do anything. Boredom became frustration; frustration became anger.

'He isn't your assistant, is he?' I faced my father one day. 'The fat man at the funeral. *He* controls *you*. You don't run the office at all, it was all a lie.'

He didn't so much as twitch, the only sign he'd heard was a deep, laboured intake of air.

'Have you been to your mother's grave since we laid her to rest?' he said. 'I think you should go. She'd like that.'

'She won't know.' Inside, I lamented my words instantly.

'I'd also like you to help me clear out her room. I think it's time. I'm not sure I can do it on my own. Please.'

I felt too sorry for him to say no.

'OK.'

'I've also been thinking,' he went on, 'that Matilda should

come and live in the house. It's a long way to the village, plus I could do with the company. It'll be lonely when you're at school.'

Straightaway I thought of Ivan. As if he were there, turning to me and staring.

'You're giving Mum's room to a *black*?'

My father looked up sharply.

'Don't ever let me hear you talk in that derogatory way again.'

'OK, the *maid*.'

'She has a name, and for your information I'm actually giving up the spare room, I shall go back next door. We all have a right to move on, don't you think?'

I thudded my mug onto the table, spilling tea, and marched inside.

It was as dim and musty in my mother's room as it had always been, almost untouched since the day she did what she did, and I was certain I could still see her waxen face set amongst the pillows.

I tore the curtains apart.

She hadn't worn clothes in ages but they were all over the chair at the bottom of the bed because my old man had gone through everything, trying to remember what her favourite dress had been for the coffin. I took them off their hangers and folded them into a pile. Everything felt like it might fall apart and I was terrified proof of her existence might disappear in my fingers.

I put her shoes alongside the bed in a row, and got everything from the chest into a single drawer and put that on the floor as well.

I was surprised by how few things she had. I was also surprised, then, to find the bedside cabinet bursting with stuff. Papers, mostly. Letters. They spilled out onto the floor. I recognized my own handwriting; it looked as if they were all here: the initial pleas, then the moans, then the lies about how good a time I was having. The memory of all those half-promises she'd made and then taken away pained me so there was little remorse when I saw the most recent letter of mine had a post-mark of almost a year ago.

On other letters I saw British stamps, from people I scarcely remembered.

. . . *'How are you?'* . . .

. . . *'We'd love to hear from you'* . . .

. . . *'It's been so long, you promised to write'* . . .

Friends. From our old life in England. The creases on the paper looked like they'd been read a million times, only clearly my mother had never responded and so in the end they'd given up.

Them, too?

'Stupid cow.' I folded the letters back with quivering fingers.

Right at the bottom of the pile I found the tattered enve-lope my mother had once tried to show me before, on the day I'd come in to ask about my grandmother. The one with the word *URGENT* written in big capitals.

I opened it up.

It was from Marjorie Downe, my grandmother's best friend.

Dear Valerie, it began. *I could never describe the sorrow it gives me to have to deliver this news* . . .

The moment was a punch. I felt hot and sick. I was nowhere and nothing mattered, and all the letters I'd been clutching fell from my hand and scattered over the floor. It didn't really matter what the rest of this letter contained because I already knew, yet I read anyway, words searing my eyes.

. . . *Your dear mother* . . . *suddenly, and regrettably for the worse* . . . *peacefully in her sleep* . . . *a small mercy* . . . *miss her terribly* . . . *no way of phoning you* . . . *the funeral will be held* . . .

Granny?

Was dead?

Why hadn't anyone told me? *When* hadn't they told me?

The letter trembled in my grasp, the date in the top corner shining like a beacon.

June 1983.

Way back during my first year at the school.

And I remembered clearly a time in my second term, calling home because it was nearly half term and I was worried my parents might pick me up late again. And my mother acting weird and distraught on the phone and my father telling me I couldn't come home for the weekend, that I should make alternative arrangements.

Your mother's had a bit of bad . . . She needs rest, he'd told me. Hiding the truth.

And I'd spent the half term on Ivan's farm for the first time, completely unaware of what was really going on.

A shape fell across the doorway.

'She'd planned to tell you. During the holiday.' To give him credit, my father didn't even try to pretend. 'She'd insisted on doing it herself. And when I found she hadn't been able to . . . Well, there was never a right time. She knew it was wrong, she just couldn't do it. I guess she never wanted to admit it was true.'

It sounded so ridiculous to me it was almost funny. I thrust the letter at him.

'That her mother had died? It was right here.'

He shook his head.

'More than that. That her lifeline had gone. I knew she had dreams of going back one day. I'm no fool. Living abroad was never *her* choice. But I wanted to be able to look after my family comfortably, you see, and it's almost impossible to do that over there where it's a struggle just staying afloat. It is with my level of salary. When Granny was alive your mother at least had hope, a light at the end of the tunnel; without her, she has . . . she had nothing.'

He made a weary gesture.

'Everyone lies. They don't necessarily mean or want to, they just do it because it's easier. I think your mother's duplicity ate her from the inside.'

I felt I couldn't stand. At long last all sorts of emotions pushed at the seams but I wasn't familiar with any of them, and I screwed the letter up before pushing past my father.

'Robert?' I heard him say. 'Where are you going?'

I didn't know. I had no idea what to do.

'What do you care? No one cares.'

'That's not true. I do.'

'Oh, sure.'

'I always did. I was just so scared of letting you down all the time because I've never had much to give.'

'Well, you've done a good job of that now.'

'I'm so sorry.'

'I hate you. I hate you both.'

It was like a bullet. He reeled.

'You don't mean that.'

'You want to bet?' I had to fire something at him because he was right, and he might have seen I knew that.

'Don't walk out. Talk to me. Please.'

'Leave me alone. Just . . . *leave me.*'

I barged through the front door and my legs started sprinting up the drive. I couldn't stop, turning left and pounding the strip road like the day the men by the statue had come after me.

I ran as much of the kilometre to the cemetery as possible. It was easy to spot her grave, the one that was too fresh to have a headstone, and I went right up to her. Of all things,

I was surprised at how much the earth had gone down and by the thick grass that was already growing over her.

I heaved agonized breaths. The clouds above were tight and heavy. I stood staring at her because I still couldn't find any words.

Then the rains broke. Huge, fat drops that pelted noisily to the ground. Only a few at first, then the downpour came. The pine trees hissed and swayed.

I swayed with them.

All I wanted was to be angry. I *was* angry. Not only about this, it was everything, there was so much that I didn't know where to begin, but most of all I just wanted her here so I could say it.

Thunder crashed. Beneath it I heard faint laughter and saw three piccanins sheltering, each perhaps six or seven and pointing at me as they flashed their white smiles.

'*What*?' I yelled, my voice drowning in the storm. Rivers streamed down my face and I couldn't be certain it was the rain. '*Why are you lot always grinning? What's so bloody funny?*'

I went to hurl a stone and they cleared off, but I fired it anyway because I needed to throw it at somebody.

By the time I left, the clouds had finished and rolled clear. I was exhausted and ready to go home.

As I turned into our drive I spotted my old man pacing up and down outside the house. His steps were anxious and short, and he held himself with his arms and muttered words over and over. His head shook and looked like a skull on a stick, his legs like fleshless pins falling out of his shorts. Where had he gone?

I was all he had now, I realized. I couldn't abandon him.

I moved forward, but as I returned to the only family I had left, Matilda appeared, despite the fact she didn't work on weekends, and she went to my old man and motioned for him to calm down. He did. She rubbed his forearms. Then she held him and kissed him in a way that was completely wrong and he let it happen. Nothing about it was right, it made my stomach churn.

I stopped again. My old man saw me and leaped back like he'd been given a shock.

He may have called out, he may even have come after me. I just started running again, the other way now, and towards town. I didn't know where to go or what to do.

So I called Ivan.

TWENTY

Ivan was lucky because he'd turned sixteen and got his licence straightaway, and his old man let him drive one of the farm pick-ups like it was his own. True to his word, he pulled up outside the hotel an hour later and hooted for me. I'd been in the bar ordering beers and smoking.

'Can I stay over?' I put my feet on the dash.

'Sure. What's up?'

'Just drive,' I told him.

'You're the boss.'

That was one of the things I liked about him.

He said he'd been going to Berg anyway that day to meet Pitters and Klompie at the movies. Now it was cool because we could all go together.

We met them outside the Kine 300 where *Beverly Hills Cop* was showing. It was the film everyone had been talking about although I didn't know who the hell Eddie Murphy was, and then the stupid nanny in the kiosk screwed up and gave me a seat on the other side of the cinema even though it was obvious we were together, and I had to go and sit right in the middle of a row of blacks.

'See you later, Jacko,' Pittman teased. 'Better not share your popcorn, you never know what you might catch.'

The film was good but I got more and more pissed off with how all the blacks in the audience kept cheering and clapping whenever something big happened, like when there was a fight scene or when Axel Foley made the supervisor in the warehouse give him some co-operation. I didn't understand why they did that. Why couldn't they just watch like normal people?

Patti LaBelle had barely started to *Stir It Up* to the end credits and I was getting out of there.

Pittman and Klompie came out with tears in their eyes.

'That was an *A* movie, man.' Pittman punched the air. 'Haven't laughed so much in my *life*.'

Klompie also punched the air even though he looked stupid when he did it.

'And I tell you, when we head home, "we're not going to fall for a banana in the tailpipe".'

'"So my advice to you is,"'– Pittman breathed all over my face – '"why don't you crawl back to your little stone in Detroit before you get *squashed*."'

Something snapped and I pushed him to the ground. Coins and Madisons flew out of his pockets and he jumped right back, nostrils flared.

'Hey!' Ivan got between us straightaway. 'What's your problem?'

'I don't know.' Pittman rubbed his elbow and his ego. 'Ask him.'

'Jacko?'

I huffed. 'It was a shit movie.'

'Why? What was wrong with it?'

'I thought it was a stupid idea with a load of stupid yanks, and I didn't like the way that Axel Foley kept eyeing up the white chicks. OK?' Ivan stared at me. From nowhere, I added, 'Mr van Hout would say the same.'

Ivan rolled it around his mouth before giving me a firm nod. He ruffled my hair, almost fatherly.

'*Ja*, you're right – *kak* movie.' He jabbed Pittman, but because it was Ivan it was OK and we were all friends again.

* * *

I gave in and called my old man to tell him I wasn't coming back for a few days. He sounded relieved, but then started stammering an explanation, and how sorry he was for everything, and where was I staying? I didn't know how to feel any more and was tired of trying to work it out, and about halfway through it dawned on me I could easily make it all go away and put the phone down.

On Sundays the Hascotts went to the Country Club. Ivan was getting excited because he knew Adele Cairns would be there and he was definitely going to ask her out, and if she said yes then he was in with a chance of finally checking out those *nyombies*.

'I swear, they're huge,' he said as we drove in convoy behind his old man. 'She's an absolute babe in a swimsuit.'

It was a hot day, and most of the kids were out by the pool while the mothers played tennis and the men sat around the bar. Adele was easy to spot. She was beautiful. She was in a red bikini, rubbing in oil and watching over her little brother messing about in the water, and I thought she was amazing. Not perfect, but that made her far better than the wax-like babes I'd checked in any edition of *Scope* because she was real. She wasn't tall and she wasn't short, and she had freckly pale skin and long brown hair which she combed with her fingers. She kept her arms self-consciously close to her chest, but if anything that just made her more alluring. Above all that, she looked kind, not barbed like so many other girls I'd met who thought they were pretty.

I felt a small stab in my chest – I was envious. I wanted someone like that. I only hoped Ivan wouldn't be able to tell.

He played it cool at first. We went to the bar and got Cokes, but as soon as we'd finished we were in the pool making a load of noise and splashing the *laaities*. Ivan made two of them cry, then play-fought me and ducked me for almost a minute, and when he finally let me up, spluttering like an arse, he was already off to make his move.

After a few minutes chatting they went inside and I was on my own.

I tried pretending I didn't mind and swam a bit more, then stood around the pool to dry off, but I didn't know anyone so I walked around the garden. In the end I just sat on the grass at the side of the Club where the workers were barbecuing steaks. One of them began talking to me, and when he asked about my mother and father I shut him up by getting him to *kife* me a free beer from the bar.

Ivan came back with a huge grin on his face.

'That chick gives.' He grabbed my beer and took a swig, although I didn't believe him because, from what I'd seen of her, I didn't think Adele Cairns seemed the kind of girl who gave quite so easily.

He looked about before taking out a Madison.

'Your old man's just there,' I warned. The men had been drawn by the smell of cooking meat.

'My old man's half-cut,' he dismissed, but thirty seconds later he was thrusting the *gwaai* into my hand. 'Say it's yours, he won't do anything to you.'

As it happened, Pa Hascott wasn't interested in anything except getting away.

'There's trouble on the farm.' His voice was strained.

Ivan checked around for Adele.

'But—'

'Don't just stand there, man, get your truck.' He turned to his wife, who was swinging as fast as she could on her crutches. 'Get a bloody move on, Gwyneth.'

We sped dangerously along the dirt road, Ivan just managing

to keep on it as we slew around corners. I had to clutch onto the side of the door. At one stage his old man's brake lights came on but Ivan didn't see them and almost charged into the back of him – he'd been watching the tail of smoke rising in the distance.

'Jesus on a swing, they better not have done.' He gripped the wheel tightly while the dust cleared. 'I swear to God.'

But they had, whoever 'they' were.

We tore over the farm boundary. Ivan didn't care now, his foot was to the floor. He even caught his old man, and then overtook him when Pa Hascott slowed at the security fence to their house, where a mob of about thirty black men were singing and doing a menacing dance that involved jabbing axes and machetes into the air. The dogs were going nuts on the other side of the wire.

The gate didn't look as though it had been breached, but Ivan knew by then that the smoke was coming from the workers' village. He sped on.

I had to stop myself from hitting the windscreen when the pick-up finally skidded to a halt, tyres digging in.

The stench of burning grass and plastic hit us immediately. The village was in chaos. At first sight only a few buildings were actually on fire, but they made a lot of smoke, and the men scampered around with buckets of water while the women were wailing in the central area where Ivan and I had once played soccer. Mothers clung onto their children. Chickens and goats were running free.

'Mastah Ivan! They came!' I could just pick out the words from the excited jumble. 'Those bad men came again.'

'They bring knives.'

'They bring fire.'

'Our homes! Those wicked Shona. Where is Baas Hascott, Mastah Ivan? You must help us.'

Before Ivan had a chance to speak his old man pulled up and they all went flocking to him. Ivan looked almost resentful.

'Where is Luckmore?' Mr Hascott wanted us to tell him but of course we didn't know so he turned to the crowd. 'Where is my bossboy?'

They didn't know either.

'Those wicked people, they set our homes alight with fire.'

'I hear you, but *where's my head workman*? Where's Luckmore?'

The crying got louder.

Mrs Hascott was helping a kid who'd cut her head and was bleeding all down her dusty dress.

'We have to call the police, Glen,' she told her husband.

Pa Hascott looked ready to hit someone. 'I can't.'

'We must.'

'What's the bloody point? I recognized at least four of them up there that *are* the police.'

'You have to do *something*.'

While Mr Hascott stood stuck, Ivan finally let out a huge cry and jumped back into the pick-up, murdering the throttle; only his old man snapped out of it and stood in the way and Ivan had to slam on anchors.

'Where the bloody hell do you think you're going, my boy?'

Ivan kicked the door open. The veins on his neck stood out. 'Mum's right.'

'Don't be so bloody stupid. You're staying here.'

'I'm getting the guns.'

'That's not the answer.'

'They're going to break into our *house*.'

'No, they won't.'

'And where the hell *is* Luckmore?'

'Most of that lot are high on beer and grass and itching for an excuse. Let them be and they'll go away. You know how they are.'

'No, Dad, I don't.' Ivan's frustration bubbled over. 'They've never gone this far before. I'm getting the—'

Before he'd had a chance to react Mr Hascott had gone up to his son, given him one around the face and whipped the keys from the ignition. The crowd hushed. Mrs Hascott rocked on her crutches while the little girl darted back to her mother.

Ivan spat blood.

'You're staying here, is what. We all are,' his old man ordered.

Ivan said, quietly and icily, 'When are we going to turn it around again and fight for what is rightfully ours? We can't let them keep pushing us around. We have to stand up for ourselves and shit back.'

'What are you talking about? We got through the war, we can get through this.'

'We *lost* the war. But we kept the farm. It's all we have left, and now you're going to let them take it.'

'*My* farm, boy. Not yours yet. If at all.'

Ivan turned slowly. 'What the hell's that supposed to mean?'

But his old man didn't say.

No one slept much.

The mob eventually drifted away and then hung about in one of the outer fields long into the night, singing gook war songs and drinking beer and burning anything they could get their hands on. When Mr Hascott went out again at first light they'd gone. Vanished.

As had Luckmore.

I got my head down for a couple of hours and woke around ten, and I crept through the house and found the family sitting in front of an uneaten breakfast. Ivan had a bruise on his jaw. Mr Hascott just kept his head in his hands. No one spoke. I'd wanted to ask Ivan to take me home, I shouldn't have been there, but he indicated for me to sit so I held onto it.

About half an hour of nothing had passed when the dogs started going crazy again, fighting their chains. Ivan's old man jumped to his feet.

It wasn't the mob, but a large black Mercedes with tinted windows and no plates that had pulled up over by the gate. A black driver stood by the open door, cool as you like. Mr Hascott was about to storm over when Ivan's mum spotted two people down by the pool house. You couldn't miss them. The woman had so much jewellery on, it almost hid the blackness of her skin, and she wore a flamboyant orange and yellow dress from which her big arse was pushing to escape. Her headdress looked like wrapping paper that had come unstuck. The man in the sharp suit was chuffing away on a cigar; each time he put it to his lips a fat, expensive-looking watch glinted in the sunlight, and every so often he would wave his arms about expansively over the pool.

'What the bloody hell do you think you're doing?' Mr Hascott demanded to know. The rest of us followed close behind.

If he'd surprised either of the intruders they didn't show it.

The woman looked Mr Hascott up and down and said something to the man in Shona. He nodded in serious agreement. Sweat glistened on his bald head like stars in the night.

'My wife says the pool is too small,' he said in punched English, as though the language irritated his mouth. 'She is right. We will need to make it bigger.'

For a couple of seconds Ivan's old man looked as though he'd been winded.

'What in God's name are you talking about?' He met the man in the eye. 'Who the hell do you think you are?'

The woman started screeching and her husband had to appease her. He sucked a mouthful of smoke and threw the rest of the cigar into the water.

'My wife is very unhappy because the pool is too small,' he explained again, sternly, as though it was all Mr Hascott's fault, 'and she knows it will cost many dollars to make bigger. I tell her I will fix this. She must have a big pool. The house she likes. How many rooms does it have?'

A line rose and throbbed down Pa Hascott's forehead.

'Get the hell off my land.'

The man gave a look somewhere near amusement.

'No, my friend. *Not* your land. Never your land.'

'I'm not your friend. I don't know who you think you are but piss off back the way you came, I've had as much of your lot as I can take.'

The man released a short, derisive laugh without a smile.

'I do not care about the words of a thief. You *stole* this land. You *murungus* took it from our fathers so we have the right to steal it back. Of course, the law says I cannot have it unless you sell. But you will sell.' He spoke slowly and clearly, producing papers from his pocket. 'And my government is kind and generous and is willing to buy what you took at a good price. Personally, I would pay you nothing, so whatever the price it is more than you deserve.'

Mr Hascott was already walking away.

'You will sell,' the man called after him. 'It would not be good for your family if you do not. And when you do your workers will no longer be required. I prefer Shona workers I can trust, not these dirty Matabele. You must tell them this. It would seem you chose unwisely after the war, my friend, for now they must leave or their families will find the same hole in the ground as your head man . . . Luckmore, did you say his name was? I am told he wept like a baby before he died.'

The man chuckled, shoulders heaving.

Mr Hascott's feet were rooted to the ground, and I swear every muscle in his body started to tremble. Everything in the world was happening right here, where we stood, nowhere else.

His eyes slid towards Ivan. 'Get the dogs.' He said it so quietly Ivan almost didn't hear him. 'The *dogs*, boy. Untie them.'

Ivan sprinted round the side of the house. Moments later the Ridgebacks came ripping and barking across the lawn. The intruders were already back at their car by then. I'd watched them walk hurriedly away, and the driver had pulled the gate to so that the dogs could only snap and jump at the wire. They were all safe; the man and his wife were back in their car and the dogs couldn't get them. There was absolutely no need for the driver to draw the gun from his jacket and turn it on the animals at point-blank range.

One shot each was all it took to bring back the silence.

The Mercedes spun away, kicking up stones and dust.

TWENTY-ONE

After the longest three weeks ever I couldn't wait to get back to school. I got my old man to drop me off much earlier than I needed to be there. It was what I wanted and he seemed more than happy to get me out of the house again.

We barely exchanged a word the whole journey. After he cut the engine the silence became awkward and he tried to give me a few more dollars than usual, but I left them on the dashboard and disappeared into Selous without looking round. When he'd gone I went back out. I was the first to arrive, the school was silent and empty. I liked it that way, with no one from the outside, both it and I waiting in anticipation.

The sun was strong for May. I sat in its glare at the edge of the car park and pushed sticks into the soft tarmac.

The more hours that went by the more convinced I became Ivan wasn't coming back, that maybe his old man had already sold and moved the family down south. So, with only half an hour to spare, one of the last things I was expecting to see was him whistling down the corridor. What I expected even less was the response we got when Klompie and I crowded him in the dorm.

'How are you?' I wanted to know above anything else.

He checked the pair of us before his bemused, almost perplexed reply.

'I'm fine. Why, how are you?'

'We heard,' said Klompie, and just in case, he stabbed an accusatory thumb in my direction. '*He* told us.'

'Is your old man selling?' I asked.

'Are you leaving?' Klompie butted in.

'Did they really do that to Luckmore? Did you tell the police?'

Ivan showed his palms.

'Guys, ease up. Yes, my old man is selling – what choice does he have? And I'm here, aren't I, so does it *look* like I'm leaving? And Luckmore . . . Surprise, surprise, the police aren't interested about him. Give me space, my arse is getting worried you've turned gay over the holidays.'

It was like nothing had happened. Like the same old Ivan.

And yet not – I couldn't say why.

Later that night, after a supper of definitely not speaking about it, I walked into the study room and saw the lamp on in his cubicle. I teased back the curtain to find him writing furiously, an open textbook lying to one side. Without looking at me he flicked over a couple of pages, with his brow knitted.

'What are you up to?'

'Got to get this finished,' he said, 'and take it up to Mark . . . to Mr van Hout.'

'You in trouble already?'

Ivan shook his head. 'It's extra.'

'Extra prep?'

'I asked for it.'

'Why?'

He thought about his answer carefully. 'O levels are next term.'

I heard Greet's voice for the first time in a long time. *Start paying more attention in class because you'll be getting nothing once Mugabe has finished with you lot.*

'But you hate History.'

'It's about how the Nazis managed to pull the wool over the eyes of the German people,' he cut me off. 'Mr van Hout chose it. Did you know they changed the names of streets and towns and buildings when they came to power, to make people forget about the past? It was a sort of brainwashing. Does that remind you of somewhere a lot closer to home? Hey? Does it?'

He scribbled a few more quick sentences. 'I've got to go.'

'When did he give you this prep?' I asked.

'In the holidays, a couple of days after you left. After it happened.'

'You came to school in the holidays?'

'Course not. He came to see me. I phoned him and told him all about it because I knew he'd understand. A good job I did because he managed to persuade my folks to let me stay on and at least finish my exams. He said he'd look after me during the term if they want to head South.'

He stopped briefly by the door.

'Oh, I almost forgot,' he said to everyone. 'Has anyone seen my calculator? I know I unpacked it but it's gone.'

In the following days and weeks Ivan became conspicuously absent and the hours were suddenly hollow. Pitters still came over but it always ended up the same, with us not talking and Pitters spraying juniors with deodorant and lighting it, or making them lick condensed milk off the tuck shop floor, or something. I was bored with his cruelty. Now and again I even lied just to be on my own, and I'd walk in the bush and daydream about things sixteen-year-olds daydream about. Invariably I found myself fantasizing about one girl in particular, even though Ivan would have killed me if he'd known.

'Where've you been, man?' We'd greet Ivan back each time like a pack of listless dogs.

But we knew he'd always been with Mr van Hout, and

pretty soon we stopped asking and just listened to his stories with the indifference of a jealous lover.

'You should check this knife he's got from the war,' or, 'He's got all these medals,' or a marvelling, 'That guy knows his shit, I tell you.'

Except when he returned angry, of course. On those days we kept out of his way.

One morning after classes we spotted Ivan with Mr van Hout way over by the amphitheatre, talking with this guy we'd never seen before who had cool shades and a look that any chick would really go for.

'That's Pete,' Ivan boasted later. We tried not to care but he had a feverish brow and he was acting really shakily. 'He's a friend of Mark's, they fought together in the Selous Scouts.'

We buzzed. Fairford even stopped whingeing about the stuff that had gone missing from his cubicle at breakfast. So it was true! The *Selous Scouts*! The Rhodesian Army's crack unit, the elite, the best . . . named after none other than the same Frederick Courteney Selous as our house had been.

'He's a journo now,' Ivan went on. 'Writes for one of those big overseas papers. They kicked him out of the country last year for stirring trouble with the government. If the police knew he was here they'd slam his arse into Chikurubi and leave him to rot.'

'How come?' I wanted to know. 'What did he do?'

'He only found out what Mugabe's Fifth Brigade have been up to, that's all.' He reached into his pocket and produced a photograph that made us forget he was talking to us as though we were stupid.

'What is it?' Klompie's eyebrows squirmed.

He was holding it the wrong way so I took it from him and turned it round.

'Jesus!' I said as it became clear that the mess of shapes was actually a pile of twisted and decaying bodies, all piled on top of each other. 'Who is this? Is this from the war?'

I handed the photo back towards Klompie but he stepped away and shook his head. Pittman grabbed it instead.

'This is *three months ago*,' Ivan told us. 'Pete took it secretly, and lots more besides. The government did this. In the south. The Fifth Brigade are down in Matabeleland killing Matabele and no one is doing anything about it or doesn't know or both.'

When no one spoke: 'This is our country, man, don't you get it? He's still fighting. Mugabe's still killing people to make sure he stays in power.'

'So he's killing blacks,' Pittman said indifferently. 'So what? And what makes this Pete such a bloody expert? Anyone could have done it, might not have been the Fifth Brigade.'

'Duh! Who else? All the blacks on the other side of the country will tell you. They're petrified of them. The Fifth Brigade does this sort of thing all the time; it's what they're there for. Jeez, Pitters, that day you climbed over the fence and messed with them . . . They would have slotted you for sure if that policeman hadn't stepped in.'

'Bullshit.'

'I'm serious. Don't you see? The war had nothing to do with politics or colour. That's what Sir says. It was about power and money. This country's rich and Mugabe wants it for himself. That's why he lets these guys do whatever they like, so he can stay at the top. Just like with the Nazis. It's all about power. He wants to scare people and wipe out anyone he thinks is against him. It's the Matabele first, next it'll be us whites.'

'He wouldn't.' Although now Pittman didn't look so certain.

'It's true. He even said it . . . Ages ago he said he had to cull the whites.'

'Bullshit,' Pitters insisted.

'No,' Klompie said quietly, looking Pitters in the eye. His hands were shaking. 'It's true. Ivan's not lying. They would have killed you.'

Someone walked past the study room and Ivan snatched and hid the photo. It was Nelson.

'Don't look in here,' Ivan fired.

Nelson hadn't been, but of course Ivan's warning made him startle and glance in, and even though he scurried away it was too late, he was guilty of doing what he'd just been warned not to do.

Ivan slapped his hand against the wall.

'Right, that's it, I'm going to teach that stupid Kaffir a lesson.'

'Wait,' I said. 'What about Kasanka?'

Ivan was already halfway out into the corridor.

'You don't understand, I have to.' And he was gone.

That evening, during prep, Kasanka marched straight to Ivan's cubicle and started kicking and punching for a good couple of minutes. Ivan didn't make a sound.

We thought he was being brave. As we found out later, it was all part of the plan.

As that winter term deepened, more and more of our stuff went missing: calculators, pens, watches . . . I thought Ivan must have suspected Nelson or maybe just wanted it to be him because he started to target him freely, regardless of the consequences. He'd hurl soap in the showers or push him in the corridor, or simply walk into the next-door study room and whack him. I never joined in, but what I did was far worse –

I did nothing. I couldn't get why Nelson never fought back, it wasn't like he was a junior and couldn't, so I told myself he was weak and ultimately to blame for what he got and probably deserved it. And sometimes Ivan did it right in front of Kasanka like he *wanted* the payback, so I reasoned there was some kind of balance.

In the middle of roll call one evening Ivan stepped out of line.

'Excuse me, Kasanka, all our things are being stolen.'

Kasanka shot him an eyeful. 'Shut up and get back.'

Ivan stood his ground. 'Someone's stealing all our stuff. There's obviously a thief in the house. Aren't you going to do anything about it?'

'I'm not interested in your stupid stuff.'

'Why the hell not? You're Head of House, you should do something about it.'

Kasanka was over in an instant.

'I'm Head of House so that I can do whatever I want and not have to listen to the likes of you. I told you, shut up.'

'Not until you sort it out.'

'I'll sort *you* if you don't hold that tongue.'

'I won't.'

'*Shut it*, white boy!'

'*No!*'

Kasanka shoved him and Ivan just came bouncing back.

'You asked for it, Hascott. Come to my study after supper.'

'Why wait?'

'What did you say?'

'You deaf? Why wait? If you're going to do it, do it. All I wanted was for you to help the house.'

'I'll do it, don't you worry. I'll do it right now.'

Ivan bolted. For a moment I thought for good but he quickly came back with a hockey stick, and he thrust it into Kasanka's hands in front of the whole house.

'Go ahead, beat me if it'll make you feel better. I don't care. I only wish you cared as much about our house as you do about stinging my arse.'

He assumed the position.

Kasanka turned about under the weight of everyone's gaze as if he were lost. If he was looking for a steer he didn't get it, not even from the other sixth formers. Everyone was waiting. He started to step away.

Only us guys closest to him heard Ivan mutter, although even *we* couldn't say what, and in a flash Kasanka pulled back the hockey stick and swiped Ivan with enough strength to send him into the wall.

Ivan fidgeted all through supper.

'How can you stand it?' I asked. 'That must be the fifth time this week.'

He grinned. 'It'll all be worth it. You wait. One day, when we're at the top, we'll be able to give it all back.'

I was going to reply but something made me stop. Instead, I just thought: the top of what?

TWENTY-TWO

I don't know how aware Mr Craven had been of the thefts but the instant they crossed his own front door he made it his business to know everything. He gathered the whole house into the common room that Saturday evening at exactly the time everyone wanted to watch *Dallas*.

When he was angry his head shook like a balloon that was being over-filled. Ivan, Klompie and I had to fight the giggles as we leaned against the back wall. But when he said he was going to confiscate the house TV until the thefts stopped and the culprit was found, it suddenly seemed a lot less funny.

Kasanka announced a house search. Everyone groaned silently, not because we necessarily had anything to hide (we weren't stupid enough to keep our smokes in the building) but because a house search usually meant a free licence for the sixth formers to 'borrow' anything of ours they liked. I'd already lost my favourite *Tears For Fears* tape.

'Don't look so worried,' Ivan told me. 'Who knows, they might catch the bastard.'

They didn't. Not on that evening, at least. Two days later a second search was called out of nowhere, only this one was for *everyone,* even sixth formers, and Mr Craven was going to conduct it personally.

Our tongues wagged as we shuffled into the common room once more, then almost spun out of our mouths when we glimpsed Bully coming into the house. The seniors joked with one another about how nervous they should be. We joined in their fun, and when Craven put his head round the door and asked Kasanka to step outside we naturally assumed it was to help, but Ivan was keen to fan some flames.

'Why *couldn't* it be him?'

'He's Head of House,' we reasoned. 'He wouldn't. He couldn't.'

'He's in power. That's where it's worst, especially with *their* sort.'

An hour later we were reeling with the hot news that, apparently, Kasanka's study had also been searched and that a box had been found under his bed, and that he still hadn't returned from Bully's office. Somehow Ivan had all the details.

'There was a whole stack of our stuff.' His arms billowed. 'Calculators, Klompie's watch, music – including your *Tears For Fears* tape – Mr Craven's radio and ZX Spectrum . . . It was all there, he was going to flog it in the holidays.'

'How do you know all this?' I asked. He cut me a look. 'I mean, are you certain?'

'Are you calling me a liar, *Jacko*?'

'No . . . I . . . It . . .'

'Bastard's been taking for months.'

'What do you reck's going to happen?' Pittman asked. He'd rushed over from Heyman as soon as he'd heard the news.

'If they've got any sense they'll kick his black arse out,' Ivan told us with absolute certainty. He got up. 'We don't need his kind.'

'Where are you going?'

He hovered at the door.

'Check you guys later. I've got something important to do.'

He went, and we didn't see him again until after supper, when he came back to the house with blood on his shirt, six stitches above his eye and a grin that slit his face.

'Boy, have I got a story to tell you guys,' he said.

* * *

'You got Kasanka *expelled*?'

I couldn't quite take it in. None of us could. The air around us was thick with disbelief, making everything seem louder. Ivan put his finger to his lips and nodded his head slowly and evenly.

'And good riddance to him,' he said.

Klompie blinked as though dazzled by a brilliant light.

'No fucking way. But that's . . . It must . . . Wait till we tell Pitters, he's going to love this. He'll be so jealous he didn't think of it first.'

'But *how*?' I wanted to know.

'All the thefts that have been happening . . .' said Ivan.

We leaned in, absorbing every syllable.

Ivan tapped himself proudly on the chest. 'Don't worry, you'll get all your stuff back. I was only borrowing it, really.' This was unbelievable, and yet he was so calm as he spoke. 'The hardest part was getting into Kasanka's study on time after Mr Bullman got his anonymous tip.'

'How *did* you get in there? Doesn't he always lock his door?'

To which Ivan dug into his pocket and dangled a key from his thumb and forefinger.

'Craven, the stupid arse, didn't exactly make my life easy, he keeps all the spares on one chain and doesn't even label them. So he can whistle if he thinks he's getting this back.'

He tossed the key into the far corner. It was a good shot and rattled to the bottom of the bin.

'But Bully wasn't going to expel him just for stealing. The government would have accused him of being racist so I had to help him make up his mind.'

'How?' asked Klompie.

This time Ivan pointed to the cut on his head.

'That, for a start. Good job Kasanka is a mean mother-fucker who doesn't need much to set him off. And right outside Bully's office, too, while Craven and Bully were trying to figure what to do. They had to prise him off me. But hey, he's a Kaffir, isn't he? They're all the same.'

He stood and rolled up his shirt to reveal the flags of yellow and purple he'd collected over his stomach and ribs and back – I was sure there hadn't been quite so many before.

'Then I showed Bully all this: everything Kasanka's been giving me. Plus the fact *he's* the racist because he calls me 'white boy' all the time, and I've got plenty of witnesses who'll back me up. Right?'

We nodded without hesitation.

'And if Bully still wasn't sure he could expel him without the government jumping on his case, that's when the big guns came in.'

We looked at him blankly.

'What do you mean?' Klompie asked the question we were all thinking.

'Mr van Hout's with him now,' Ivan explained. 'Talking to Bully about his idea.'

He let it hang, teasing us.

'Which is . . . ?'

'To let more blacks into the school, of course. He told me about it a while ago. Bully's been trying to open the doors to more of them for ages and so keep the Inspectors out, only it's never enough, and Kasanka as Head of House was only going to appease them for a short time. When they hear he's going to be kicked out the Inspectors will be back here in no time, interfering, telling Bully what to do, messing things up. So Mr van Hout's suggestion is to get *local* blacks in, from the village.'

We were shocked into silence.

'But they couldn't possibly afford it.' Klompie wiggled his finger in his ear, like he always did when he was really confused.

'That's the clever part. They wouldn't have to.' Ivan sat back down, his bruises forgotten about. 'The school could offer cheap education. Dirt cheap. Free. Allocate a set number of bursaries for *day* scholars. The school would only soak up minimum costs because we wouldn't ever include them as an integral part of the school but on the face of it they'd be getting the same education as us in class. The government go away happy.'

'You mean . . .'

'And Bully gets commended for making Mugabe look good, like he's actually done something to deserve that phoney degree he got.'

'"For services to education in Africa",' I remembered.

'Exactly. And who knows? Maybe Mugabe will even come here personally to kiss Bully's arse.'

He stopped to think about what he'd just said. He was thinking hard while we took it all in.

A moment passed before I asked: 'So you and Mr van Hout have been planning this together? We thought you were doing work.'

Perhaps there was something in my question Ivan didn't like because his lips tightened.

'Sir says Kasanka is a rotten apple in a flourishing orchard,' he told me with blunt words. 'He cares about this school. He believes in keeping standards, as we all should. We don't want his sort at the top, it isn't right, so whatever it takes to get him out.'

And in the seconds following I could feel the air getting heavier around us until Klompie unknowingly swished it away.

'I don't get it – did Kasanka take my watch or not?'

We laughed.

'What happens now?' I asked.

'Ngoni Kasanka won't be coming back to this school ever again, you have my word on that,' Ivan said simply, smiling again. 'Anderson will take over as Head of House, which is where he should have been in the first place. And of course I've got some catching up to do.'

'Catching up what?'

He gave my shoulder a gentle pat and stepped out into the corridor to show me.

'Ndube!' His voice resounded. 'Nelson Ndube! Come here.'

A moment. Then Nelson appeared.

He edged closer, afraid. He knew exactly what was going on, and when he got there a simple question tumbled out.

'Why? Why do you hate me so much?'

It made me think of me and Simpson-Prior the day he'd run away, and I stayed back.

Ivan took a knife he must have stolen from the dining hall out of his pocket. He ordered Nelson to hold out his hand then gripped his fingers so that they were straight and couldn't move. He slotted the blade between Nelson's middle and index finger, right in the V. I knew this one well, Greet must have done it to me a hundred times: the person keeps a tight hold on the fingers and starts twisting the knife; very quickly your skin there is raw and screaming. If you're really unlucky it'll split, though that only usually happens after about the twentieth turn.

'Evening, boys.' Mr Craven suddenly appeared from nowhere, oblivious to what he'd disturbed. 'Are you having fun?'

Ivan slid the knife back into his pocket.

'Not yet, sir,' he replied.

Nelson had already made a hasty retreat. For the moment, he'd escaped.

Ivan must have been pleased at that point in time, it was going so well. But all that was about to change, and when it did I daresay even Ivan didn't know quite what had hit him.

TWENTY-THREE

Less than a week had passed since Kasanka's departure and the jokes and rumours were still fresh. As it happened, we were laughing about it on our way to History after break, but it was a lesson that was never going to take place.

We were over by the chapel when we heard the commotion. It was coming from Mr van Hout's classroom. Instantly we knew it must be serious because if it had been a couple of boys fighting it would have drawn a crowd, but the guys who were close by took one look and moved quickly away.

We picked up our pace.

The shouting suddenly got louder and a cloud of papers burst from the open door. Darkness fell across Ivan's face. He dropped his books and ran, the rest of us dutifully on his tail.

We crushed our bodies around the door. I could see the back of Mr van Hout's blond head, while at the rear of the classroom Mr Mafiti stood with fear all over his face.

'*Get out of my classroom,*' Mr van Hout yelled at him. '*I'm fed up with you messing up my blackboard. Go on, get out!*'

Only Mr Mafiti *couldn't* get out. If he went left, Mr van Hout mirrored him and cut off his path; if he went right, Mr van Hout went that way, too. Eventually our chemistry teacher made a bolt for it anyway down the side, but white hands snagged his jacket and pulled him back in.

Mr van Hout spun him and held his lapels. For a couple of seconds Mr Mafiti's feet even left the floor.

'How many times do I have to tell you?' Mr van Hout

glowed with rage. He didn't care that he was spitting into the other man's face with each word. 'This classroom is *mine*. It was given to *me*. You do not belong here and I don't want you interfering in here *ever again*, you stupid . . .'

Numb, unable to move, I could sense what was coming and I willed him to stop as other teachers began to near.

Mr van Hout shook Mr Mafiti hard. The chemistry teacher's eyes searched desperately towards us for help.

'. . . gormless, grinning . . .'

With each word, Mr van Hout shoved Mr Mafiti against the wall.

'. . . stinking, dirty . . .'

Someone was pushing behind us. Mr Dunn, trying to get through, but it was too late. A sound stung the air – Mr van Hout had hit Mr Mafiti with the back of his hand, and behind it came an unstoppable surge.

'. . . *Kaffir*.'

There was a sharp intake of breath. I don't know which of us it was, but there was one thing we certainly all knew: the shining light we'd enjoyed during the otherwise drudgery of classes had just been extinguished.

TWENTY-FOUR

We gathered for the emergency assembly.

The silence was absolute as Bully walked slow, funereal steps down the middle of the hall and onto the stage.

Before he began he coughed into his hand, finding his voice, making sure it was still there.

'I'm not,' he began, already hesitant. 'I'm not going to recap on the ghastly events of yesterday morning. I will, however, quell any rumours and fill you in on the details. Mr van Hout is no longer considered an employee of this school and is currently being detained by the police. What will happen to him is a matter for the law; what I know for sure is that he will never be welcome here and shall not return.'

He paused. If he was expecting an interruption of whispers he didn't get it, the silence continued to hum.

'For those of you who witnessed Mr van Hout's actions, I advise you blot it from your minds after the police have asked their questions. The rest of you: I advise the same. Haven School needs to move on from this dim chapter, and as quickly as possible, or else . . .'

Bully wiped his mouth with a handkerchief. The words wouldn't come.

We sat literally on edge. Or else what?

' . . . Or else we . . . That is, assuming they don't . . .'

Ivan, especially, looked like he might burst: *What?*

'I am pleased to announce,' Bully said instead, 'that Mr Mafiti was not badly hurt and will return to teaching duties tomorrow.

We should remember him in our prayers and thank the Lord things weren't more serious than they were.'

And in case the Lord or we had temporarily forgotten who it was that had stepped in, Mr Dunn sat straight in his chair and lifted his head above the other staff members.

It was weird going back into the classroom. It felt strange to think Mr van Hout wasn't going to step through the door and surprise us all in some way or other. We missed him already.

On the other hand, it was as though he hadn't actually gone anywhere, although I didn't know that yet.

Bully was going to stand in and be our history teacher from now on, at least until a replacement had been found. He sat at the desk with a weary slump.

'Someone tell me where in the textbook Mr van Hout had got to.' He opened his own copy as if something horrible might fly out.

Fairford volunteered an arm. 'Mr van Hout didn't really use the textbook, sir.'

Bully merely looked at him.

'He said books like this are full of rubbish, that we would only learn how much of a wan . . . how unclever the author is. Sir.'

Bully waited, then sighed.

'"Unclever" isn't a word. Turn to chapter four and copy out paragraphs one to five, then eight, ten and twelve. I seem to remember there's some good information there. If you finish, get on with some reading. *No* talking, Osterberg. Yes, Hascott?'

Beside me, Ivan had raised his eyes from his desk, though only just. His skin was pale.

'Can I be excused, please, sir?'

The same question at any time in the past would have got Ivan a Task, maybe two strokes. Now Bully simply wafted his hand in the air and told Ivan sure, he could do what he wanted, and we didn't see Ivan again until I found him deep into the afternoon.

He was down at the Cliffs. I hadn't doubted for a second I'd find him there. He was sitting right on the edge in a patch of sun with his feet dangling over, occasionally throwing stones out into the drop.

He didn't acknowledge me. In the end I had to say something.

'Are you OK?'

He made me jump by snatching two envelopes from his pocket. One of them had, I thought, Mr van Hout's handwriting on it. He put that one quickly back and showed me the other.

'I got this from my folks this morning,' he spoke into the open air. 'My Old Queen says the sale has gone through. They'll be packed up and gone to my aunt and uncle's in 'Maritzburg by the end of the month.'

He let that hang.

'Blacks have stolen our home and no one gives a shit, because *Mugabe* made it legal.'

I could find absolutely nothing to say.

In the end the best I could do was, 'Are you going with them? Is that it, then?'

To my relief and amazement he shook his head.

'I told you, I'm staying for as long as I can. I have to. Don't you see?'

See what? I thought.

'What will you do? At exeat weekends, I mean.'

'I'll have to become a sad-o like Button and drift around here like a lost fart. I don't care. And I can stay with Klompie sometimes, his aunt and uncle are loaded. Maybe I'll even come out to the sticks with you and your old man, if you ever ask me. Come stay in your spare room and keep you two company. I guess it must be lonely for you guys. You know, since your mum died.'

But Matilda now lived in our house, and the thought of Ivan finding out about that terrified me. I was scared for myself. More than that, and despite everything, I suddenly felt an overpowering need to protect my father. So I acted like he was cracking a joke.

'What do you reckon will happen to Sir?' I asked.

Ivan threw a big stone and we watched the rings it made fan out across the water. His eyes were intense.

'That guy's an idiot. Pulling a stunt like that, after everything he taught me. He might have ruined everything.'

'Yes, but—'

'I won't make the same mistake.'

He wasn't making any sense.

His voice softened. 'Jacko?'

'*Ja?*'

'How do you know if you're ready for something? If there's something you know you want to do, only you've never done it before, how do you know you'll see it through when the time comes?'

I could only imagine he was talking about exams.

'You just have to tell yourself you can do it,' I told him, pleased to be offering him help for once. 'And test yourself, of course, that's the most important thing. The more you do it the easier it gets.'

And with that I saw the trace of a smile.

'*Ja.* I thought so too.'

I couldn't have known it then, but he wasn't talking about exams at all.

* * *

From my first days in the house I was often plagued with a dream I never told anyone about, in which I would wake up in the dead hours and see a load of seniors, all of them looking like Greet, rushing into the dorm and beating people up, and I'd be powerless to say or do anything except wait my turn.

On this occasion the nightmare was disturbingly different.

The shapes came slowly this time, smooth and silent, drifting like ghosts. I had to blink to make sure I'd seen them, but when I looked directly at them they seemed to blur and appear somewhere else. I knew on some level that this was another dream, but a bit of me wondered.

The intruders spread through the dorm, hovering over the sleeping shapes of the other boys. Something about them terrified me so I hid and lay still, praying desperately they wouldn't come to me. When the fear got too much I dared a peek over my blanket.

The shapes knew at once and turned where they stood, and I saw faces I recognized: my father, my mother, Matilda, Mr van Hout, the Ambassador, Mr Bullman . . .

I squeaked and ducked back under the covers. My breath swelled.

Then I heard it, the first *whump* of someone getting it. Hard and heavy. And again. And another.

But then came a different noise, a soft sliding across the polished floor. This sound of dragging followed every hit, and when it had all gone quiet I ventured another look to find the shapes had gone. All the other boys had vanished too, their bloody sheets and blankets ripped and strewn on the floor. I was completely alone.

I woke with a gasp.

The night was deep and black. That time where people shouldn't be.

Only someone was. I heard movement in the corner where

Ivan's bed was. A rustling of clothes, the indistinct glow of a white shirt being removed.

'Is that you?' I whispered.

He paused, and then came a step closer. Now I could see his face through the gloom. I thought, though couldn't be certain, there was a smudge down the side of it.

'*Ja*, it's me,' he said. 'Go back to sleep.'

'Where've you been?'

'Nowhere. Shut up and go back to sleep.'

In the morning, a sleep-drugged Anderson ambled down the line, calling out names and warming his balls with his spare hand.

'Ginn.'

'Yes.'

'Hodges.'

'Yes.'

'McGill.'

'Yes.'

About halfway down there was a pause. A gap.

'Ndube,' he repeated, irritation quickly replacing the boredom in his voice.

He glanced up. Nelson Ndube wasn't there.

'Someone go upstairs and kick his lazy arse and tell him he's got a Double Task.'

'He's not there,' one of the Agostinho cousins told him.

'Well, where the hell is he?' Anderson demanded to know.

Christos Agostinho shook his head. No one had seen him, his bed had been empty at rising bell. Nelson had just gone.

TWENTY-FIVE

At first everyone thought Nelson must have headed out for an early run and lost track of time – his watch was still in his locker.

By start of breakfast he still wasn't back, and Mr Craven worried he'd gone for a run and hurt himself so he sent a group of boys to go looking along the usual cross-country routes. There was no sign, and when chapel had finished and the start of classes had failed to bring him back it was decided that he must have simply run away.

If that was the case he deserved all the ribbing he was going to get for turning his back on the school, we concluded.

All through breaktime, Ivan sat reticently in his cubicle. After ten minutes he threw his pen down and swatted his mug to the floor.

'Can't you guys talk about anything else?' His feet crunched over the pieces. He was self-consciously touching his face. What I'd thought had been a smudge was actually a fresh scratch running two inches down his cheek. He said he'd done it to himself in his sleep. '*Jislaaik*! I'm trying to write to Adele and all I can hear is your jabber about Nelson bloody Ndube. Just *lorse* it, OK?'

He slammed the door behind him.

We thought it must have been because of the guilt, seeing as it was Ivan who'd picked on Nelson the most.

We didn't hear anything more and assumed we probably wouldn't, that Nelson had made it home and his parents weren't going to force him back like some did. But eight days later we saw his folks going into Mr Craven's.

Was Nelson back?

Apparently not. His mother cried constantly, occasionally breaking into a wail, while his poor father had gained a decade.

So where was he?

'Who gives a monkey's?' Although Ivan looked nervous as he said it and for some reason he wanted to stay in the dorm that afternoon. 'What's with all the concern? He ran away and got lost, and now they can't find him. It's his fault. Was he your bum chum or something?'

The winter dragged on through July, day after day of an insipid sun in clear skies that pulled at our shadows.

Bully was a fresh air freak who insisted on opening all the windows for class so we had to sit shivering. If that wasn't bad enough, his lessons were a mountain of boring. He didn't do anything, just made us read while he sat and stared out the window. When the bell eventually rang Fairford or Rhys-Maitland or someone had to break his trance and ask for dismissal because it was like he hadn't heard and would keep us in there forever.

One day Osterberg finally dared to ask Bully if he was going to start giving us prep. We hadn't written an essay since Mr van Hout, the academic year was passing and O levels were at the end of next term in November, and that was less than four months away.

Bully winced like he'd been stung.

'What's the bloody point?' he said, and then perhaps realizing he was speaking out loud: 'Yes, prep. Read chapters fourteen and fifteen. Make some notes or something. There won't be a test.'

'Are you sure, sir?' Osterberg was apprehensive.

'I was once.' It was a hollow voice. 'Today, I can't be sure of anything.'

He worked out a deep breath. 'Boys, you need to know I won't be headmaster of this school for much longer. I think the time for me to retire has come. I always said when I went it would be on my own terms, and I intend to keep it that way.'

A hush blanketed the classroom.

Someone's pen clattered to the floor and it sounded like crashing rocks. It was Ivan's. He bent down to retrieve it, his eyes unusually open and skittish. I could see he was thinking fast and yet not really thinking at all. To me he looked like someone who was in a strange, panicky place and desperately looking for a way out.

When lessons were over he didn't come back with us to the house. Instead, and without a word of explanation, he headed straight for the Admin Block and up the stairs to Bully's office.

'Bully's decided to stay after all. But there are going to be a few changes,' he told us when he returned to the house. 'Changes for the good, in the long run, you have to remember that.'

'What have you said to him *this* time?' we asked in wonder, but he wouldn't be drawn on what any of the changes would be.

'Come. I need some air.' He was already walking up the corridor, wrapping on his scarf. He meant only Pittman, Klompie and myself, of course, no one else. We followed close behind.

'Let's go to the Cliffs,' said Klompie.

'*No!*' Ivan snapped. Then more quietly: 'No. Not the Cliffs. We're always going there. Somewhere else.'

The cold air tugged sharply that afternoon but there was something about the day that made us believe summer could return. Ivan led us around the squash courts and onto the path that led to the workers' village. As we got close some piccanins who'd been playing with toy cars made from wire and Coke bottle tops started running around us, the younger ones laughing hysterically as the older ones showed off and braved it to within a couple of metres before scampering away again.

'Herro, sah. Herro, baas,' they trilled. 'How do you do?'

We went under the cover of the pines and Ivan took out some *gwaais*. When we'd all lit up, using the glow of tobacco to try and warm our hands, he started to tell us more.

'They're going to be watching us like hawks, now,' he said.

Klompie and I both nodded, understanding. It was Pitters who spoke out.

'Who?' He looked suspicious.

'The government, of course. Who do you think? First Kasanka, then Mr van Hout. Now Nelson. It's too much. They don't like us private schools as it is, we remind them of the past. Too many whites in one place, and they have too little control.'

'So what? Let them watch. What the fuck can they do?'

'They can close us down,' Ivan said, eyeing Pitters levelly. 'Or give us a government-appointed teacher to keep an eye on what we're doing. I've told Bully he needs to get someone in to replace Mr van Hout quickly. A black teacher. One who's managed to climb their way out of the township or whichever mud hut they came from and made something of themselves. A living example of independence. A white one wouldn't work.'

Pitters stabbed a tree with his smoke.

'Jeez, man, students *and* teachers? We already have Mr

Mafiti. Whatever happened to standards? What are you trying to do to our school, Hascott? It'll be more wanked than ever.'

Ivan threw his own butt at him. Pitters' eyes flashed angrily.

'It's about *integrity*,' Ivan told him. Told us all. 'All I want is to uphold the integrity of the school, and to ensure it remains open. It *has* to stay open, we *mustn't* let them close it. This is the best school in the country. If we have to make a few sacrifices to keep the government happy then so be it.'

'We should be kicking more blacks out, not letting them in.'

'Don't you see? It's the only way.'

'Only way for what?'

'To stop them closing us down, or taking us over. Because of what's happened.'

'They can't do that, it's not theirs.'

'They can do anything that bloody pleases them,' Ivan said, 'and if it's not the law now they'll *make* it the law. They mustn't close the school. Not until after we've left.'

Pitters had already come forward, but as Ivan spoke he'd backed off again, hands in pockets. 'Why do you care so much, Hascott? Why the hell do you care when you want to leave at the end of the year anyway?'

Ivan twitched a smile.

'That's the other bit of news. I'm not leaving either, I'm going to sort it with my folks and get my A levels here. I plan on staying right to the end.'

He glared.

Klompie tried to break the tension with a high giggle. 'We'll be surrounded by them,' he laughed. 'I never realized you liked Kaffirs so much, Ivan.'

Ivan grabbed Klompie by the shirt, holding him firm. Their noses almost touched.

'Don't you ever, *ever* say that again. You hear me?' His eyes, his cheeks . . . his whole face was a storm. He punched Klompie and dropped him. 'I hate them. They took my country, they took my home. We lost Sir because of one of them. You will never say that about me again. I . . . hate . . . *them*. Got that?'

Klompie mumbled. 'Sorry, Ivan.'

'Got that?' He turned on me.

His intensity had rooted me, I lifted my hands and surrendered. It was that easy.

He started hunting for stones. The piccanins were still in sight, playing up by the corner. Ivan launched his missiles in quick succession and the kids squealed with delight, dodging and enjoying the game.

'Cheeky bloody . . .' Ivan snatched more stones up, bigger ones this time. 'They're laughing at us. Are you just going to sit there and let them take the piss? Look, they think we're a joke.'

He dropped the stones at our feet.

The children howled with glee.

'Well? Or are you bunch of gays going to stand there and let them do what they like? We wouldn't have let them get away with it in the Old Days.'

It was enough. Klompie and Pittman took a handful and started hurling. Ivan clapped approval, and then all three turned and stared at me not joining in, as though I wasn't one of them. As though I didn't understand what it was like to be them.

I snatched a stone from Ivan's hand and chucked it hard. It hit one of the little piccanins right in the head. He stopped dead and covered his eyes and screamed while the others scattered. All at once the game was over. For them, at least; for us it had just begun as we chased them through the trees, throwing and cheering and howling like a bunch of fucking animals.

UPPER SIXTH
1987

TWENTY-SIX

When I woke, the sun was full on and shooting straight into the backs of my eyes. The sound of U2 gently messed up the inside of my head, tormenting me with images of angels and devils and a burning cross of shame.

Grimacing, I twisted my head and wiped heat from my chest. The combined effects of weed and beer, which had seemed such a good idea at the time, had worn off but left me with a serious *babbelas*. My head throbbed, my tongue was dry and swollen and scraped across the roof of my mouth like a slab of biltong. Inside, I was screaming for relief. Outside, the body refused to move and attempted to cling on to sleep, but behind the veil was the faint aftertaste of a nightmare I didn't want to go back to.

With a surge of effort I hauled myself upright.

The sun pounded, ricocheting off pale slabs. A few feet away the cool blue of the pool beckoned but any other movement was too much, so I just stayed like that until I was ready, feeling the jarring rhythm of my hangover beat in time with the music.

All the other sun loungers were empty now, a couple of discarded towels the only sign that anyone had been here. The pool was calm and flat. For a brief second I wondered if I'd slept through to the next day then dismissed the idea. No, it was still the same.

Everything was the same.

Still hiding out at the hotel pool. Still under a hot spring, September sky. Still wasting my holidays when I should have been at home revising for final exams. Home, however, wasn't a place I liked to spend much time in case Ivan rang again, wondering why I wasn't with the gang, questioning why I wasn't there to go out on one of their 'walks'. The truth was I didn't like their 'walks'. I never had. Not that first chase through the pines after the piccanins over two years ago, and definitely not when they suddenly started getting worse. But I didn't see how Ivan would ever accept the truth so it was far easier to stay away and hide.

I pushed my feet and clipped an empty bottle, sending it bouncing and spinning across the stone. I waited for it to break, but amazingly it didn't. I retrieved it and placed it on the table, still in one piece. I turned off my cassette player and began the walk back home.

I was almost at the front door when I caught the sound of an engine. Something about it made me stop.

I turned, and beyond our drive I saw a dirt-white pick-up leading a trail of red dust as it came near. I urged it to carry on past, for it to be just any old pick-up, but already I knew it wouldn't. Sure enough, it turned in.

Ivan had come to find me.

'Shit.'

I didn't have time to think. I ran round to the side of the house. Straightaway my old man looked up from his newspaper.

'What's happened?' he startled.

'Dad. Hi,' I said, feigning calm words very badly. 'Where's Matilda?'

'What?'

'Matilda,' I urged. 'Where the bloody hell is she?'

'Now look, Robert, there's no need to be like that. I thought we'd got through all your issues about your stepmother.'

'We have. I like Matilda. But this has nothing to do with her.'

Although that wasn't completely true. It did really.

Out at the front of the house, Ivan's brakes squealed to a halt.

'Never mind, it's too late. Just stay here, OK?'

'Why?' he tried to crane forward. 'Who is it?'

'Please, stay here. And Matilda. Trust me on this.'

And I ran back round in time to stop Ivan getting out from behind the wheel.

'Howzit,' I said, all cheerful.

Ivan looked out and took a long swig from the Coke bottle he held between his knees.

'So this is what your house looks like,' he said at last. 'And you're not dead after all. I'm disappointed, because that can only mean you've been *choosing* not to see us.'

I laughed. Ivan didn't.

'I've been revising,' I explained.

'That's what you always say.' Another slow swig. 'What's your problem, Jacko? You've stopped seeing us in the holidays and at school you haven't been out with us in bloody months. You're missing all the fun.'

'I don't have a problem.'

'So why don't you join in any more . . . you know . . . with the games?'

Games, I thought. *Is that what the past two years have been to you?*

I shrugged. Out of the corner of my eye I saw my old man standing on the grass, looking at us. Then he turned and said something to someone out of sight. It could only have been to Matilda.

'OK, I'll come now,' I told Ivan hurriedly.

He seemed pleased by that.

'Really?'

'*Ja*. It'll be fun.'

'Well about bloody time. Go get your stuff.'

Relieved that he didn't even try to move from the car, I darted back towards the house.

'And hurry the hell up,' he called after me. 'Five minutes and I'm coming to get you.'

I was out in four.

TWENTY-SEVEN

Most of the boys from school came from rich families but you never really thought about it, it just was. Klompie's aunt and uncle were slightly different because you couldn't help notice they were *seriously* rich.

Their house was in Borrowdale for a start, and it was one of the best. Two storeys sitting contentedly in a massive garden on the gentle undulations of the capital's most desirable suburb, with tennis court, swimming pool and sauna, and the main gate was an electric one you could control from the car – you didn't have to wait for the houseboy each time. The garage doors, all four of them, were automatic as well, although they were closed and locked most of the time; you rarely got a glimpse of the dazzling BMW, Range Rover and Mercedes paintwork and even Klompie was only allowed near one of the two VW Golfs parked in the drive.

This was a white man's paradise, and everything my father had ever pointed an accusatory finger at. It was lavish and exclusive, out of reach for the majority, yet I'd always had the feeling the ten-foot wall right around the perimeter was as much to keep us in as it was to keep people out.

I went through the French windows and collapsed onto the sofa in the lower living room, overcome by tiredness or the crushing boredom, I couldn't tell which. I'd wanted to go to the *Graceland* concert playing at Rufaro Stadium that weekend but I was here now. It wasn't just music, it was anti-apartheid, and in Ivan's eyes Nelson Mandela should die in prison and Paul Simon was nothing more than a shit-stirring Kaffir-lover, so that was that.

In the other living room, Klompie and Pittman were at the bar with their forearms locked together and deep in drunken concentration. They were playing their favourite game, the one where a lighted smoke is placed in the crack where two arms touch and the first one to flinch has to drink.

Upstairs, in one of the five bedrooms that had become his own during the holidays when he wasn't seeing his own folks, Ivan was with Adele making noise. I buried my head under a cushion and tried hard to imagine it wasn't Adele up there he was doing it to, that it was somebody else, anybody, but it was no good.

It was like nothing had changed. This was no different to any of the holidays before when I'd come to stay. No wonder I'd wanted it to end.

I threw the cushion into the corner.

'I'm going to Dairy Den. Who wants?'

And in case anyone heard I quickly slipped out.

Beyond the gate, the tarmac road was a furnace under my bare feet, but already my head was starting to ease. At last: change. For the briefest of moments I was free again, and I wallowed in it.

When I got back the house was quiet. The bar area was deserted. I went down to the lower living room for a smoke.

I got to the coffee table in the middle before I realized Adele was there too, lying on the sofa.

I started, my cheeks instantly warm. Adele's mouth pulled upwards and sideways as she sat up and I blushed even harder. As far as I could see she only had on a towel wrapped around her, and she struggled slightly to keep it closed while keeping her cigarette away from the cushions. It was clumsy, but I yearned even more – Christ, *anything* she did looked sexy.

'Hey, Robert.' She took a drag and blew soft smoke towards me. 'I knew it was you. You have a much gentler step than Ivan.'

'Oh,' I smiled, feeling stupid, and then I couldn't talk any more because nothing would come.

'It's nice, I like it. I've missed you being around. I borrowed your lighter, I hope you don't mind.'

'Sure. *Lekker*. Help yourself.'

Ivan had a lighter she could have used and yet she'd chosen mine.

'Want a smoke?'

'Thanks,' I reached and our fingers touched. At exactly the same time our eyes touched too and now *she* started to blush. It made me braver so I sat beside her, guilty and excited.

Adele didn't move away, only pulled the towel over a yellow-green bruise on her thigh.

'Where is everyone?' I asked. 'It's like a scene from *Ghostbusters* in here.'

'They've gone to the store. Ivan said we needed more beers.'

'I didn't see them on the road. Mind you, with Klompie's driving they could be anywhere. If they're not back in half an hour we'd better send out a search party, hey?'

Adele giggled and came a little closer. 'Robert, you're so bad. Shame.'

'I know, you're right. Sorry.' I counted to five. 'Better make that fifteen minutes or we might never see them again.'

'Shame, hey!' I got a playful slap. 'You'll get into trouble with them.'

'I'm eighteen. I think I can take care of myself.'

I could have sat there with her forever, I never wanted it to end. I pushed for something else funny to say but all of a sudden something dark fell and before I'd turned round I knew it was him. He was back.

Ivan was a few steps into the room, his corporals flanking his sides. He was bearing down with a look I knew only too well, the only difference was that sometimes I'd been up there with the other two when it happened. I leaped and moved away.

Gradually, Ivan came in and took my place. He grabbed Adele's legs and pulled them so they were across his lap, stroking them like he was rubbing down wood while the other hand massaged his upper lip – he'd taken to growing a moustache in the holidays that wasn't as thick as Mr van Hout's but looked just like it.

'Howzit, sweetie,' he said, still checking me out. I lit my smoke again, acting normally while inside I felt my stomach melting. 'What are you guys up to?'

'Nothing,' she replied calmly, but her eyes flicked me a look and I saw she was just as scared. 'You know . . . talking. Just talking.'

'I saw. What about?' He scraped his fingers lower and began bending her toes.

'Nothing,' she said again, the one answer I'd hoped she would and wouldn't give because 'nothing' was a guilty admission. Anyone who went to school knew that.

Ivan's hand stopped. 'Do you want to fuck him?'

I blurted smoke. Adele's eyes opened wide and she slapped his arm – not too hard.

'Hey!'

'I'm serious. Do you fancy him? Because I reckon you're the one Jacko thinks about whenever he locks himself in the toilet.'

I hid my hand because it was trembling so hard. Adele teetered on the edge.

A laugh burst from Ivan's mouth. 'Oh, man!' he clapped his hands. 'You two should check your faces. You're hysterical. I was joking!'

Klompie and Pittman joined in. I put on a dutiful smile

while Adele just stared at a spot on the floor. She could barely hold onto the tears and, keeping her towel tightly around her, she stood and fled the room.

'Jeez, can't you take a joke?' Ivan yelled after her. 'Jacko's a virgin; a painted wall is enough to get him shooting off.'

A door slammed.

He rolled his eyes. 'Chicks! Who wants a swim and another beer? We got heaps, and I made the Kaffir get us real coldies from the back. May as well get pissed before we hit town seeing as I won't be getting my oats again today.'

Another night, another bar, another club.

'Where are we going?' I asked with disguised sarcasm. 'The Causerie? Flagstaff? Captain's Cabin? Or maybe some place we *haven't* drunk dry before?'

Ivan sat back, arms wide across the back of the sofa.

'You haven't had a night out with us in ages, so you choose'– he nodded at me – 'and I'll get the first round for cracking a joke at your expense. Because you wouldn't dare fancy my girl, would you, Jacko? Hey?'

I didn't care where we went so I chose The Causerie.

Adele said she could see the funny side of Ivan's joke and apologized to him, but as soon as we got there she spotted some schoolmates and went straight to their table. Ivan gave the finger as she went.

We grabbed the table in the corner. The waiter took five minutes to come, by which stage Ivan was furious and told him to get lost; he didn't want *him* touching his beer. He made me go to the bar instead, and when I got back he and Klompie and Pittman were in a conspiratorial huddle. They looked serious. I couldn't hear a word because the music was too loud so I necked my Depth Charge and went back to the bar.

I was happy to stay there this time. As the music thumped and the mix of beer and mint liqueur worked its magic I started to relax. Ivan and his gang could have their secrets, I was content to keep away from whatever they were. Doubly so when the DJ started spinning *True Faith*, because Adele couldn't resist the call of her favourite song and flocked to the floor. Watching her dance made me fall in love with her again. There wasn't a single guy who wasn't checking her. I wanted to make eye contact but she wouldn't quite turn my way, she kept her eyes down and hid behind her hair, biting her lip. She was *trying* to ignore me, and that made me feel good.

She waved towards Ivan when she caught him looking. He didn't react, just kept glancing over his shoulder at her, then at me, making sure.

I wished I could leave. I wished I had the courage to walk out and keep walking and never come back. Instead, I simply moved to the end of the bar and ordered another drink.

I lit a smoke. The match broke up and hit my leg, I jumped and smacked it before it could burn a hole.

'Hey! Watch it,' said the guy on the next stool, drawing his beer in and rounding his shoulders. 'Spill my drink and I'll kill you.'

I'd barely registered he was there until then. I started to apologize, then stopped the instant I checked his face. I stared. It was all I could do.

'What are you gawping at? Keep eyeballing me and I'll kill you.'

It was Greet.

True, he didn't look much like the senior boy I'd last seen four years before; he had mullet hair and the skin on his face was heavier, but it was definitely him. And age wasn't the only thing he'd gained: a sagging chin and a belly overhang that smothered the top of his draw-strings showed me a young man who was serious about protecting his beer. Plus I couldn't get over how much shorter than me he was now when he'd always been a giant. Above all that, he looked tired. Tired, worn out and utterly harmless.

Where had the monster gone? Or had I just stopped believing in monsters?

'I said, what the bloody hell are you—'

'Howzit, Greet,' I said. I felt completely calm.

He looked me up and down, taking a long sip. He was very drunk.

'Do I know you?'

'You went to Haven School.' Then: 'Selous House.'

'Tell me something I don't know.'

'You left in eighty-three.'

'Were you a squack?'

'Robert Jacklin,' I told him.

Greet met the news with a shake of his head. How could he not remember?

'Did I beat you?'

'Once or twice.'

'Good. I'm sure you deserved it, you look as though you were a little poof. Give me one of your smokes, I'm all out.'

How could *he* not remember *me*? The taunts. The beatings. Day after day, my life of living hell.

My heart began to race. The music pounded. Lights flicked red, green and blue, then the sharp, stuttering white of a strobe that flashed snapshots of his whole face, with each one a new memory coming back. After all these years, the stinging pain. I could feel every swipe.

'What are you up to these days?' I asked, taking a Madison out of the pack. He ogled it, licking his lips.

'Ach, you know, man. Bit of this, bit of that. Security. Farm help. My old man got me jobs pushing papers but I jacked them all in. Too boring. I've been between jobs for the last six months. Maybe something good will come along soon. Hurry up with that *gwaai*, man.'

He held out his hand. I leaned in closer.

'That's tough. As you say, maybe it'll come good soon. Or maybe you'll never find a job and die a sad and sorry death.' I made sure he got every word. 'There can't be much out there for a sadistic, shit-for-brains dickhead like you.'

I dropped the smoke into his beer. He blinked at it for a good five seconds, open-mouthed, before turning to me.

'What are *you* staring at, you ignorant prick?' I said. 'Have you remembered me yet, or are you still trying to place the Pommie squack you used to put your cigarettes out on?'

I stood over him and buried the glowing cherry of my smoke into his arm.

Greet yelped and jerked back, catching his beer with his elbow and sending it flying. The glass crashed to the other side of the bar.

He jumped up from his stool.

'What the . . . ?'

He lurched and grabbed my shirt but it didn't take much to swat him away. With rolling eyes, he swayed and fought for balance.

'You're pathetic, Greet,' I yelled over the music, enjoying the words. 'You're not even an excuse.'

He came again. His fist caught me on the side of the head, but it was badly aimed and went too far, and he ended up falling. It didn't hurt at all, though I suddenly had a dead weight pushing against me. I tried to shove him back only my legs got caught up with the stool behind, and the next thing I knew I was on the deck. The bouncer had Greet with his arms pinned behind his back.

Klompie and Pittman were there, pulling me up, while Ivan dealt with the bouncer.

'It's OK, they're friends,' he tried to explain.

Friends? I thought.

The bouncer wasn't listening. There were fights every night at The Causerie and he just wanted us gone. He bundled us all together and we all fell out of the doors.

The night was warm and still: a sanctuary. I stood on the walkway and breathed in clean air, and the rush in my head quickly started to ease.

'Hey! Where are you guys going? Let's just go home,' I called out when I realized Ivan and the others weren't stopping. I followed them down the steps and across the car park, then into a dark alley along the side of the hotel. They half carried, half dragged a loping Greet and dropped him into bags of rubbish.

Ivan emerged back onto the street.

'What are you waiting for? This is your chance.'

'For what?' I replied, although I knew.

'To get your own back.' He waited. 'You made a good start, now finish it off. Well?'

'I'm not so sure.'

'Shit. Whatever it is, Jacko, you'd better snap the hell out of it. Don't you want revenge? Stop acting so gay.'

Klompie and Pitters stood behind him. Pitters already had blood on his knuckles.

At the end of the alley, I could see Greet with vomit and grime on his face trying to crawl. Beyond, I caught ourselves in one of the large hotel windows, and in that reflection I was one of them again. Four boys dangerously close to the edge of manhood, together.

When we were done, and as Ivan drove us back through the sleeping city, I felt the familiar mix of emotions I'd often felt after one of the *games* come seeping back. Shame and joy, nausea and relief. I was all powerful, top of the school, and all I wanted right then was to be back in the comfort of the house where I really belonged. I was safe there, I was a somebody, while out here I was just Robert Jacklin that nobody knew. But we were going into our last ever term, and, with the image of a bloody and gibbering Greet still vivid, I was suddenly being haunted by a whole new thought.

I *was* Greet.

When I was with Ivan like this I became what Greet had been. Whether I secretly claimed to dislike it or not, I'd still done it, and all those other times before, I'd consumed the thing I'd despised and I spewed it from my position of power.

Then, more terrifyingly: What was there for me *after* school? What purpose? Where was I heading and how was I getting there?

Back at Klompie's I jumped out and immediately chundered into the flowerbed.

Ivan slapped me on the back and laughed. Apparently he didn't worry about such things.

TWENTY-EIGHT

Pulling from the main road. Through the stone pillars that bore the school's name. Moving slowly along the willow-lined drive.

But this time, because it was the last first day of term I'd have, I made my old man drop me at the gate. I sat in the silent car and gazed across the fields and at the buildings that had been my home – my true home – for the past five years, and I wondered: Was this what it was like to get old? A sudden, heightened awareness of your surroundings and of the things that really matter?

My dad made the usual gesture, pulling out notes from his wallet. I surprised him by ignoring the money and shaking his hand instead. It felt like the right thing to do.

'Thanks,' I said, holding him.

'For what?' he asked, surprised.

How could I answer that in such a short space of time?

'All this,' I told him. 'It means a lot.'

He frowned, perhaps wondering if there was a trick.

'Is everything all right?'

'You once said, after Mum died, that you'd only wanted the best for me. Well, I got that. You gave me the best. This place has taught me so much, and I don't mean just in the classroom. It wasn't always good, but now, today, I think . . .'

I grappled with words, not quite knowing how it would end, so I just said, 'It's taught me a lot. So thank you.'

'I tried,' he said.

'You did.'

'But you realize it doesn't stop here.'

I liked that I could have predicted his response, it felt familiar and secure.

'I know, I know: still one last term to get through. I promise to keep pressing on until exams are over, Dad.'

He smiled.

'I meant the learning, Bobby,' he said. 'That never stops. Not for any of us.'

As usual I was earlier than I needed to be. I stood and watched my old man drive away through the early summer heat and then drank in the silence.

I bottled the moment, making a promise to myself that I would never forget this place. Of course, I never would, but as I stood motionless there I didn't know the lasting memories would be born from an instant other than this. I was completely unaware of what was coming, and that in a matter of weeks I would be running along this very road for my life.

In the sun's full glare, I pulled on my blazer (now with the white edging of Full Colours, for continued excellence within and successful captaincy of the Rifle Club) and began to walk. It was a slightly different journey from what it had once been thanks to the new boarding house being built close to the upper tennis courts, almost complete. The school was expanding and looking to the future, not wilting and dying as Bully had once feared might happen. The rumour was that the house had been another of Ivan's ideas. I didn't know if that were true, but at the very least I was certain he'd had an influence with its name.

Mugabe House.

Of course! What better way to win favour than by flattering the country's leader? What better way to protect the school than by making *him* part of it? One thing was for sure: it wouldn't go unnoticed.

Ivan had known what he was doing, all right.

Within the first week we had a special assembly, but it was Reverend Kent who was waiting on stage, not Bully, and sitting alongside him were a doctor and a priest who'd driven in from town to tell us about a new deadly disease called AIDS that was spreading rapidly around the world.

The priest stood up and talked about how this was clearly a message from God, warning us against the perils of homosexuality and multiple partners and delayed marriage.

The doctor seemed embarrassed by that and explained how no one knew quite where this disease came from, possibly monkeys in Africa, but the one certainty was that there was no cure. It was A Killer. To the sound of much amusement, he went on to demonstrate the practice of safe sex with a condom and a banana.

It was unfortunate that the very next lesson was History. Ivan had barely sat down before he opened up a salvo on Miss Marimbo.

'They reckon it came from monkeys.' He slouched in his chair, spreading his legs wide.

'Yes, that's what they say.'

Miss Marimbo spoke English without a trace of an accent. She was young and had travelled all over Europe, so she didn't look like most of the local black Africans – she straightened her hair, for a start. She'd also seen enough during her teacher training days in London to know how to handle the likes of Ivan.

'Isn't that a bit unfair, miss?' he went on, grinning.

'How do you mean?'

'Well, with you teaching us. Aren't you putting us at risk? You might gush a period and bleed infection all over us.'

Miss Marimbo's light brown skin flushed but she managed to stay calm. She walked to the door and pulled it open.

'Get out.'

'What?'

'I said, get out. If you can't be civil then there's no point you being here.'

Ivan leaned back on his chair and stretched. 'You can't do that. I'm Head Boy.'

'I'm well aware of your status. All the more reason for me to dismiss you – leadership is by example. Please leave.'

Ivan looked at her, then round to the other six of us in the class. I kept my head down. In the end he had no option; he kicked his chair back and swaggered slowly out, lurching at the last moment and putting his face right into Miss Marimbo's.

I knew how he'd be.

Sure enough, when I got back to the house Ivan was lying on his bed, hitting a hockey stick against the wall with feeling. Klompie sat on the seat by the desk fiddling with the cassette player and Pittman stood in the middle swinging a cricket bat. It was like I was that new boy again, walking in to make tea for Greet.

As soon as he saw me, Ivan stopped and swung his legs to the floor.

The other two waited. Klompie turned off the tune. I wanted to walk straight back out.

'That black bitch pissed me off. We're going for a walk down past the village,' Ivan told me. 'Coming?'

I'd known it was coming. I reached for the first excuse I could find.

'I have to clean out the rifle room this arvo.'

'You're captain of the club; get a squack to do it.'

'I have to supervise.'

I could see bubbles rising.

'What's the matter with you, Jacko?' He came up close. Not quite as tall as me, but still giving the feeling he was towering above. 'I thought we'd been through all of this. Why are you avoiding us?'

Behind him, Klompie and Pitters both grinned in a way I wanted to forget instantly.

'Like I said, I've been busy.'

'Busy being a poof. I thought we were buds.'

'We are.'

'You're not acting like one. *Why* don't you want to come? And how come we never get to play games with the blacks around *your* house in the hols? Are you bored with us?'

'No.' It was a half-lie – the truth was I was bored and a bit scared.

'Maybe you want to poke my missus.'

'No ways!'

'Why not? Are you calling Adele a dog?'

He was in that sort of mood. I just shut up.

'Well, maybe we'll get bored with you, Jacko,' he went on, 'and we won't want *you* around *us* in future.'

If only, I thought, but it wouldn't be that easy.

'So?'

'So, what?' I said.

'So are you coming with? You've been missing out, we play different games now. Much better than before.'

Games.

His eyes glinted like cold steel.

'I told you, I'd like to but I can't.'

He turned. I thought to go back and lie on his bed but

instead he plucked his mug from the desk, gripped it like a base-ball player then launched it straight at me. I saw it coming and I ducked to one side. The mug exploded behind me in a shower.

'See you then, *Jacko*,' he sneered. 'Jacko Jerk-off.'

He laughed at his own joke, and the other two quickly joined in.

The rifle room was actually overdue for a clean but that didn't matter, nothing I did could sweep away the gnawing sense of guilt as I hid out in the small and lightless room. In the end I tossed the brush into the corner and sat mulling in my chair.

I thought we were buds.

I'd wanted to get away from him, absolutely. Now that I was, however, I didn't know quite what to do, like a dog that had struggled to slip its lead and finally won. The truth was they were my only friends in or out of school. I had no one else. Yes, Ivan had chosen me ages ago, but I had let it happen, I'd desperately wanted to be a part of him, and so before they'd had a chance anyone else had been demoted to the level of 'just someone I knew'. Even the other boys in the rifle club, most of whom were younger than me anyway. Bizarrely, other than the gang, Jeremy Simpson-Prior and Nelson Ndube had come the closest, except those friendships hadn't lasted long. Ivan had seen to that.

Did I want to be cast completely adrift? What would it be like?

That thought of having no one and nothing was too much to bear.

I locked up and went back to the house. They still weren't back, still out on their 'walk'. I definitely did not want to do that, but maybe I didn't have to. Why *couldn't* I just be their friend without having to join in all the time? I could explain. We weren't kids any longer, surely they'd understand?

I decided to go and meet them, excited by my sudden awareness and ability to make sense of things – I was growing up. I put on my whites for a run and made sure my route took me down by the squash courts, then onto the path towards the village because I knew they'd be there.

The rains hadn't started yet that summer and October's afternoon sun was strong and uninterrupted. I was ready to stop when I thought I glimpsed them ahead. I skirted round the edge of the compound where children had once played so freely and went on to the smoking spot.

I paused to catch my breath. The insects buzzed. Under the cover of the pines the air was dark and obscure, something about it made me not want to go in there.

I thought I caught a faint whiff of cigarettes.

'Hey! You guys in there?'

I got nothing back. Did something scamper across the ground?

'I thought I'd join you for a *gwaai*.'

Now there was definite movement, but the glare of the sand around me made it hard to see beyond a few feet. Above, a scurrying sound through the dense branches.

I glanced up and saw something coming down at me. Then again. Huge pine cones started to land around me, thudding to the ground as I jumped from side to side.

The scurrying sound again, only these new missiles were being thrown much higher, hitting something else up there. Almost instantly the air was filled with a different noise altogether. At first I couldn't place it – rasping, grating, singing. Then I spotted the hive the size of a man's torso swinging from a bough and I knew.

As I watched, the hive detached itself and fell, and when it struck the ground it disintegrated into a swirling cloud that rose like a departing spirit.

The bees were on me. At first all I could feel was them bumping into me, and I remember thinking, *Is that all?* They were harmless. Maybe it was panic, because very quickly I started to register the sting that came with every hit. In no time the swarm was all around, all encompassing, black shapes whichever way I went. A suffocating cloak. I ran faster, and they were still there. I darted left and right, and they followed as though they were part of me, attacking my arms, my legs, my neck . . . any bare flesh they could find. I slashed at them with my hands; they stung my fingers, which started to swell. My breath laboured in my throat, a strangled cry escaped. With every new attack the energy sapped from my limbs until, in the end, I did the worst thing and stopped to fight them.

Their noise crescendoed. I could feel them everywhere: under my shirt, up my shorts, smothering my face, working through my hair. Stabbing, always stabbing. Their sound was deafening as they flew into my ears. I opened my mouth to cry out and they got in there too, pricking my tongue with their poison.

I spat and started running again, slapping every part of me with each new flare of pain. And then I realized the pain must have got too much because they were still around me only I couldn't feel them any longer.

My feet dragged in the sand. My chest wheezed as I struggled for any breath I could get, and with every step I could feel my airway closing and closing until finally, inevitably, I couldn't breathe at all.

This time there was no resistance. My legs buckled and my body sagged, I could feel myself going horizontal but the point at which I hit never seemed to come. And as the light dimmed I could have sworn I heard the sound of human laughter through the angry buzz.

TWENTY-NINE

At first the darkness was where I wanted to be, but gradually I fought with it, and a mingle of wood smoke and gentle voices I couldn't understand began to break through. When I finally opened my eyes I saw a colourless ceiling of corrugated iron. The voices stopped and the face of a man filled my view.

He grinned hugely.

'*Mhoroi, shamwari.*' Hello, my friend.

My body was aching and tired; it took all the energy I had to winch myself up onto my elbows. The gloom was thick in here – wherever here was – the only light coming from a dim, naked bulb, but it was enough for me to see I was in a small room with no floor, just dirt, and that the walls were the same rusting metal as the roof. Along the far side, a time-beaten armchair and a set of decaying dining chairs around a table, while the mattress I was on was grime-grey and full of holes.

From somewhere else I heard the high guitar twang of *Jit* music, the Bhundu Boys or someone like that, the sort of music we wouldn't have been caught dead listening to.

The man pushed back on his haunches and sat in the armchair. He was slight, with a wide and cheerful face that shone unstoppably beneath an uneven sea of hair. His temples were silver, so perhaps he was older than he looked, and I couldn't help noticing how long and slender his hands were as he held them, like a vicar about to deliver a sermon.

He unlocked them briefly to take a swig from a bottle of cream soda and said something towards the open door. A small child appeared with a bowl. Keeping his head down so I couldn't see his face, he placed the bowl on the table and hurried out again. Something about him disturbed me.

'My son is most shy.' The man beamed an apology. He leaned forward again and rested the bowl on my stomach. 'You must eat more. It is goodness for you that will make you bett-ah.'

I flinched as he came near. 'What is it?' My throat was still swollen, my voice wasn't my own.

'You must eat,' he gestured. 'This will help you, for sure. Number one *muti*, make you bett-ah bett-ah one time.'

It looked like black porridge and tasted bitter and sharp like mulched leaves. I tried spitting it out but he gently kept the spoon in place so that I had to swallow.

He chuckled softly to himself.

'You feel it here?' He rested his comforting palm flat on my chest.

I did. Almost straightaway my heart began to pump hard and fast, and my strength ebbed back.

'What is it?' I still wanted to know.

'This is number one *muti* against the bees. Makes you bet-tah in quick-quick time, you will be straight back to school like nothing has happened. You feel it?' he said and sat back, looking pleased. 'You are ver-ry very lucky, you nearly died.'

I pushed myself upright.

'Where am I?

'You are in the workers' village still. This'– the man gave a proud wave – 'is my home, Mastah Rhrob-ett.'

I looked at him. 'How do you know my name? Do you know me?'

'I do not know you other than your voice, I have heard it ma-ny many times before.'

'When?'

'On the tellyphone, of course. I know the voices of all the peoples.'

'Weekend?' I said, relaxing at once.

'The one and the truly.'

'What are you doing here?'

He found this amusing. 'It is my home. But we have not spoken for a long time, my friend, I have missed you. Why is it that you are not tellyphoning anyone? Your father? A ladyfriend?'

'I don't have anyone I want to call,' I answered.

'Ah, yes. But maybe perhaps if I had a tellyphone that would let you talk to those in the sky . . . ?' I realized he meant my mother. 'I was most saddened when I heard this news. You must miss her.'

I didn't answer.

Weekend's son came back and hovered by the door, daring himself to peek half a face then snapping quickly out of sight whenever I looked.

'How's your wife?' I asked.

'They are well, but sometimes . . . sometimes they fight so very much that I cannot hear myself thinking what is going on in my head. Always they want money, or a new hat, or to know where are the children.' The grin came marching back. 'I have three daughters now. Tuesday here is the big brother to them all. He is seven years.'

'You must be very proud.'

'For sure. And tired! Always tired. Tuesday sleeps in here with me, the other children sleep next door with their mothers.'

For a moment I thought he was joking.

'You should ask the school to fix you up with a bigger place.'

'There is no need, my friend,' he told me, coming forward to share a happy secret. 'Soon I will be moving. I will leave the school and we will have all the space we need.'

'Have you bought somewhere?'

'No.' He laughed loudly and slapped his knee. 'I have no money!'

'Where are you going?'

'I do not know.'

'*When* are you going?'

He shrugged again.

'But you're definitely moving?'

'For sure.'

'Then . . . how?'

'He has promised it,' came the simple response. I knew who he meant: the Prime Minister, of course. 'He told us. I was there when Mr Mugabe came to the stadium. He said one day we would all have land, that this country now belonged to Africa and the Africans who have struggled for so long without it. I do not hate the White Man – I do not hate *any* man – but when they first came they did steal what was ours. They must share, it is only fair. And when it is my turn I am going to have a farm, and I am going to grow maize, *sterek*! So much maize. I am going to be a rich man, and my children will be happy and so will I because my wives will stop shouting at me.'

I thought of the man who'd taken Ivan's farm, the government minister with his big Mercedes and his big cigar.

'What if you *don't* get any land? I mean, what if Mugabe gives it to someone else?'

'*Every*body will have it. Black and White. You and me. We will all be rich with land of our own. He has promised.' Then his voice became serious. 'I, for one, cannot wait to leave, for the sake of my children. This is not a good place to be living any longer. Bad things happen.'

'Demons?' I patronized.

He shook his head. 'Only the demons inside of the men that do those bad things.'

He gestured to his son. Reluctantly, the little boy obeyed, and Weekend sat him on his knee. At first I thought it was just the poor light, then I saw what it was about him I'd found strange: one eye flicked nervously at me while the other was in permanent shade, missing, his scarred and wrinkled lid sealed over a hollow of sightlessness.

'You see?' Weekend spoke with calm emotion. 'He does not speak about when this bad thing did happen, but other children say it was white boys throwing stones.'

My heart raced again. This time it had nothing to do with the home-stewed medicine I'd been given.

'Does he know who it was?'

My mouth had gone dry.

'He does hardly speak at all, not since that day. More than two years now.'

Tuesday stared at me. I felt ill and wanted to leave.

More than at any other time in my life, past or future, I hated myself. I loathed every little thing I'd done, for allowing it to happen.

'I'm sorry,' I said. And then, quickly: 'For Tuesday, I mean.'

Tuesday squirmed on his father's knee until Weekend put him down and he went running out. I gazed at the space where he'd been long after he'd gone.

'I am sorry, too,' Weekend said. 'But I thank God that is in the sky that I have him still.'

'He almost died?' I practically wailed.

'No,' came the sombre response. 'But others . . .' His hands wrestled. 'Come, Mastah Rhrob-ett,' he said. 'I will show you.'

He was right, his medicine had worked quickly; all I felt was tiredness in my limbs as I moved. It was still light outside, if only just, in the west the sun had started to set in a screaming sky, I can't have been there much more than a couple of hours.

Weekend took me through the middle of the compound,

where everyone stopped to look. It was hard not to feel like a prisoner on parade – I deserved to be, and a lot more besides, but Weekend was constantly by my side like a best friend.

About halfway down he pointed to another shack, and to a group of children younger than Tuesday playing. One was clearly different from the rest, the skin of her cheek and neck pink and raw.

'Fire water,' Weekend explained, 'like that in your laboratories. They threw it at her as she walked home one day.'

On the other side, a teenage boy battled for a football. He ran holding his left arm because whenever he let it go it flapped, and much of the hair on the back of his head was missing. The other boys seemed to let him score a goal easily.

'They whipped Philip and beat him with sticks until he could no longer stand.'

And there were more. Drifting through the compound he pointed to another five children: burns, scars, a permanent limp . . .

I couldn't look.

This wasn't me, I wanted to tell him. *I had no idea. If I'd known* . . .

But *hadn't* I known? Deep down, hadn't I always realized how sour the milk had turned? What Ivan and Klompie and Pittman had been doing? The long walks, the jokes, the innuendos, the whispers of shared secrets . . . Why else had I chosen to stop going with them?

'And then there are the children who do not return.' Weekend finally halted near the point where the bees had attacked me. 'One day they went and never came back. I still cry for their mothers and fathers.'

In the dying of the light, I saw tears welling in his eyes.

I looked to the path that would take me back to school. Across the distance I heard the house bells ringing, calling for showers, calling for roll call, calling for life to continue. But now I saw how life – my life – had been detached from reality with its own sick laws and cruel order, and how I had willingly been a part of it.

'This is not a good place,' Weekend told me again. 'Bad things happen here. But soon . . . soon I will have my land. He promised us. And I will farm. And I will be happy again.'

THIRTY

I stared at Ivan all through supper, watching him fill his face up on top table and laugh with the other prefects.

What have you done? I kept thinking.

I broke my gaze to find Klompie and Pittman smirking and sniggering at me.

'Hey, Jacko,' Pitters threw a balled lump of bread, 'what'you get up to this arvo, you poof?'

'Looking a little off colour, Jacko.' Klompie chewed meat with his mouth wide open. 'Anything the matter?'

'Like what?'

'I don't know. Maybe you dropped a grade and got a C instead of a B for your essay. I know how much you like *bees*.'

I pushed my plate and walked out.

I didn't go back to Selous at first. Instead, I found myself in Burnett House, staring at the photograph of the young Mr van Hout as he sat in his Haven uniform. His smile cut his face at a cruel slant, his eyes buried deep into me.

'Why couldn't you have just stayed away?' I heard myself say.

His smile remained, unfaltering, mocking.

Above all else, I needed to get rid of that picture. Then maybe everything would be all right with Ivan, like it had been in the beginning. I didn't care how I did it, I'd break the glass if I had to, but right then a group of younger boys returned from supper and checked me with my hands about to punch forward.

'Evening, Jacklin,' some of them greeted subserviently, confused and probably slightly afraid.

'Howz,' I said.

I was sweating. I wiped my forehead and left.

Perhaps I should say something, I wondered. I should confront him, hear him deny it.

But I didn't see Ivan in the house at all the whole evening. I didn't know where he was, just that it couldn't have been good because his two sidekicks had gone with him.

By the following morning I'd managed to convince myself I was making something out of nothing, merely an overactive imagination going crazy. It was Weekend. It was his fault. He hadn't done me any favours.

Then, during History, I noticed Miss Marimbo straight-away. She was ten minutes late, for a start, and she spent the whole lesson locked in an invisible cage: nervous and timid, scarcely looking up to the class and completely unable to meet Ivan in the eye. When she spoke, her voice wavered and cracked. Her hands trembled so much she couldn't write on the board.

Ivan seemed to be relishing her discomfort, splaying his legs wide, occasionally giving his crotch a meaningful grab.

When he got up at the end of the lesson, Miss Marimbo practically jumped into the corner.

And I just knew. For the first time I understood who Ivan really was.

But I still needed to prove it.

Ivan spotted I was taking my twice-a-term privilege earlier than usual.

'What's so important you can't take your weekend with the rest of us?' he wanted to know. 'You avoiding us?'

I shook my head perhaps a little too vehemently.

'I need to get some heavy revision in,' I replied. 'Plus there's a shooting club I want to check out near home. You know, for after we've left school.'

He sucked on this. 'Sure. Whatever you want. But when you get back I want to have a serious talk.'

A serious talk.

I'd never been so pleased to get beyond the school gates.

Home weekends never lasted long so I didn't waste time.

'Hi, Adele.'

'*Bobby?*' A long pause. The phone felt hot and slippery against my ear. Then: 'Hi, how are you? What are you doing?'

Being out of school or taking this risk?

'I was hoping to talk to you. It's important.'

She hesitated. 'O-K.'

'Not on the phone.'

'Well . . .'

'Please. Ivan doesn't need to know. Today?'

'Well . . . A bunch of us are heading out to Mermaid's Pool this arvo.'

I mouthed a curse.

'You can come if you want.'

'Sure,' I said. Anything. 'I'll meet you there.'

I went straight into my old man's and Matilda's room to hunt for the keys to the car. I was planning to be long gone before they realized.

Everyone knew Mermaid's Pool. About forty kilometres out of town on the Shamva Road, it was an oasis in the bush where nature had crafted one of the best playgrounds in the country.

The pool itself was a huge gouge in the rock, black with depth so you could easily dive in without touching the bottom. There was a rope swing and a zip line, but the best part was the twenty metres of steep granite you could slide down in fast water because the place was on a hillside.

I saw Adele straightaway sitting towards the top of the slope. She was alone. I sat beside her and she reacted as though I'd been away for minutes, and for the next quarter of an hour we chatted about nothing. I was happy to delay what I'd really come to say.

'Do you . . . That is, has he . . . Does he ever . . .' I took a breath. 'Does Ivan ever hurt you?'

I sensed Adele retract. She finished her smoke and grabbed another.

'How do you mean?'

'I mean, does he hurt you? Physically. Does he grab you, or play too roughly?' I remembered seeing bruises on her legs. 'Or hit you?'

'Of course not. You're not being very nice, I don't think I like you at the moment.'

'I'm not trying to make you uneasy.' I moved to put my hand on her shoulder but she wouldn't let me. I'd gone too far. 'I'm sorry, I didn't mean to.'

'Why are you being like this, Bobby?'

'Because. Because . . . He's been acting strange recently.'

'Ivan's always acting strangely.' She bit her lip. 'Isn't that what everyone likes about him? Why did you come here?'

'You're the closest one to him.'

'Am I?' she turned, looking hurt. 'You could have fooled me. He thinks far more about his *gang* than me.'

'Yes, but you're closer. You know what I'm trying to say.'

'*Ja*, I know. And I've a good mind to tell you to *voetsek* and mind your own bloody business.'

'I'm not trying to pry.'

'Yes, you are, that's exactly what you're doing. Why don't *you* tell me something, Bobby?'

'What?'

'Does Ivan know you're here today? With me?'

'Of course not.'

'Any reason I shouldn't let it slip when he phones tonight? I didn't invite you, I've done nothing wrong.'

Now *I* was nervous.

I watched a couple of kids slide by and smack the water at the bottom. Suddenly I saw how bad an idea this had been.

'I should go,' I said. 'My old man will be shitting mangoes about the car.'

At last I got a smile.

'You know you shouldn't have come.'

'I know.'

'But I'm glad you did.' Her warm fingers briefly touched my hand. 'I was so bored. And it's nice having someone I can talk to.'

'Where are your friends?'

'Not here.' She began playing with her hair. 'Sharon wanted to bring her brother, and if Ivan found out . . . It's less complicated to come on my own. And then you phoned anyway. I told them I wasn't feeling good.'

'Oh,' I said stupidly and stood up.

'You're not really going, are you? Stay a bit longer.'

'I wasn't joking about my old man.'

'I'm quite thirsty. Can you get us a Coke? Stay and drink with me, and we can talk properly.' She shaded her eyes from the sun. I thought: *Marry me.* 'Please? I'll answer anything you like – *apart* from that – and I promise I won't be such a bitch.'

'Are you sure?'

'It'll be good.'

I walked down to the store and didn't even wait for the change from five bucks. But as I got back up the slope I saw Adele wasn't on her own any more. Some guy had taken my space, and an icy shiver gripped the skin around my neck when I recognized the back of Ivan's head.

My feet rooted to the spot.

They were about thirty feet away. I was coming from the side, and fortunately he had his back turned. Adele was smiling and looking at him with surprise-wide eyes, and even though she must have seen me coming she did that thing of looking by not looking.

They stood. I shrank into the bushes. Now they were walking away. Adele had picked up her towel and her bag, and they were moving down the edge of the rock towards the car park, Ivan making her hold his hand.

Had he seen me? Had she told him? Was she telling him now?

No, I decided.

But *what was he doing here*?

I watched their cars reverse out and move off into the distance, sunlight glinting. I could taste blood and felt a hole I'd chewed in my lip.

I gave the Cokes to a couple of piccanins playing by the side of the road, and when I tried to unlock the Peugeot I dropped the keys three times because my hands wouldn't keep still.

THIRTY-ONE

I lay on my bed and smoked all night. I didn't feel I'd slept but I guess I must have done because suddenly the unwanted day was pushing against the curtain. As the sun broke the horizon I was already out of the house, walking the road to the cemetery for the first time in a long time.

I found my mother's grave and sat beside it.

'Mum,' I said eventually. The word sounded weird yet strangely comforting. I'd missed it. 'Sorry I haven't been to see you for a while.'

For once I went back to school as late as possible, moving silently through the house while everybody was showering and getting ready for supper. I went to my study and closed the door behind me until, all too quickly, the shout for roll call came.

Ivan was already at the head of the line preparing to read off names. I stood close by. It was going to be another hot evening, although that probably had little to do with the damp hair matted against my brow.

'Howzit.' He flicked his eyebrows.

He looked serious. Or did he always look like that?

'Howz,' I said back.

'Good weekend?'

'Not bad.'

'Club any good?'

For a moment I fumbled. Then I remembered. 'Place was wanked, reckon I could find better.'

He seemed happy with that.

I didn't see him again for the rest of the night, not until after ten, when most of the house was asleep.

I was sitting at my desk when he came, in the dim pool of light that my lamp made. Books lay strewn and open though I was finding it hard to soak up a single word. I'd spent hours gazing out through the window. The cicadas screeched and my head pulsed noisily, sometimes I couldn't tell which was which.

I hadn't heard my door open or Ivan coming in. He was just there, sitting on my bed, removing his tie and playing with it in his hands like a hangman might play with a noose.

I didn't speak. On a normal occasion surely he would have found that strange? I thought. But this wasn't a normal occasion, and he just sat and toyed with the fabric serpent between his fingers.

'So,' he spoke at long last. 'Town was good, was it?'

He knew. He knew very well.

I swallowed. My throat clicked.

'You mustn't blame Adele. I was the one who asked to see her. I insisted.'

He didn't respond.

I couldn't take the silence. I couldn't take the gloom either and I moved across the room to turn on the main light, but Ivan must have thought I was leaving because suddenly I was being propelled the last few feet. My head hit the door and bounced off. Stars flashed in my eyes. The next thing I knew I was back at my desk, smashing against it, pain flaring up my legs as Ivan leaned me further and further until I was sure something would snap.

I gave in. Now I was on my back and helpless, lying over my books with Ivan pinning an arm across my chest. I could barely see his face, he was an outline as the lamp blinded me, coming closer, its heat getting stronger and stronger until the searing bulb was eating into my skin. I shouted out, twisting. Ivan's hold was too heavy and my cheek burned.

'You picked the wrong chick to steal, Jacko,' he said over my cries. 'A fine mate you turned out to be.'

I spluttered. 'I didn't . . . I wasn't trying to . . .'

The heat vanished. He hauled me up and tossed me onto the bed. Two quick punches and I was curled in agony.

'Don't bullshit me. Why else would you have gone there? Tell me. What were you doing if it wasn't to try and take my woman?'

What could I say? The truth?

He backed away. Almost as an afterthought he lurched forward and slapped me several times around the head.

'I trusted you. Despite my better judgement I took you in and made you my friend, and this is how you repay me. Why, Jacko?' He kicked my feet. 'Tell me why. What have I done to you?'

I groaned.

'I wasn't . . .'

'Don't *lie* to me,' he yelled. 'I *knew* you were lying. I didn't want to believe it, I was willing to give you the benefit of the doubt, but you had to go and screw it all up. And I'm the idiot with egg on my face for opening the door and inviting you to come and be one of us. Well, not any longer. You can fuck off and die. You'll regret this, I promise you. I'm Head Boy, you have no idea how miserable I can make your final days here.'

He headed out. At the door he paused without turning.

'Don't you get it? You needed me. You could have been part of something great. You still need me, but now you're going to find out what life's really like.'

Since then I've gone over and over those words in my head, poring over the irony of how it was actually completely the opposite of that. For what he had planned, *Ivan* needed *me,* and he'd known it. He was in far greater agony.

THIRTY-TWO

I probably could have made it.

Despite everything they threw at me – the names, the jibes, the stares, ants' nests in my bed, glass under my pillow, the shit smeared on my study walls, even a snake in my wardrobe – I reckon I could have kept my head down, focused on my studies and got through relatively unscathed.

The problem was Weekend.

Every night I saw his face as I tried to sleep, and I'd hear the words again and again, always the same.

And then there are the children who do not return.

In my dreams I saw the piccanins with burnt and acid-scorched skin – and Tuesday, of course, with his missing eye – and I would invariably wake chasing a cry into the darkness. I didn't like sleeping any more, so I didn't mind that, increasingly, I couldn't. But my studies were suffering too, and all I could think about was Ivan.

In the week that marked the mid-way point, with half term approaching, I returned from class to find my study turned over again, although this time was slightly different because it was as though they'd been looking for something.

What did I have they could possibly want? I thought as I put the room back together.

My heart beat faster and faster when I realized I couldn't find the keys to the rifle room.

I heard Ivan's study open. There was a murmur of voices and a snigger before they drifted off. I dared to crack open my door; off on one of their walks, by the looks of it, Klompie and Pittman each with a hefty stick.

And then there are the children . . .

I gave them another fifteen seconds before slipping out in their wake.

My stomach rolled as they headed straight for the rifle room. But they didn't stop, instead carrying on through the classrooms, past the woodwork shops, right on out of the top gate. Now they were on the dirt track there, a popular back-route for smokers because it was rarely used and, more importantly, it met the main road right opposite the Zama Zama bottle store, far away enough from the school's official entrance not to be spotted.

They veered off the track and hovered under a *msasa* tree to light up, and when they were done they moved on again, digging out coins from their pockets.

Just coming for a smoke, picking up more illicit supplies. That was all.

Zama Zama was little more than a concrete block under a tin roof, the front wall splashed red and white by a giant Coca-Cola logo. The coast was clear. Ivan stole into the gaping black mouth that was the way in while the other two hung about round the side. Apart from them the place was deserted, it was too hot, everything was still.

I watched and waited.

Eventually Ivan emerged with a couple of bottles. The store owner was right behind him, also carrying beers, and Ivan indicated for him to go ahead.

'*Mazviita, shamwari.*' Thank you, my friend. 'You are Number One.'

The owner – a short man of about sixty with eager eyes

and a boyish face – beamed. He'd be making a buck out of this, maybe even two.

He walked on.

Out of the man's sight, Klompie and Pittman were waiting, tapping their sticks on the ground, getting ready for something.

Ivan let the man get to within a few feet of the corner then paused to quickly put his beers down. Now he crept up on the storekeeper's back.

I didn't like it. This wasn't right. I looked around for anything and found it.

The stone hit exactly where I wanted it to go: not at them, they would have known for sure it was me, but into a stack of wooden crates. Sound ricocheted and instantly the three of them were scampering into the bush, scarcely pausing to glance at the bewildered store owner. By the time they passed me, heading back to school, they'd started to laugh and joke.

Would they have actually done anything? Was it all in my mind?

Yes, I decided as I ran back, and no. In that order. And I had to do something about it.

Bully looked over his half-moons and I knew I was wasting my time. I hadn't really expected anything else. Ivan wasn't just Head Boy, he'd been Mr Bullman's outright choice. An attack on Ivan was an attack on Bully. Bully was, in short, in league with the Devil, a fact made more terrifying because he had no idea.

He sighed.

'Our head pupil,' he said, 'harassing local Africans at the bottle store. And workers from the village.'

His chair made a sound like grinding teeth as he leaned back.

'And the keys to the rifle room – over which you, the Captain, have responsibility – have gone missing.'

'Yes, sir.' I felt the ground falling away. I saw myself as he saw me: red-faced and covered with sweat and grime.

'Do you realize how ridiculous your accusation sounds? Ivan is Head Boy, and he has proved himself to be nothing more than an exemplary example of such to me and the rest of the staff. He has helped this school tremendously, so to have you here today telling me these things . . . Well, I'm surprised. I thought you and Ivan were friends.'

'We were, sir . . .'

Slowly, he removed his glasses.

'I see. You've fallen out.'

'No, sir. I mean: yes, sir, but that's not why . . .'

'These things happen between boys, Jacklin, I understand, particularly at a time of exams when pressure is high. But that is no reason to make matters worse by creating fanciful stories about the other.'

'But, sir, I'm not making it up. You're not listening. You have to believe me.'

Mr Bullman was Headmaster and he didn't *have to* do anything unless it was the government that told him. The glasses went back on. The battle was lost.

'I'm not expecting to find anything, but I shall look into these allegations of yours,' he said. 'In due course. Right now, with mere *days* to tie up preparations for a Speech Day that will be engraved into the school's history, I'm too busy. In the meantime I advise you to focus on what you should realize are the most important examinations of your life.'

'But, sir . . .'

Bully threw his pen onto the desk, where it lost itself in a river of papers. Briefly, I saw official letterheads and the government coat of arms and the word SECRET stamped in big red letters.

'I am *busy*, Jacklin. I have very important matters to address, arrangements to make. If the keys to the rifle room *are* lost – not stolen or missing, lost – then recover them.'

He waved me away.

As I reached the door he added: 'You know, I am not only surprised by your appearance here today, but sorely disappointed. If you and Hascott have fallen out, then there are other ways to rectify the situation.'

I waited, but there was nothing else.

I left and found Ivan coming down the corridor towards me. He eyed me up and down.

'Jesus, you're a mess. You been playing in the dirt with your friends again, Jacko?'

His heavy shoulder clipped mine, spinning me round. I watched him saunter down to Bully's office and go in without knocking.

THIRTY-THREE

Half term came to release me.

My old man met the announcement that I wouldn't be going anywhere over the whole weekend with little surprise.

'I've been meaning to ask: whatever happened to that friend of yours?' he asked. 'Ivan, I think you said his name was. And the two others. You used to talk about them all the time.'

'Exams, Dad. My studies are more important at the moment,' I explained.

'If you don't know it now you never will. What have you been doing for the last five years?' was his response.

'Dad!'

'Sorry. Just joking. Maybe you'll have time for a game of cribbage later?'

'You bet.'

I thought it would be different – better – but I felt as much a prisoner at home. More so, because at least at school there were people to talk to, even if it wasn't about what I *wanted* to talk about any longer; here, there was only my old man and Matilda, and I couldn't tell them, so I had no one. I was alone.

A dozen times, possibly more, I picked up the phone to dial Adele's number, though could never quite turn the last digit. What was the point? She'd be with him. And what would Ivan do this time if he found out?

What *would* Ivan do?

I thought of our meeting at Mermaid's Pool and worried. I hadn't seen or heard from her since that day.

On the back of a lie about wanting to catch some movie, I took the car and drove into town, but instead of keeping straight for the centre I headed towards Avondale and parked under lilac shade at the top of Adele's road, fully aware that if Ivan was around I was dead. It was a chance I was willing to take. I cut the engine and waited, heat and jacaranda pods tapping on the roof.

After two hours I saw her, a brief glimpse as her mum's Datsun Cherry emerged from the gates. Adele sat meekly in the passenger seat, head low, hair shielding her face. There was something different about her, a change, she seemed so small and fragile that I almost didn't recognize her. And when she lifted her face to slip on dark glasses was that a bruised smudge beneath her eye? Or just the light?

My fingers dug into the seat. What had he been doing?

I fired up the engine, pushed first gear and started to follow. By the end of the road I saw what I was doing and how impossible it was. I couldn't confront her, not again.

I would have to find out another way.

'Sorry, Dad. It was a long movie.'

I turned right and headed out of town, and as fast air blasted at me through the open window I wondered for the first time: *What* exactly was I hoping to find out?

An hour later I was through the school gates and parking up outside Selous. It was locked, of course.

I walked round to Mr Craven's front door. I didn't know if he was more surprised to see me or by the fact that I'd caught him with a cigarette in his hand. I was shocked, but I supposed teachers had to be human some time.

I fed him a line about having forgotten a book and that I'd left my key behind, and he handed over his bunch of spares.

Inside, the bone-rattle of keys echoed loudly along the corridor as I tried each one in turn. My palms were slippery. Finally, the lock turned and Ivan's door swung open. The room was dim and unwelcoming, as though it knew I shouldn't be there.

Now what?

Hurry. Hurry up, before . . .

. . . Before . . . ?

I went through every drawer, between every item of clothing, under every loose piece of flooring. I even reached up the chimney.

Nothing.

No rifle room keys, and not a single piece of evidence to prove he was far from the model Head Boy he pretended to be. I stood in the middle of the room and exhaled, a part of me relieved.

As a final check I went through his rubbish and found exactly that, and in frustration I kicked the wastepaper bin to the other end of the study. The tin clattered loudly as paper strew all over the place. I regretted the action instantly and rushed round to collect the mess, wondering if anyone had heard, wondering if Ivan would notice the difference. It was with the last piece in my hand, however, that something made me stop to look at what I was retrieving.

An envelope.

Addressed to Ivan.

With a South African stamp.

Nothing remarkable about that, it could have been from his folks. But I noticed the Nelspruit postmark and *his* parents were all the way down in Pietermaritzburg; they weren't anywhere near the Transvaal.

The envelope had been ripped open in a way that made me picture frantic, eager fingers. I turned it over, and the sender's details shone out in a heavy, angular hand I'd seen before.

MvH, PO Box 3447, Nelspruit,
Transvaal, South Africa.

MvH.

Mark van Hout.

It had to be. It could only be. All this time . . .

I delved back into the bin, but of course the letter itself was nowhere to be found.

I swayed, adrift yet again. My eyes fell on the collection of toy cars the piccanins made from coat hangers and bottle tops. It had grown along Ivan's windowsill over the months. It was as though I was noticing them for the first time. You could buy toys like this anywhere, a few cents on the side of the road, but was that likely? Ivan?

I picked one up and remembered children playing down at the workers' village, and a shudder gripped me.

There was a noise.

Outside, I saw Mr and Mrs Dunn as they walked between the houses. Dunno glanced up and I stepped quickly out of sight. He didn't spot me and carried on walking, now moving across the grass and heading towards the Admin Block.

I left the house and made sure he was out of sight before following his trail, stopping short of the school's main building to check the rifle room itself. Using my own spare, I released the giant padlock and checked inside for the hundredth time. Everything was still in order: all rifles present and standing correctly, all bullets accounted for. Again, I questioned if I hadn't simply mislaid or lost the keys after all, maybe Bully was right. Or maybe they were just playing with my mind. Or maybe . . .

. . . Maybe, maybe, maybe . . .

In the cool of the windowless room I slumped to the ground with my head in my hands and reminded myself repeatedly that there was only half a term left to go, fighting the other voice that told me that was still half a term to endure.

More footsteps. I sprang to my feet and got out of there, and just managed to snap the bolt shut before Miss Marimbo emerged down the steps from the dining room. She was barely a foot away when she spotted me lurking in the doorway and she startled with a small shriek. Any other teacher might have then asked why the hell I was here, over half term; Miss Marimbo just turned and walked the other way, her feet breaking into a trot.

'Miss Marimbo. It's me, Jacklin.'

She knew perfectly well who it was, though: Robert Jacklin, aka Ivan's Friend, aka One of the Gang. Hadn't I seen that same look on so many faces over the years?

I went after her. 'Miss Marimbo.'

'Stay away from me.' Her voice was high and thin. She looked around to find we were the only two people in sight. 'I'm warning you.'

'Miss?'

'What are you doing here? Is he here with you?'

'Who?' I asked flatly.

Miss Marimbo stopped.

We'd reached the Admin Block. Upstairs, Mr Dunn appeared at the staff room window. Naturally, he looked surprised to see me. Miss Marimbo hovered with one hand on the door, visibly reassured.

'What are you doing here, Jacklin?' she asked again.

'Ivan and I,' I told her, '. . . we're not friends any more.'

She seemed to relax more.

'That's not what I asked.'

'I came for something.'

'What?'

The heat of the afternoon pressed around us. We were both still conscious of Dunno's gaze. Miss Marimbo smiled up and he went away.

'I'm not sure,' I said.

Miss Marimbo began to push open the door. She opened her mouth and for a moment I thought she was going to tell me what I wanted to hear.

'You are young,' she said instead, 'and I believe you're actually a decent person. Ivan? He isn't like you and, if you must know, your friendship with him always mystified me. Finish your exams, leave this place, then forget it and forget Ivan.'

She started to go.

'Wait.' I held her arm, and immediately let go again. 'Has something happened? Has Ivan done something? Please, I need to know.'

And when she didn't reply.

'You can do something. You can tell Mr Bullman. The police, even.'

'Neither of whom would believe me. Me, an African woman, whom Mr Bullman has employed as more than a maid only because he's scared the government will shut his school down. He still *treats* me as a maid.'

'But the police—'

'Are all Shona tribe. I am Matabele. If they thought I was under threat they would be happy. Police and soldiers mistreat the Matabele all the time and everyone looks the other way.'

'They wouldn't do that,' was all I could offer. 'They're all . . . You're all . . .'

'Black? African? In Africa, that doesn't count for much. Please, go home.' She went inside. 'If you really want to do something, forget you ever came to this school and get on with your life. It's what I shall do.'

THIRTY-FOUR

'Whatever it is you're doing, stop it.'

My chest was thumping, so to make it easier I kept my eye on the First XI. It was the last match of the year. I'd waited all week for an opportunity when I could get him alone without actually being alone, and the edge of the cricket field was the perfect place. Masters and parents gently edged the oval.

Ivan loathed cricket. He shuffled on the bench with mild astonishment.

'What are you gibbering about now, Jacko?'

'I spoke to her.'

'Who?'

'You know who.'

Ivan eased back, stretching his spine into a confident arch.

'Jesus, I thought you'd be pleased. I don't want her any more, you can dump your muck now. She's a crap lay anyways, not that you'd know the difference.'

I struggled to keep my voice under control.

'I'm not talking about Adele. I spoke to Miss Marimbo.'

'What has *she* got to do with anything?'

I turned to him.

'She's terrified. What did you do?'

He casually cracked his knuckles.

'Marimbo needed to learn respect. Kicking *me* out of class . . . ? That sort of thing would never have happened in the Old Days.'

'She wouldn't even have been allowed to teach in a school like this in the Old Days.'

'My point exactly. What's she going to do about it anyway?'

'She can go to the police. They'd have a thing or two to say about it.'

'She wouldn't dare.'

'That's where you're wrong, because she's thinking about it.' It was a stupid thing to say. I had his full attention, but it scared me. More than that, I was scared for Miss Marimbo. 'You belong in the Dark Ages.'

'Don't be so naïve. The first rule of nature is inequality. Sir didn't make that up.'

'Inequality in the sense we're all different, not what he wants it to mean. Can't you see how he tried to twist things?' He flicked impatiently at me. I ignored it. 'And still is. I know he's been writing to you.'

He paused.

'Sounds to me like someone wants to play with the big boys and has been snooping around.'

'What's he been telling you?'

'Shut up and listen, Jacko. If anyone's got it wrong it's you. Ask anyone, we all think the same way and we want the same thing. You're not from here so what would you know?'

'I don't see anyone else fighting. As far as I can tell you're on your own – you and your trained chimps.'

'Don't get bloody cheeky, Pommie.' He moved in closer. 'Have you ever lived through a war? Hey? Of course not. *I* have. This whole country has, for fifteen years. Fifteen *hard* years, because when you're fighting Kaffirs you're not dealing with human beings, that lot do things *dogs* would think too cruel. Folks had had enough of fighting, they wanted to be able to breathe again, but if you think they've given up dreaming of how it used to be . . . If there was even half a chance they'd have their country back, you see if they don't.'

Around the edge of the field the scattering of spectators, all white and dressed from another era, applauded a boundary. They drank tea and ate cakes and dismissed black staff without speaking.

'You lost the war, your country's gone. It's in the past now. Colonialism is an outdated ideal and it was never going to work – you can't simply plant a flag and claim rights over someone else's land.' My father's words but with my voice. 'Accept it and move on.'

'Never. The war wasn't lost, it was stalemate, and if we'd been allowed to hang on a bit longer the blacks would have fought one another into the ground and we'd still have a nation that *means* something. But the Poms had to interfere, and now we have a leader who's going to ruin everything. All that bullshit he talks . . . Mugabe doesn't care about us or anyone, he's only after two things: money and power. Power and money. He'll burn this country to get both. Sir said.'

'How can you believe that?'

'*Because he's already started doing it.*' Heads turned to look. Ivan didn't even notice. 'He's taking land, he's messing with our school, he's slaughtering Matabele. I don't care that he's killing blacks, but he said he'd cull the whites too and he will. I'm telling you, it'll happen. Mugabe's hatred hasn't just gone away. He's still fighting the war only no one can see it. We have to fight back or we're fucked. And not just us whites, it's everyone who isn't waving his banner and licking his arse. We're not safe until he and all his lot are wiped out.'

In that moment I sensed what it might have been like to have been Miss Marimbo the night he'd got her.

'And that means cracking heads down at Zama Zama?' I said. I wanted to keep him talking and conceal my nervousness. 'The children in the village?'

'We have to fight back. Don't you see? Exactly as Sir said. I want you to understand. I hoped maybe you would. You were part of it, remember? You were there too.'

It was true. I was.

I couldn't take it any more. I stood and walked quickly away. Ivan came with me. His arm snaked over my shoulders.

'Hey, come on, Jacko. I never wanted us to fall out, you know.'

It was a trick. I said nothing, just kept on walking.

'I hope you're not going to do anything silly. You wouldn't do anything like that. Besides, you'd be in trouble too, I'd make sure of it, and you'll just end up wasting that gift of yours. Don't throw it away.'

I didn't know what he meant.

'Go away.' I pushed him off.

'Hey, Jacko . . . Bru.' A hurt plea. 'Don't be like that. Look, if I upset you I'm sorry, I was just a little pissed off. But that's all right now, friends are more important than chicks. Adele and I are through. Come on. We can still use you.'

Use me?

'I don't care about you any more.' We were round the back of the new boarding house, I saw buckets and paint tins and other building materials all around us that had been hidden for the official opening. What I couldn't see any more was the cricket field. We were completely isolated. 'All our games . . . *Games?* They're not games, they're barbaric, the things we've done. Cruel. We hated what Greet and Kasanka and the others used to do to us yet we're happy to dish out the same. No, *worse.* It's not right and it never was. We have to stop. *You* have to stop.'

'So I'll stop.' He waved his arms. 'OK?'

'All of it.'

'I swear. Cross my heart. I've missed you, man, we all have.'

He smiled in his way, and just like that I believed him. Not because he wanted me to, but because we were alone and I was too afraid not to.

'Shake.' He offered me a hand.

Hesitantly, I took it, and as I did so there was an almost undetectable shift. His smile grew wide.

'You weren't really going to say anything to Bully, were you?'

I shrugged. 'Maybe.'

'You would have been wasting your breath. He's got enough on his plate sorting out Speech Day tomorrow. That sad old oak will do anything to make sure they don't close the school down and the last thing he needs is you whingeing in his ear.'

'Why is that so important to you? You used to hate this school, why does it matter whether they shut it down or not?'

His lips pulled back.

'You'll find out,' he said. 'But I could tell you now if you want, it's not too late. We've got one more game to play.'

I let go and pulled away.

He quickly closed the gap. 'Think about it. Have I really been doing anything that bad? They've taken my country and my home, all I'm doing is trying to survive. And people will thank me one day. I'm going to be a hero. Don't you want to be a part of that?'

I tried to move past and he grabbed my shirt.

'What are you talking about?' I said.

'Come back into the gang. Be a part of something special.'

We stared at one another for what seemed like minutes. Yes, I thought. I could go back, and it could be like it was before it turned.

'The truth is,' he went on, 'as far as I was concerned you never left. Don't you see? You're just like us, wanting the life you think you should have had, the life that someone took away.

Sir spotted that about you straightaway, even before your mum died. And there's nothing wrong with wanting. Why shouldn't you? It's your life. And you know what? You *can* do something about it. Shit back! You can take control, make it happen. We're your only friends, stay with us and we'll help you.'

He nodded, willing me to copy.

The same old Ivan. He would never change.

I forced myself to look away and stepped around him.

'This is your last chance, Bobby,' he called after me. 'Stay with us and it'll be worth it, I promise you.' And then: 'Come on, stop being so staunch. After everything I've done for you, the least you can do is give me something back. You owe me. Klompie and Pitters . . . They're OK, but you're better. Come on, man, I need you.'

I walked faster.

'You're being stupid, Jacko. You can finally make something of your sorry excuse of a Pommie life. Don't go and ruin it now. Bully will never believe you anyway.'

Now I started to run because Ivan was running too, his feet slapping the lonely path that narrowed and curved. A high wall on one side and a hedge on the other – there was nowhere else for me to go. Why had I come this way?

I sprinted, a push of panicky air escaping my lungs. The bend was relentless and the end always out of sight. My legs pressed and pressed but a nightmare was coming to life, and a heavy hand grabbed my heart and pulled it down as the trap closed in.

Then, thankfully, a couple of boys appeared around the corner. I allowed myself the taste of relief.

'Hey! You guys! Stop him!' Ivan yelled at them. The bark of a Head Boy losing his grip.

I ran harder towards them.

Then my heels were digging into the ground, skidding,

trying to stop myself from going any further as Derek De Klomp and Sean Pittman loomed into focus.

Ivan was ripping through the air. I turned and saw him for just long enough to register the length of building wood swinging from behind his head before my world went black.

The ache in my head brought me out of it. I'd been dreaming about watching a dawn rising, and the brighter the sun grew, the greater the pain, so I was surprised when I opened my eyes and found night.

The moon was sharp through the window and showed me a room I'd never seen before. Yet instinctively I knew I was in the new boarding house – in one of the study rooms – the smell of plaster and fresh paint thick in my nose. I also realized my hands and feet were bound, and that Ivan had made this happen. He'd hit me unconscious, carried me to the nearest hiding place and would come for me later. I knew these things with total, absolute certainty.

What he'd do next, however, I couldn't say.

Rolling onto my back, I gnawed at the rope around my wrist. The knot came undone with ease; I could only guess Klompie had been left in charge of that little job. Struggling for balance, I tried the locked door and then moved across to the window. The catch had been glued down but I managed to rip it free and then slipped out onto the lawn.

I waited, listening.

The school was eerily quiet. Lights were on so it couldn't have been late, yet as I wandered through, the place felt like a ghost town. I saw no one. Prep? The houses were empty, the study rooms void. Supper time? Only kitchen workers occupied the dining hall, clearing the last remnants of the meal.

Out of the corner of my eye I saw someone striding across

the grass. Bully was moving with determined steps towards the theatre hall. He'd no doubt called everyone there to make an announcement about tomorrow.

'Sir!' He didn't hear. I ran past the dining room, down the stairs. 'Excuse me, sir!'

I wasn't fast enough. He slipped through the doors and into the back of the hall. Bent sore and out of breath in the foyer, I heard everyone on the other side standing to attention, then sitting again, then Bully's cigarette-raked voice begin.

'Tomorrow,' he said, and in my mind I could see him standing upright and rigid, 'brings with it a very special day in the school calendar: Speech Day.'

I should have just gone in. I should have torn through the doors, made an entrance and told them all. They would have listened to me then and Ivan wouldn't have been able to do a thing.

'As ambassadors of the school, your behaviour and appearance will be unblemished. You will be walking examples of the kind of model pupil that this education establishment prides itself on turning out.'

But I didn't go in. There was something that made me want to listen. With the fascination of someone watching a crash, I wanted to hear what Bully had to say.

'These are the things I want and expect, you know me by now.'

I moved right up to the door and pressed against it, and through the thin crack I made I could see the boys at the back. Ivan was there with the other school prefects. I pushed a fraction harder and I could spy Klompie and Pitters two rows in front.

'But I call from you your sense of duty and pride more than ever before, for tomorrow holds importance that raises this above all Speech Days of the past. Yes, it is the school's thirtieth anniversary, and, yes, it will include the official opening of Mugabe House, the single most important statement to our new government of our determination to look to the future. The one thing that truly heightens the occasion, however, is the acceptance of our invitation to open the House by *Prime Minister Robert Mugabe himself.*'

Excited whispers through the hall.

A few feet away, I watched Klompie and Pittman look round with strange smiles on their faces. Ivan gave an imperceptible nod, a secret sign that no one else would have noticed, and they turned back. It was at that point, as when a heavy cloud rolls clear of the sun, that I began to see.

'I'm sure you can appreciate,' Bully's voice went on, calming the ripple, 'why I've been unable to tell you before now of these plans. Security has to be at its highest, our leader's aides instructed that I make the announcement as late as possible and to facilitate a curfew under the watch of the Prime Minister's own soldiers, who must ensure no terrorist faction takes advantage of our VIP invitation. They will be patrolling the school grounds all night. Under no, absolutely no circumstances must you step beyond the inner ring road. The soldiers are under strict orders to protect, at any cost, and I warn you now they are unlikely to ask questions first.'

The ripple turned into a buzz.

Ivan moved his head sagely up and down. None of this news was a surprise to him. Of course it wasn't.

'Our honoured guest is scheduled to arrive at ten o'clock, shortly after which he will commence speeches and prize-giving. Parents and government officials will take priority over the seating, naturally, so all junior boys will collect chairs from the classrooms and arrange themselves *in an orderly fashion* on the grass. Sixth formers not receiving prizes will be up in the gallery. The Prime Minister will speak second, after the Head Boy.'

Ivan had planned this. Him and Mr van Hout, coming up with a way to lure the Prime Minister into the school. All these years, I thought.

'Following on from this, the Prime Minister will be invited for coffee at my home together with the Chaplain and the Senior Master.'

Waiting patiently. Making plans together. Looking for ways to achieve the impossible dream.

'At one o'clock, boys who have been selected will gather for the formal opening of their new boarding house.'

Plotting. Lining up the pieces. Biding their time.

And now that time had come.

We have to fight back.

Ivan's words swarmed around me. Like the bees. Stabbing, always stabbing.

If there was even half a chance they'd have their country back, you see if they don't . . .

. . . People will thank me one day, I'm going to be a hero . . .

. . . Don't you want to be part of that? Klompie and Pitters . . . They're OK, but you're better . . .

Sweating, winded, I staggered from the door.

A low rumble rose beyond the glass. I saw lights by the Admin Block as three army Crocodile trucks trundled into the car park. They lined up side by side, then a jumble of soldiers with red berets poured out with rifles. They lit up smokes and spat. One urinated into the storm drain.

'So now you know.'

The words floated gently.

I spun round, and he was standing there. Just him and me at opposite ends of the foyer.

A few quick steps and he was on me.

'You could have been part of it but you turned your back on us.'

'You can't be serious,' I said. 'Assassinate Mugabe?'

He launched his forehead and pain exploded in my nose. A powerful jab and I was down, gasping for air.

'Shut up. You're the only one who can get in the way and I've waited too long to let a stupid Pommie ruin it.'

But I wasn't the only one. Not really.

He read my face.

'I think you and I need to go for a little walk. We'll pay a surprise visit to Miss Marimbo before she opens her ugly black mouth, sort the both of you out at the same time.'

He grabbed my hair, but right then the doors to the main hall blew open and suddenly the foyer was flooded with boys. Ivan's grip dropped and I took my chance, I elbowed him and jumped into the current.

When I dared a glance, Ivan had been joined by the other two. They were looking for me, tracking my path. I started running and dived into the thick, warm night.

'Jacko! Run, Jacko,' Ivan yelled. *'I'm telling you, you'd better run* hard *cos we're coming to get you. Gonna slot you, one time. You're dead.'*

THIRTY-FIVE

I was aiming for the main gate, and as far beyond it as I could get, but even from a distance the moonlight was enough to show me the outline of a closed barrier. The cherry of a soldier's smoke flared red.

I veered from the road and cut across uneven ground. I stumbled over loose rocks and soil, then slammed into the fence because it was much nearer than I'd realized. Up the line I heard the sound of a rifle being readied.

'*Eweh!* Who goes?' came the gruff voice.

I pulled myself over and down onto the other side, and headlong into the pines.

At the road, I ran down the centre lines until my lungs burned. I sat in the ditch, crying and heaving for air. There were no cars, no lights. I was alone and miles from anywhere. Anywhere but here.

Then a voice, and it wasn't Ivan's.

Forget you ever came to this school and get on with your life.

Miss Marimbo.

A light wind grabbed me from nowhere and it made me cold.

Scared eyes through the gap. A chain kept the door tight.

'What are you doing here?'

She didn't know; they hadn't been yet. I'd never felt so relieved about anything.

'Miss Marimbo, you have to get away from here, it's not safe,' I told her. 'I think he's . . . I think he could . . .'

She knew who I meant.

I heard noises and glanced over my shoulder. 'There might not be much time.'

Her expression paled. She let me in off the stoep and locked the door behind me. Inside, I vaguely registered the naked living room and the boxes piled against one wall.

She noticed me looking.

'I am leaving tomorrow, as soon as speeches are over. I cannot wait until the end of term.'

'No, go now,' I said. 'It isn't safe.'

She stared at the cut on my face. 'What has happened?'

'All sorts. I can't explain everything now, but Ivan believes you might go to the police about what he did to you.' She looked at me, terrified, and I hated myself. 'I told him we'd spoken. It's my stupid fault. Can you drive us out of here?'

'To where? There are soldiers all over, the headmaster has warned us that we must not . . .'

'Please. Right now.'

Miss Marimbo stood, dazed, wanting and not wanting to understand.

I told her what I knew.

'Ivan's planning to kill the Prime Minister tomorrow.'

She didn't laugh, or rebuke me, or even ask me to say it again.

'OK,' she simply said at last. 'We'll go now.'

There was a sharp crack against the window and the curtain puffed into the room. Miss Marimbo jumped and frowned at it, then at the pieces of glass on the floor, but already I understood. Before I could warn her a second crack sounded, and this time the stone smacked into the shade hanging from the ceiling. The bulb exploded.

Miss Marimbo screamed. I grabbed her hand, pulled her to the kitchen and shut us in, killing the lights. I slid the table across as a barricade while heavy feet smashed into the front door.

I pushed the window.

'Is that your car?'

Miss Marimbo nodded. She grabbed keys off a hook.

'Get out and start it. Quickly.'

'What about you?' she wavered.

A loud thud against the kitchen door. The table rammed in and for one horrifying moment Ivan's face was there. I leaped and made him disappear and wrestled the barrier back into place.

Miss Marimbo was halfway out.

'Robert.'

'Just go.'

'But—'

'*Now!*'

With a sob, she vanished, and long seconds later the engine roared to life. Headlights flooded the kitchen. With a last shove, I jumped and scrambled headfirst out of the gap and rolled to the ground. The car wailed, then Miss Marimbo's scream rose above it. Pittman was on the passenger side slapping at the door while Klompie had managed to get the driver's side open and was lunging in.

Without thinking, I dived at Klompie, tackling him to the ground. He slashed his arms while I pinned him face down. Pittman picked up a rock and aimed at the windscreen.

I reached out my foot and kicked the car door shut.

'*Get out of here!*'

Miss Marimbo didn't need telling. With one quick movement, she pulled the car into reverse and sped through a narrow gap between the trees, leaving Pittman bathed in blinding headlights and swinging his rock at fresh air. He was almost clown-like in the way he spun and collapsed to the ground.

Now the car was on the track. Miss Marimbo straightened up and the tyres dug deep. Above me, Ivan leaned out of the window. Without looking back I scurried the only way I could and didn't stop until I was over the perimeter fence, away from the retreating glow of the car and back out into the safety of the bush.

The night stalked me. I felt I'd been going for hours, my limbs aching and hot.

The stars were hidden now and every few seconds the clouds glowed silver as a battle ravaged the sky. Angry murmurs rumbled in the distance. I wasn't sure where I was going, but I needed to stop and think so instinct took over and put me on the path to the Cliffs. I also needed to shelter because the rain had started to fall, instant and heavy.

I shuffled under the overhanging rock close to the drop. Initially I cursed how the storm trapped me there but secretly I was comforted by it. I felt safe, the sound of it a reassuring blanket. As long as it was there I was certain they wouldn't be hunting for me, so I pushed myself further beneath the granite and lay with my head on the earth.

Sleep was fitful, and in my dream I saw that Miss Marimbo had made it and released the news, so that when I went back to school it was all over. Soldiers and police were everywhere. Ivan and Klompie and Pitters had been arrested and the Prime Minister was safe. And I was welcomed back as a hero. Then the dream turned and Miss Marimbo *hadn't* made it, so I had to smuggle my way back, get past the soldiers and disable Ivan myself. Only I couldn't find him. And I could hear the Prime Minister's motorcade getting closer and closer, but however hard I tried to tell them, the lines of boys and masters and parents in the chapel sat blankly and unhearing like dummies. They couldn't even see me. I screamed at them, I shook them. They did nothing. And now the Prime Minister was here, coming through the huge doors at the far end with all his bodyguards around him. The light behind him was so bright he was faceless, an apparition devoured by silhouette.

Snap, the bolt of a rifle echoed.

Klompie was at the altar and aiming his gun down the aisle.

Snap.

Pittman, in the pulpit, rifle butt nuzzled against his cheek.

Snap.

Ivan, suddenly right next to me, ready for the shot.

My eyes burst open into the murk of pre-dawn. The rain had stopped, the air was heavy and still. It was too early even for the birds.

I pulled myself out.

I hadn't been to the Cliffs in ages – this was *their* domain – and the whole area seemed different somehow, smaller. I remembered the night I'd saved Klompie, the day of Nelson and the scorpion . . . So long ago. It could have been another lifetime. It *was* another lifetime, I'd been so many different people.

They obviously still used the place because there were patches on the ground where fires had been lit. Then I noticed the marks in the bark of a tree, all our names and a date. I picked up a rock and started to hack at it, wanting to erase every sign, past or present, that they existed and that I'd had anything to do with them.

And then I stopped. The rock slipped from my fingers.

Something hidden through the bushes.

Nothing very remarkable, just mounds of earth, each no more than a few inches high. They hadn't been there before, I was certain of it. They looked out of place because some of them had grass or plants on them that weren't growing anywhere else, while a few were completely bare.

Just long-drops, I told myself. Ivan never liked people shitting near the camp.

And then there are the children who do not return.

The light crept and shapes emerged from the dark. All of a sudden this was a very bad place to be.

I inched forward until I was at the first line of raised earth, one of the fresher ones without any growth. I didn't want to touch it so I broke off a stick and started to rake over the top. When I eased the end down it went in easily, and kept on going until it met resistance. A rock? Too soft. Elastic, almost. I prodded my way around until I was underneath whatever it was, then levered back. The top of the mound breathed, but whatever was down there was too heavy for my length of wood, and as I pulled harder something gave and a popping sensation raced to my hands. A rancid smell hit my nose.

I let go instantly and stumbled. I fell. The bush suddenly came to life as birds woke and cried and flapped. I watched them overhead, a flurry of shapes against the pale sky, and I wondered what evils they were fleeing, and what they had seen in the past.

Finding my legs, I ran.

The soldier must have been watching me the whole time as I struggled at the top of the fence, trying to unhook my shirt, because as soon as I hit the ground he stepped from behind the trees. He held his Kalashnikov in one hand, in the other he had a length of sugar cane which he tore at and shredded with his teeth. His uniform buttons were mostly undone and his eyes were heavy and red. I caught alcohol fumes as he swayed.

'Who are you?' he demanded. 'What are you doing?'

I threw up my hands. 'I go to school here. I'm a pupil.'

'What are you doing?' he said again, spitting out bits of cane. He jabbed me with the barrel. 'This is Prime Minister's day, you are trespassing, *murungu.*'

'No, I—'

He held the gun in both hands.

My throat hitched.

'I'm a pupil. I was just going . . . for a run. I didn't know we weren't allowed to move around still.' His finger wavered over the trigger and my words garbled. 'I'm sorry I didn't know I'm really sorry. Please.'

He stopped chewing. He believed me, but that didn't mean anything and he dug the butt of his Kalashnikov under my ribs. I collapsed with a groan.

Laughing, he stepped over me for a second helping when a voice boomed across the athletics field.

'What the bloody hell do you think you're doing? Leave that boy alone.'

Dunno was marching towards us, his lips so tight they'd disappeared.

'You can see perfectly well he's harmless. You so much as lay another finger on him I'll have you reported for malicious intent.'

The soldier trained the weapon on him.

'He must not be here. We have orders to protect the Prime Minister. I say he is wrong. *You* are wrong.'

'And I say you're nothing more than a thug in uniform,' Mr Dunn told him.

'I am a war vet.' It sounded like *wovit.* 'I fought for this country.'

'With the likes of *you* in a position of authority, God help us. And don't you bloody point that thing at me.' Dunno swatted the rifle away.

The soldier had to do something. To my relief, he backed down and walked away with a tut and a sneer.

Dunno helped me up.

'Thank you, sir,' I managed.

'Don't thank me, you're a bloody idiot. But *that* lot . . .' he smouldered. 'You know you're lucky to be alive. What the hell do you think you're playing at? And at this hour?' He noticed my clothes. 'What have you been doing, boy?'

I struggled for words. 'I found . . . I think there's . . . Sir, I need to tell you something. It's important.'

But I'd already lost him. His eyes burnt holes into the back of the ambling soldier.

'It'll have to wait,' he told me.

'Sir, I—'

'I said, not now. I've been up all night and I'm in no mood. Not after what's happened.'

'Happened?' I didn't like this. 'Is it something to do with Hascott, sir?'

'*Hascott*? What are you talking about, boy? It's Miss Marimbo,' he said, jaw tensing. 'That poor woman. They said she wouldn't stop, that they tried to wave her down. They said she was driving aggressively and that they were only obeying orders. She was trying to *leave*, for Christ's sake, not get in.'

Each word a solid punch.

'The filthy gook bastards . . . They shot her. They *murdered* her. And the government will brush over this like it never happened. I'm telling you, someone should shoot him. If this is the kind of game our Prime Minister plays then we're better off without him.'

THIRTY-SIX

I started to cry. As Dunno spoke everything caught up with me and I lowered my head and bawled. I didn't know what to do now.

Neither, it seemed, did Dunno.

'Boy? Are you all right, boy?' he asked.

I wanted to tell him everything, but when I tried it felt like needles were stabbing the back of my throat. I couldn't talk. My knees buckled.

Mr Dunn caught me and half-led, half-carried me back to his house, and hastily made his wife take over while he went to try and deal with the mess. Mrs Dunn was from the same cast as her husband, but she was also a mother of some twenty years and still had an instinct.

'Don't you worry, my boy,' she said as she laid me onto a bed. I was dazed. Numb. I stared at nothing. 'It's Robert, isn't it? You look in a terrible state, Robert, but you'll be fine. It's been a great shock. Try to get some sleep.'

'Will they cancel Speech Day?' I croaked, surprising her. 'Do you think they'll stop him from coming? He won't come after what's happened. Will he?'

Ma Dunn gazed at me, frowning. The glow of the rising sun coming through the window was unable to melt the stony set of her face.

'It's an important day,' she replied, 'for the headmaster *and* the Prime Minister, they both have a lot to gain. I don't think either man would let something like this hold them up.'

And then she turned.

'You look tired. Shame. Try to get some rest, hey.'

It was so easy.

Lying there in the Dunn's spare room, staring at the colour-less ceiling, I told myself there was nothing I could do. It was out of my hands. Besides, it was what they all wanted, wasn't it? The Whites, the Matabeles . . . So maybe it really *was* for the best. What if Mugabe really was as bad as they said, and not actually the great man my father insisted he was? His soldiers had killed Miss Marimbo without thinking about it, so they probably had killed lots of other innocent people for him in the past, just as Ivan told us they had, and would keep on killing in the future.

After all, it wasn't my country, so what the hell did I know? All I had to do was lie here and do nothing, let the hours run dry. Whatever the outcome, one way or another, it would all be over. And it would have nothing to do with me.

I felt the lump on my head, the scratches and bruises on my body. I closed my eyes wanting only to come out on the other side, but beneath the shroud I met Ivan.

Ivan at the bottle store.

Ivan at the Cliffs.

Ivan in a darkened alley with an inert Greet bleeding at his feet.

Ivan by the workers' village.

Then I was dreaming, and I was in the chapel next to Ivan with the Prime Minister coming towards us again. This time Ivan didn't take aim. Instead, he was handing the rifle – *my* rifle, from the club – to me, and as I took it he said, grinning and nodding: 'Klompie and Pitters, they're OK . . . But you're *better*. I need you . . .'

*   *   *

The sound of the bullet echoed and I jerked straight. It came again – *crack* – but it was just the jacaranda pods exploding as the heat grew. There was another noise with it, and when I looked out across the playing fields I saw cars.

The morning had moved on, people were starting to arrive.

THIRTY-SEVEN

I like to think there was a moment in Derek De Klomp's life in which he considered everything he was about to do and re-evaluated his part. If he ever did, it was as he stood, smiling and proud, in the car park with his relatives and glanced across to see me running like a thief towards the house. I stopped, and for that moment there was a glimpse of uncertainty as a line of complete understanding passed between us. Not regret, exactly, or guilt, rather the genuine fear of someone who'd found himself in a place to which he'd willingly gone but didn't like now that he was there. And there was no way out and he knew it.

His aunt pulled him round to straighten his tie, and the moment was gone. He lifted his head once more to me, though now the look of deviance and loathing Ivan had taught him was back.

By now everyone was beginning to notice what a state I was in. I finished my dash for the house while the De Klomp family joined the flow that headed for the chapel.

I called for a squack from the junior dorm as I changed into my clean uniform.

'Where's Hascott?'

The squack shook his head: he hadn't seen him all morning.

Through my study window I checked the state of the procession. The De Klomps were still in view but Klompie himself had broken away and was moving briskly round the back of the tennis courts and towards the new house, constantly checking over his shoulder.

In the distance I heard the siren wail of the Prime Minister's motorcade.

I knew Klompie could only have been the failsafe. The back-up. The last-chance-shot should things not have gone to plan. He was too stupid for anything else. Simply lie still, wait for Robert Mugabe to step up to the decorative ribbon and then pull the trigger. Even a monkey couldn't miss at that range.

I don't think Klompie really believed he'd be required to make that shot, or maybe he just hoped it would all be over before the cloud of VIPs got anywhere near him. Whatever the reason, it obviously hadn't dawned on him that by running through a mound of cement dust outside he'd leave a trail of footprints that led me up the stairs and right to the chair he'd used to climb up into the attic. The stink of cigarette smoke hit me straightaway. He hadn't even bothered to pull the cover across after him.

I eased myself up. He was squatting uncomfortably on the rafters, gun against the wall. His line of sight was through ventilation bricks. Even with just my head and shoulders pushed through I could feel the instant heat. Klompie was having to wipe sweat and keep his fringe out of his eyes, and when he realized I was there he squinted several times to make sure he wasn't seeing things.

'What are you doing here, Jacko?' He sounded worried. Then, angrily: 'What are you *doing*?'

He leaped. There was a hollow sound as his head connected with the beam directly above him and he went straight back down. The gun slid and fell, and with a stretch I grabbed the end of the barrel.

Too late, he saw what was happening and reached for the butt with panicky hands. We wrestled briefly for control, and for one terrible moment I saw his fingers snatching close to the trigger, but I managed to kick out and when he tried to regain balance his foot slipped and punctured the ceiling.

He looked stupidly at what he'd done. Unbelievably, even for him, he pushed the other foot down to try and get himself out and made the hole even bigger. His face melted into a look of absolute dismay as he sank to the waist.

'Hey, man . . .'

His clothes were caught and snagged so he couldn't go up or down. He was helpless. Trapped. Like a movie villain in quicksand he gasped and struggled, as I emptied the gun's chamber and took out the magazine.

'You're crazy, De Klomp,' I said, actually feeling sorry for him now. 'You let him talk you into something you could never get away with.'

He grunted. 'We knew we were never going to get away with it, you idiot. Not at first. But maybe one day, when our guys take over power again . . .'

He laughed at me.

'And even if they kill us we'll be heroes.'

'That's lies. How can you believe that?'

He suddenly stopped squirming and looked at me squarely. Because it was Klompie, the sincerity and intelligence of his response startled me.

'If you were in front of Hitler with a gun, wouldn't you squeeze the trigger? *Why* wouldn't you? I'll tell you why: because you're a coward. You're a coward who doesn't even belong here, you're not one of us. You don't understand.'

For a moment I did nothing, just stared, then I smashed the rifle into the wall.

'Why don't you piss off back to Pommieland,' he growled. 'This is our country.'

I climbed back down.

'That's Ivan talking.'

'So what if it is?' he shouted after me. 'He was right. And Mr van Hout was right, too. Can't you see? Kaffirs will destroy our country. Ivan's not the liar. *Mugabe* is. *He's* the one who has to be stopped. He'll destroy us all.'

From inside the study only Klompie's legs were visible. He started to kick.

'*No*! You can't. You'll ruin everything. *Everything*.'

'If anyone's going to ruin anything it's Ivan. I'm only trying to make things right.'

Only some might say that that never happened: I *did* ruin it, I screwed up big time.

Limping slightly, I ran out and towards the chapel. The bell had started to ring, I had to hurry.

THIRTY-EIGHT

The Prime Minister's cars were taking up the entire space outside the Admin Block. I knew he was up in Bully's study because six bodyguards were posted around the building while another three stood on the stairs. Boys and parents and masters were answering the call of the bell and filing into the chapel.

The bodyguards began to jostle nervously. The Prime Minister must have been ready. It was only about ten metres to the chapel entrance and the area was too open. Ivan and Pitters had to have been inside.

I pushed my way forward and went in through one of the side entrances. A quarter of the pews were already full while sixth-form boys were taking their places up in the gallery. I looked hard. Where were they? Behind me the choir had taken all available positions around the altar, the only vacant seats there belonged to Bully, the Prime Minister and his entourage.

Where were they?

Mr Hodgson came in and settled at the organ. After a few seconds, the towering collection of pipes wheezed into life and Mr Finklater had to come over and tell me to stop loitering and get up to the gallery. Parents were looking at me like I was going to make an announcement.

I moved slowly, still scouring faces. Mr Hodgson's prelude continued, and it was difficult not to notice his slightly erratic performance because he always prided himself on perfection. I let myself be distracted by it and watched Mr Hodgson's face crease with agitation as notes slipped from his fingers.

One note in particular, in fact, and each time he glanced up at the culpable pipes.

Something was wrong. Something, I wondered, or someone?

Mr Finklater made a grab but I was too quick, darting across the altar to the vestry door. The choir watched with mild confusion as I passed. I'd never been up to where the organ pipes were. If you got caught up there it was instant expulsion. I figured that didn't matter any more.

The steps were narrow and near-vertical; the higher I climbed into the lightless room the harder the music pressed.

Pittman was waiting for me at the top, emerging like a ghost. He grabbed me and pulled me up and threw me further into the room of tubes and pipes. I bounced between the unmoving metal and skidded to the floor. Ahead, I could see Pittman's gun lying flat.

'Ivan should never have trusted you.' Swinging his shoe into my ribs. 'Who cares if you're a crack shot, you're still only a Pommie.'

He landed on my spine and drove the air from my lungs. Then he turned me over and leaned forward.

'I hope I only injure him and get the chance to make him die slowly.'

I tried to push his face out of mine. His teeth bit into my hand. With an agonized thrust I pushed forward so that my finger went all the way in and scraped the back of his throat and he fell off me, eyes bulging. He made a retching sound as I quickly faced forward and crawled. All I could see was the gun. All I had to do was get the gun.

Pittman came again.

I grabbed the rifle in both hands, quickly pulled the bolt without him seeing and swung. Pittman stopped, the barrel digging into his stomach.

'It's over, Pitters,' I told him over the music.

'What are you going to do? Shoot me?' He grabbed the barrel and stuck it under his chin. The trigger strained dangerously against my finger. 'Go on – shoot! Do it.'

I did nothing, of course.

'You're such a poof, Jacko. You would never have done it. I knew that. You might be good but all you can slot are squares of cardboard on a range.'

He whipped his fist and I caught it on the cheek. Fire erupted.

A second swipe and the world slipped away. My eyes rolled. *Help* . . .

I could only think the words as my mouth slurred something vague and incoherent.

Please . . .

Even if I'd called it no one would have heard, and as my dark cloud descended I sensed movement out in the main chapel. The sound of the main doors. I heard a wave roll through the congregation, from front to rear, and through small gaps between the organ pipes I saw heads turn and bodies stand. Mr Mugabe had entered and was walking down the aisle.

And there, on the end of the last pew right at the back, was Ivan, watching with more intent than most and with a distinct grin on his lips.

THIRTY-NINE

He probably saved my life. That's the irony of it.

By coming in when he did, Mr Mugabe inadvertently made Pitters rush back into position instead of finishing me off. Maybe Pitters thought he'd done enough, or that Ivan would somehow know he wasn't getting on with the job. Either way, Mr Mugabe saved me by making himself the target.

The organ rose, a forceful heroic piece of music which I'm sure the Prime Minister had insisted upon. He wasn't a big man, in fact he was dwarfed by the giants behind that were his bodyguards. True as that was, there was a something that made him impossible to ignore. He wore an impeccable light grey suit, and he came slowly, in his own time, his face high and unflinching as he looked out from behind those TV-screen glasses at the sea of mostly white faces.

What was everyone thinking? In hindsight, I've often asked myself this. Whatever it was, he met their gaze with the un-wavering tenderness we'd only seen on posters, across television screens, in papers. Paternal, almost. He was their ally, it said. Their guardian. Once an enemy of the white government, true, but now an equal friend to black and white alike. They had nothing to fear because he meant no harm, he wanted what was good for them and the country. It had been over seven years since the end of the war, so surely they could see that by now?

Pittman could see everything that was going on, staring at it down the barrel of the gun as he kneeled on one knee like a soldier. Mugabe grew steadily larger in his sights. He had a clear line, he could take the shot at any time, but he wanted to be sure. He also wanted it to look good. He'd let him get right to the front, turn, face the congregation, then . . .

'Pittman.'

Pitters blinked like he was coming out of a dream: had he heard something?

He lowered the gun.

He turned to me, or to where he'd left me. And then, realizing, to where I actually was, right over his shoulder. His eyes widened with genuine surprise, his mouth forming a silent O. Quickly, quicker than I thought he could, he moved to regain firing position but already my arm was in motion. It arced though the air, followed by an abrupt stop.

Pittman's head bounced against the wall. He snarled like an injured animal, pulled the trigger, slumped, and finally collapsed forward without resistance.

The Prime Minister's head bowed as he went down, one hand flashing the shape of the crucifix across his chest.

Pause.

Then he was up again, his Catholic duty in front of the altar fleeting. Bully showed him to his seat.

Behind the pipes, I bowed my own head to the bullet still in my hand. If Pittman had seen me take it from the chamber, all it would have taken was a quick back and forward of the bolt to bring the next round up. But he hadn't realized, and so with those few seconds of extra time I'd managed to return the favour and save Mr Mugabe's life right back.

I took the rifle from under Pittman's inert body, removed the rest of the ammo, damaged the firing pin, and left him to wake up in his own time into whatever nightmare he would find.

I slid out of the vestry door and made room for myself at the edge of the choir stalls, sorting out my shirt and tie and cleaning my face. The boys there stared though they didn't say anything as Bully worked his way into the proceedings.

'. . . and it is of course with extreme pleasure and gratitude that we welcome our esteemed guest today . . .'

I eased forward to snatch a daring peek at Ivan. His face was buried under an impatient frown as he peered up to the organ pipes. His lips moved soundlessly.

Come on, come on . . .

His eyes dropped to me, and it must have been written all over me because he seemed to understand exactly what had happened. His face transformed, but for the first time I wasn't scared. I was shaking loose.

His mouth flat-lined, hard and straight.

'. . . I know I speak on behalf of everyone here when I say we are – truly – thankful, Prime Minister, that you have been able to find time in what I know must be an extremely busy and important schedule . . .'

Ivan looked lost for a moment. Like his world was falling away from beneath him. But then, slowly, the corner of this mouth started to rise again and any uncertainty on his side had gone. I tried to pretend it hadn't but I could *feel* it happening. My own self-assurance ebbed. What could he do? I wondered. There was no one else.

Was there?

Ivan's smile was broad. For one last time, he seemed to know what was going on in my mind and peeled open his blazer enough to reveal the handle of an automatic pistol sticking out of his pocket, no doubt the exact one he and I had fired a million lifetimes ago on his farm. He'd held it back, stolen it from his old man . . . He'd planned this day for too long to let it slip him by.

'. . . So without further ado I now call upon Head Boy, Ivan Hascott, to start the speeches and officially welcome our special guest.'

Bully moved aside and ignited the applause.

The Prime Minister uncrossed his legs and stood.

Ivan pulled his blazer tight, buttoned it, and finger-combed his hair.

I had no time to think. I'm not even sure it was a conscious decision to jump to my feet and walk forward, I simply did it.

Bully was the first to notice me coming and his expression suddenly became a very different one, somewhere between surprise and extreme annoyance, but he kept on clapping because the Prime Minister's bodyguards didn't know better, and nor did Mr Mugabe himself, who was looking at me with his arm outstretched. I could see Bully wondering what to do about this but already it had gone beyond that as I accepted Mr Mugabe's hand.

His fingers enveloped mine, his hold firm, and as he took control of the movement, pushing my arm down subtly yet surely, he noticed the state of my clothes and face. Even so, his stance was unwavering, and without letting go he spoke under the applause.

'I have heard many great things about you,' he spoke softly. 'I am told you are the son of a farmer.'

I nodded.

He leaned in closer and smothered my hand with the both of his as he smiled. And I winced.

At the far end of the chapel, a cry permeated the air. Soft at first, growing louder. The clapping petered out until there was only the cry, rising from the depths of Ivan's hell.

Everyone turned.

Ivan was running down the aisle, one hand reaching into his blazer as the word resonated.

'*Nooo!*'

He came quickly and aggressively, shouting. My mouth went dry as I took an involuntary step in front of Mr Mugabe, but now the bodyguards were spurred into action and closed a tight circle around Ivan before he even had a chance to reveal the gun. They grabbed him with rough hands and managed to bustle him back and out of the main doors without his feet touching the ground.

All the while, Ivan shouted and kicked and screamed.

'*Get your filthy hands off me. Let me go. Don't you see? Put me down, you black . . .*'

The exit was shut and his voice cut off. There was the noise of a scuffle, the bellow of one of the bodyguards, then nothing.

A mutter gradually filled the chapel. Robert Mugabe brushed down his suit, discarded me and returned to his seat. He managed to appear as though nothing had happened yet I caught him blaze a look at Bully that could have melted rocks.

Mr Bullman broke out into a sweat.

'Ladies and gentlemen.' He raised his hands, shaking visibly. 'Please, ladies and gentlemen, everything is under control,' he said, because he thought it was.

They dragged him down the chapel steps, across the sun-bleached grass and away. They'd already vanished from sight before I managed to get outside. I only knew where they were from the disbelieving gazes of all the juniors.

I raced after them, not knowing what I was going to do, only that I had to.

Behind the library I found two of the bodyguards crouching while the third lay panting in the dust, clutching his groin. He groaned and yelled, and the other two yelled back. None of them seemed worried about Ivan, only I was as he darted across the lower playing fields. He was getting away.

I kept on chasing. He didn't get far, though, because a soldier was running from the other direction to cut him off. He made Ivan kneel in the middle of the grass. When I caught up I saw it was the same soldier who'd confronted me earlier, already jabbing the Kalashnikov at me, too, as he tumbled from whatever he'd been smoking and into a swirl of paranoia.

'Down! Get down!' His hands didn't know who to point the gun at. Then he seemed to remember my face and settled on me. 'Do as I say do as I say!'

I obeyed without hesitation.

'He's got a weapon,' I tried.

The soldier looked confused and split his guard between us. Ivan grabbed his chance.

'He's lying. *He's* got the gun. He tried to kill the Prime Minister. He did it.'

'No, he's the liar. Check his pockets if you don't believe me.'

'Don't believe him. Look, they're all after him.'

From one. To the other. To the other. In the end the soldier chose me and shouted.

'*I am watching you.*'

'No, I'm not the one . . .'

'I will *shoot.*' He raised the Kalashnikov. 'I will shoot and kill you dead.'

Ivan began to stand.

'*Both of you.* Stay still.'

'But I'm innocent.' Ivan raised his hands. 'You've got the right guy there.'

'I am warning you.'

'But . . .'

'*Stay!*'

Ivan turned on me. 'This is all your fault.' He took a furious step, coming between me and the soldier. 'I could have done it by now.'

Behind him, the soldier hopped to keep me in his sights.

'Why did you stop me?' Ivan thrust a finger in my face. Was all this another ruse? No, the anger was genuine, he couldn't have faked that.

'Out of the way,' the soldier ordered.

Ivan ignored him.

'Well, I'm not giving in. I have to do it. I have to go back and get him. Don't you see? It's what everybody wants,' he told me. He took a deep breath, and then the smile returned. He gave me the Ivan Hascott wink and I saw his hand reaching into his pocket. His fingers wrapped around metal. 'But first this stupid Kaffir deserves a hole in the head, don't you think?'

He turned quickly.

'*No!*' I yelled.

The bullet hit the soldier with enough force to knock him down, his arms spinning. His Kalashnikov flew through the air. He wasn't dead, though, and he rolled onto his front and started to drag himself with eyes bulging. He made short gasping noises.

Ivan stood over him. Over on the edge of the field I was aware of people running, getting nearer.

'You see? *Kaffirs*: too stupid. If he was white I'd quite rightly be dead by now.'

He pointed his gun at the back of the soldier's skull and braced himself for the shot.

I'm not sure I remember actually picking up the Kalashnikov from the grass, just that it was in my hands with smoke drifting from the barrel. The echo of an explosion was in my ears, and Ivan was staggering backwards as though he had been yanked by something invisible.

He gazed at me stupidly with a thousand and one questions in his face. Then at the small hole in the shoulder of his blazer. A second later, a small spot of dark appeared on the blue material, expanding slowly.

'What the—' the pain started to creep in on him – '*fuck?*'

My head spun. The metal of the Kalashnikov was searing and cold against my fingers.

'I can't let you do it,' I told him.

'But . . .' he grimaced. The pistol hung limply from the end of his lifeless arm, he grabbed it with his left hand and waved it about to make his point. 'Don't you get it? After everything I've told you?'

'Yes, I get it. I get everything. You're the one who doesn't.'

He let my words sink in, then twisted his mouth and pointed his pistol straight at me. I could see right down the barrel. It was deep and black. Sweat ran into my eyes.

'I almost admire you, Jacko. But you're fighting for the wrong side.'

'There are no sides. Not any more. Can't you see that what you're doing is all wrong?' I said. And I remembered what a friend of mine by the name of Nelson Ndube had once told me. 'Wars should be about putting an *end* to a wrong, not making a new one.'

His head shook from side to side. He reasserted his grip around the butt of the gun and held it steady.

'Stupid Pommie bastard.'

A second crack punctured the air.

I stumbled, expecting pain yet finding none. I looked up, and it was Ivan who was tottering on his feet. His mouth was wide open. He blinked slowly, looking at me, though I think he'd worked out what was happening before I had, a glimmer of sadness drowning in frustrated, undiluted anger. Because that's all it ever was: anger, with no place to put it.

'You . . .' he started.

The bodyguard shouted as he charged near. Ivan swung the gun that way, and the bodyguard dropped and fired another shot. Ivan folded at the hips as a flash of red flew out of the back of his blazer. Now there was only disbelief in him. He turned, barely in control yet managing to get upright.

'. . . You . . .'

The bodyguard readied himself again, one eye closed, but his gun clicked harmlessly onto a jammed chamber.

Ivan landed his sights on me.

The Kalashnikov jumped in my hands and the final bullet punched into Ivan's chest. He fell backwards and landed on the ground as if at the top of a sit-up, with legs straight and arms limply by his sides.

His head nodded, fading.

'You should have let me do it,' he whispered. 'You'll see.'

Then no more words came, just a strange gurgling as his head dropped and his chin tipped closer and closer to his knees until at last it stopped. After that, he didn't move at all. Not even as they pulled me off the field to some waiting car. As far as I was concerned he stayed like that forever, bowed to the tall bodyguard at his feet, his fringe moving lightly in a sudden breeze that somehow gave no relief.

ZIMBABWE
Today

FORTY

The school is closed now.

I already knew that. There were no surprises as I pulled from the main road and up the drive to find a heavy chain hanging from the gate like an ill-disciplined tie. Even so, it took me a long time to leave the car.

Tell me about your school days.

From my wife, my friends, my colleagues. The bullet I've excelled at dodging.

'Here it is,' I could reply for the first time. 'This is the place.'

And I climbed out beneath the huge summer clouds.

The chain rattled its empty threat as I climbed the fence, but at the top the past came spiralling towards me, and in the next moment I was slipping down the other side, fingers raking metal, into a cloud of dust.

Jacko! A shout came as I hit. *Run, Jacko. I'm telling you, you'd better run hard cos we're coming to get you. Gonna slot you, one time. You're dead.*

The school is closed now, but that has nothing to do with what happened back then, with what we did.

As the bodyguards had pushed against me in the back of that car, the Guest of Honour had gone on to finish his speech and open the new boarding house as planned. He'd then been driven away – in blissful ignorance, I'm sure – and I doubt he gave that day a second thought as he returned to his eventful working life as Prime Minister, then President, then Tyrant and Oppressor. The school closures (for Haven was by no means alone) were a part of that life and had made international news, a stabbing punctuation mark amid all the sorry and sadistic stories of Mugabe's determination to run this forsaken country into the ground. Unheard cries – a country is burning yet no one will tackle the flames.

You should have let me do it . . .

Leaning against the fence, I looked around to see who might be there watching. No one was. Just me with a whole load of ghosts.

I turned and faced the empty road, a view that had evoked so many emotions, good and bad, in the past. Those emotions weren't there for me any more. A relief: truly, I was no longer the boy I'd once been. Surely.

I walked on around the ring road. Heat bounced off the tarmac in waves, and I paused to peel off the boots and damp socks from another hemisphere and continued barefoot, exactly as we had done as children in Africa. Everywhere, grass lapped at buildings like a hungry sea.

The lower playing fields opened up to my left. Beyond, out there somewhere beneath the level-topped canopy, the bush hid the Cliffs, haunted forevermore by the shallow graves that had been discovered there, Nelson Ndube's amongst them. All the action of some Crazy from a neighbouring village, apparently, or at least that had been the conclusion of the lazy police. But I know.

I know.

The sun drowned beneath slate, dark patches bled and became one.

You should have let me do it, the voice came again. *You'll see.*

His voice, reaching and grabbing me just as it had always done, making me do things I knew I didn't want to do. For one horrible moment I thought I saw him there, as I'd seen him so many times in my dreams. I couldn't go on. It wasn't going to work.

Dread filled my legs and I slumped to the side of the road.

I've no idea how long I was like that before the old man wheeled slowly past me on a bicycle that creaked and groaned as if every turn of the pedal might be its last. He gazed unemotionally down on this pale white man (and somewhat covetously at the boots by my side) before wobbling to an inelegant stop.

'*Eweh! Shamwari*. What is happening?'

His voice sounded stern but the lines of his face gave him away. He was just curious. He scratched at thin patches of hair, and his large brown eyes swam in a yellowy sea of age. Sad, tired eyes. No election fever there. Once upon a time, maybe, not any more.

When I couldn't find a response I thought he might move on, but I was too much for him to ignore. I was *murungu*. A white man. What on earth was the likes of me doing here? It wasn't safe.

With a touching diligence, he put his bike to one side and sat close by. I noted his clothes: flannel trousers, shirt, jumper and tweed jacket despite the heat. All hopelessly old and beyond better days, yet he brushed off splashes of dirt as though he couldn't see the decay that covered each item like a rash. He didn't have any shoes on, probably because he didn't have any shoes. I was hit with wood smoke and musty body odour.

He stared and produced a smile of gaps and gums.

'My friend. You are crying many tears, you must be most unhappy. What is this that you are feeling most unhappy about?'

I was touched. I liked him.

I wiped the tears I hadn't realized were there, then picked up a rock and focused on it.

'I was at school here. Many years ago.'

'Ah! For sure?' He met the news with delight. 'But this

school, it was ve-ry very good. The teachers, they were ve-ry very good. You are luckyman. You have nice clothes and a nice watch. You are lucky. I think this was a *good* school for you.'

'Let's just say I didn't leave with the grades I should have had.'

'There is a lot more to an education than what happens inside the classroom.'

I sat up.

'Very true, *shamwari*,' I said. 'Very true.'

Not realizing the importance of what he'd said, his eyes flashed over my blue-white skin.

'You have come long way, so I believe you must like it here very much. You are young man. It cannot be so long ago, you must remember it well.'

'A little too well.' I flung the rock and it fizzed into the grass. 'Do you work near here?'

He laughed.

'*Shamwari*, there is no work here. The Old Man took it away. He lied and took everything for himself. The White Man can be blamed for many things, but the Old Man must also be blamed. Mugabe was *tsotsi*. *Mambara*. Because he was a thief without care who stole our hope,' he lamented. 'And now I am old man, too, the arms and the legs are verr-ry very slow now.'

The air rustled through the trees. Thunder rolled in the distance.

'The afternoon rains are on their way and I do not want my new jacket wet,' he announced. 'My wife will not be pleased. My girlfriends will not be pleased, either.'

'It's never good to upset your wife. I did, over and over. And my daughter.'

'Ah! A little one. How many years?'

'Three next month.' With a longing for the absent I was glad to feel, I showed him a picture of blonde bunches and dimpled cheeks.

'I know this!' he burst. 'I know this pride that a father has for a little one such as this. I had *seven daughters*!'

The smile became fuller, richer. It was the sort that belonged to someone marvelling at a setting sun: a moment of privilege and pleasure as you behold a sight so beautiful you never want to lose it, knowing you must.

'Now I have none. This country . . .' He gave the photo back, its light fading for him. 'It is not a young person's country, for it will never let you get old. I am old, but I am luckyman. My children . . . Now there is only my son. His name is Tuesday. He is half blinded. I pray that he can see only half the evil spirits that are surrounding us here.'

Already the tears were coming again because I *knew* what he would then say.

'My name is Weekend.' He offered me his coarse hand.

I took it and held it tightly, and, as with our common memories, never wanted to let it go.

'Yes,' I said. 'Yes, it is.'

But I could no more tell him I knew him than I could tell anyone about my school days and what we'd done back then, and what *I'd* done.

So I stood and said my goodbye and watched him clamber onto his bike, though not before I'd passed over my watch and boots and all the money I had in my pockets. Perhaps it was wrong, but he gave me something all those years ago for which I never repaid him, and yet I took so much.

He rode inexpertly away. I watched and let the first droplets smack against the tarmac around me before rounding the corner to Selous House.

Ignoring the rain, I stood under the gaze of those louvered windows. There was no spark of recognition in them. No emotion of any kind. All of that was on my side, it plagued me like the swarm that had once pushed me so close to the edge. Sweat pricked my scalp.

I found another stone.

It gave me no pleasure to hear the shattering of silence or to see two strips of glass disappear into my old study beyond, but there was satisfaction of a sort. Leaving this place had been a voiceless moment, there'd been no anguished cry or even a look back in anger as they'd driven me away, and I hadn't uttered a word all through my arrest. In the end they'd had to let me go: I'd helped save a soldier's life, thank you very much, be on your way and forget about it. That's what they said they would do. But from that day until the time I finally left for an alien life in England I never felt fully alone: cigarette smoke from parked cars, passers-by in inappropriate suits, strangers with a knowing look . . . Ivan – my friend – had brought a gun to within spitting distance of the Prime Minister, so I don't believe they ever stopped watching me, hungry to protect their corrupt leader.

'There goes a great, great man,' my father had told me as we'd headed towards my first day at Haven. 'He's given the people freedom – what could be a greater achievement than that?'

But you can't give freedom. Freedom must be found.

The wind was gusting now, the rain strong.

You should have let me . . .

The voice that has been with me without mercy for over twenty years.

I tipped my head and let the downpour wash through me, and suddenly I was fifteen again, in history, with a teacher called Mr van Hout asking the question.

'If I stood you in front of a man, pressed the cold metal of a gun into your palm and told you to squeeze the trigger, would you do it . . . ?'

Unlike then, I had an answer.

'Yes.'

Because I'd already done it, and Ivan was dead because of it.

But the country I'd come back to was one I scarcely recognized, a mere remnant writhing in a swamp of persecution and corruption, of anger and hatred, of death, misery and disease. Families are destroyed by starvation and AIDS and preventable illnesses every single day. Mobs of henchmen terrorize the countryside with impunity, intimidating folk – black and white – and drive them from their homes. While up at the top the Big Men and Women still sit and watch it all happening around them, the cronies who carved out a position of obscene privilege for themselves and sucked the life from a once-bountiful nation.

And all, ultimately, the legacy of one man.

So was I right?

Or should I have let Ivan do it?

Should I?

Should I?

It was a question for which I'd hoped to find the answer, only it wasn't here, and I realized in that moment that I'd *never* find it. Which was answer in itself.

If I stood you in front of a man, pressed the cold metal of a gun into your palm and told you to squeeze the trigger, would you do it?

No, sir.

Are you sure?

Of course, sir. No ways!

What if I then told you we'd gone back in time and his name was Adolf Hitler? Would you do it then? Would you? Would you?

'I'd want to ask him: *Why?*'

*　　*　　*

When I looked again the rain had stopped and the charcoal ceiling was giving way to the blue.

I listened hard.

The door to Selous beckoned but I didn't go to it. I sensed there might not be any need, and instead I turned and walked the other way.

The playing fields were empty. At that moment the shade evaporated from them and a warm sun pressed against my back.

I listened again and still there was nothing. Ivan had gone.

From amongst the trees that hid the workers' village I saw someone move and imagined maybe it was Weekend. I raised my arm, but already I was alone again, waving a farewell to faces that weren't there any more, in a silence I hadn't heard for a very long time.

As I went back through the school I suddenly noticed things weren't quite how I'd remembered them. Smaller, of course, and crumbling in places. But it's still strong to the core. It's a hideous waste yet at the same time I see hope, for maybe one day things will be different and the school can open again. History – the *course* of history – is never set.

I reached the gate, scaled it and sparked the engine of my car back into life. I moved slowly away without even a glance in the rear-view mirror, in and out of shadows down the willow-lined drive and beyond huge stone pillars that bore the school's name.

At the end I turned west into the softening African sun. The storm clouds had gone and I was going to meet a shifting sky of wonderful, impossible colour.

ACKNOWLEDGEMENTS

For the priceless help, insight, belief, support and hard work given during the writing of this book, my heartfelt thanks to: my agent, Carolyn Whitaker; my editor, Charlie Sheppard, and all at Andersen Press; and Margaret Barton.

OVER A THOUSAND HILLS I WALK WITH YOU

HANNA JANSEN

'At its heart the Rwandan tragedy was profoundly personal. This novel captures with great poignancy the terrible cost to the youngest and most vulnerable.'
Fergal Keane

'This is an extraordinary and devastating book. Like *The Diary of Anne Frank*, I will never forget it.'
Emma Thompson

Jeanne is a typical school girl: bickering with her little sister, teasing her brother. Then, in one horrifying night, a torrent of violence is unleashed. Jeanne's family flees their home and tries desperately to reach safety. They do not succeed. Jeanne is the only survivor of her family's massacre, and this is her story as told to her adoptive mother. A story that makes unforgettably real the events of the 1994 Rwandan genocide.

ISBN 9781842706732

£6.99